George Robertson, Alexander Hamilton Robertson

An Outline of the Life of George Robertson

George Robertson, Alexander Hamilton Robertson

An Outline of the Life of George Robertson

ISBN/EAN: 9783743333178

Manufactured in Europe, USA, Canada, Australia, Japa

Cover: Foto ©Raphael Reischuk / pixelio.de

Manufactured and distributed by brebook publishing software (www.brebook.com)

George Robertson, Alexander Hamilton Robertson

An Outline of the Life of George Robertson

GEORGE ROBERTSON.

AN

OUTLINE OF THE LIFE

OF

GEORGE ROBERTSON,

WRITTEN BY HIMSELF,

WITH AN INTRODUCTION AND APPENDIX
BY HIS SON.

"And this (publication) I desire, not in the vain hope of posthumous fame, but in the belief that it may be my best legacy to my descendants, useful to surviving friends, and of some service to my succeeding countrymen."—GEORGE ROBERTSON.

"Do you not know how strictly we should guard the homes of the dead, since they cannot do it for themselves?"—MARLITT.

LEXINGTON, KY.:
TRANSYLVANIA PRINTING & PUBLISHING. CO.
1876.

CONTENTS.

INTRODUCTION.

The name of every member of society, certainly of every well-known man, is, at all times, impleaded before a tribunal, august, by reason of its power, the number of its judges and the gravity of its issues, for the most part honest, but fallible and irresponsible, whose laws are unwritten, whose jurisdiction is unlimited, whose proceedings are irregular, and which never adjourns; from whose decision there is no appeal, and from whose police there is no escape; which wields a might above the sway of Church and State, and grasps, not only the functions of a civil service—commission to try and to sentence every holder of a public trust, but also the authority of that God-appointed and private censor, Conscience, and that far-off hierarchy who sat in judgment of the dead.

Its name is Public Opinion.

These pages may be accepted as the final report, filed in that inevitable Court, of the manner in which he had discharged his obligations to his fellow-men, and his duties to himself, by one whose term of service upon earth was about to close. Putting yourself in his place, do you ask what good it will do you to be remembered with kindness, or, at all, after you are dead? The question is unanswerable. The wish to be so remembered, even if never fulfilled, may shape your course, and work out your welfare, here and hereafter, and if accomplished, may make your example of infinite value to others.

The philosophy of practical life, which adapts means to ends, has vibrated between two great motives. The creed of a generation whose last survivors are fast passing away, may be summed up in the well known words: A good name is rather to be chosen than great riches. Its effect was to moor many a true and drifting soul to sure and steadfast rules, which had their outgrowth in plain manners and in the performance of every social duty. The substance of the faith which now prevails, may be favorably condensed into the expression: Property is respectability, or the chief good is wealth. Would you see its fruits? Behold this age and land, matchless in the profusion and variety of their material advantages, but strewed with moral wrecks!

The low plane of the sensual offers few objects of pursuit that are not within the reach of both **wrong means** and wrong subordinate motives and right ones. **Its** rewards are also bribes; its incentives to good **are** temptations to evil. The voyage **of** the Apostle and **the** cruise of the pirate are steered by the same star. The love **of** approbation may beget grovelling arts and counterfeit presentments. It is not the desire of praise, but the desire to be worthy of praise, that regenerates. A name to be good must be true. Public integrity must denote private virtue. The one is the flower, the other the **root.**

This volume **is** the profile of a single life. **Its** author was acquainted with the leading characters **and** the great social **and** political movements **of** the progressive times **in** which he lived, and especially **with** the controlling minds **and** the written and oral history **of** his native **State.** His familiar discourse was often enlivened by fresh and racy sketches of men and manners, which, if extended and written out, would be as entertaining and **instructive** as the diary of Evelyn, the memoirs of Barrington, **or** the **full** length portraits of Clarendon. But his purpose, in this posthumus publication, was not to give a retrospect of his **own** . times. He knew that could not be done impartially **and** without offense until not only he, but all those whose motives or actions entitled them to notice, had passed for**ever** from the scene. Without, as his words often, and his conduct always declared, valuing that widespread and indiscriminating notoriety which may be the offspring of a prostituted press or party, **or** the bastard **of** accident, he did earnestly desire that the witnesses **of his** conduct in the various relations of life, and most of all, **those** who had confided private or public trusts into his hands, might be able to **say** with truth, if not with gratitude, **after** he had gone from among them, Well done, at all times and in every place, tried and faithful **man!** And **with** unshaken confidence in his own probity, **if** tested by the highest human standard, he left this memorial of his motives and his deeds, his sorrows and his joys, his weakness and his strength, with the hope **that** it might guide other travelers along the rugged, treacherous and bewildering path which he had safely trod. In these last lines, dictated or approved when the shadow of coming oblivion **was** settling fast upon him, he speaks words of good cheer, now sealed by death, to young men, especially those of humble birth and fortune—the class from which he sprung, and to which he ever extended an open hand. He shows that without being "pensioners on the dead," or parasites of the living, without advantages derived by descent or obtained by marriage, or by any of the windfalls that irresolute Micawbers ingloriously await, strong will and lofty aims may reap harvests of their own sowing, and "repose beneath shades which they themselves have planted." He points to his own sturdy and unaided growth to prove that lack of help may be the mother of self-reliance and the stern nurse of untried power, and adds one more example to the old lesson, so seldom learned until the recitation is ended and the refractory pupil about to be dismissed,—that the vicissitudes of life are the frosts and thaws of a disciplinary winter, intended to weed, mellow and strengthen the mind and heart, to produce plenteous and golden fruits. Unlike parvenues who disown their origin, he claims to be the shoot of an undistinguished but brave and honest stock, and quietly takes the place which by sympathy, manners and association, he ever held among plain people of moderate means, pure morals and good sense. It was among such that he found his earliest, latest and most faithful friends. And he felt sure, if it conferred no merit, it was neither a reproach nor misfortune to be bred and trained in the ranks of the common people—that mighty infantry, without pennon or device, who, though often led astray and often betrayed, shattered and driven back when in the right course, had from the days of the unlineal Elijah the Tishbite, in every succeeding age, in every free country, and in every field of useful effort, wrought most of the memorable deeds and produced most of the great names that have blessed mankind.

He teaches that the only place at which to begin is the one which has been assigned us; that the best place to attain may not be the one which we most desire, or for which we are best suited, but that which is best fitted for us; that the best place at which to end is where, after having employed every talent, and performed every duty, with exhausted strength, and with harness on, we fall. He shows, inferentially, that great powers of action and endurance may find large scope for their exercise in any place; that the humblest place may be exalted, and the proudest place degraded, by its occupant; and that the skeleton of the guard

found standing at his post, near the gate of the disinterred
city, still holding aloft the lantern, which lighted for all
but him the way of escape, tells the story of a grander
place, because more grandly filled, than the imperial seat.
Finally, he shows that no place upon the quicksands of
Time can satisfy the infinite longings of a thoughtful soul.
His career affords a cud for both the Pelagian and the
predestinarian. He does not assert that he achieved any
extraordinary share of that material and external advancement which human short-sightedness elevates as the
only standard of success, but only claims to have received
such returns of that kind as any one may reasonably
expect in this world, of uncertain and unequal rewards, for
doing his duty. He leaves the enigma of his own, and every
other life in which the conflicting forces, free-will and necessity seem to co-exist, to be solved, if ever, in a state of
being, where the evidence is clearer, or the discernment is
more acute, than in this. If he rose above difficulties, sorrows often rose above him; and his history reveals that pure
intentions, leading to good actions and amiable affections
devoted to worthy and attractive objects, may not prevent,
but may be the means of producing temporal afflictions more
severe and lasting than those which commonly result from
debased appetites, directed to selfish and ignoble ends.

If this result of an upright life tends to prove that it is a
failure, it creates a far stronger presumption, that it is unfin-
ished and will find its complement hereafter. And, therefore, every such example points, it may be, through mists
and clouds, to this truth as the guiding star of human destiny.
That the only measure of a man, which can stand the tests
of time and change, is not the adumbrations which he casts
before men, nor what he has, but what he must think of himself when his thoughts and deeds are squared by the "shadow
of God," which is the light within him. And that "wisdom,
as it refers to action, lies in the proposal of a right end, and
the choice of the most proper means to attain it; which end
doth not refer to any one part of a man's life, but to the
whole as taken together. And that, therefore, he only deserves the name of a wise man, not who considers how to be
rich and great when he is poor and mean, nor how to be
well when he is sick, nor how to escape a present danger,
nor how to compass a particular design, but he that considers
the whole course of his life together and what is fit for him

to make the end of it." A fit motto for this book would be: Act well your part; a fit moral or conclusion: Live for others.

Reticence is not a fault of this narrative; blunders are admitted and merit is claimed; disappointments and sorrows under domestic afflictions, which neither faith nor reason could assuage, are disclosed; incidents that might be trivial, if anything influencing character is so, are told. He tells of his hurried education, of the straightened circumstances (*angusta resdomi*) of his early married life; of his addiction to cards, and his other shifts to earn and make money, and of his provincial rusticity, "By forms unfashioned, fresh from nature's hand," and want of *savoir faire* that led him, when a member of Congress, uninvited, to drink the wine of a Commodore. That there are no confessions, like some of Rousseau's, and many by De Retz, is because he was not a less candid, but a purer man than the erotic sentimentalist or the reckless Cardinal.

Complete self-knowledge is impossible, and the author of these pages may have done himself more or less than justice. In the judgment of those who knew him best, his failings, like the bending of the stalk of well filled grain, were the re sult of his goodness.

This autobiography was originally written by the author's own hand, and was more succinct and connected than now. During the last years of his life, when blind and helpless, he dictated many interpolations, some of which, perhaps, he would not have approved, had his health been vigorous. Whatever may be its faults, it contains no word of reproach, and the grave has closed the ear of him who was both its author, its subject, to the voice of censure and of praise, and to the dull, cold silence of indifference—facts that will bespeak for it a forbearance that might be less willingly conceded to a more aggressive work, or to the autobiography of a living man. Toward the matter which has been appended to the narrative, by one who had no other qualification for the task than long acquaintance with the author, may be supposed to confer, and under circumstances which rendered the task imperative, far greater indulgence is needed and besought.

This book is only a meager outline. If a full and just biography of Judge Robertson should ever be written by a competent hand, it will show a heart almost incredibly pure and amiable; a will always earnest and active; a mind that

could not only master the most difficult subjects, but also
capable of great and original thoughts, and able to organize
knowledge; a citizen watchful of his country's interests, con-
ceiving with the wide and prophetic vision of a statesman,
speaking with the force of strong convictions, advocating and
opposing with the fearlessness of a patriot; a jurist, who
soared to a height above the dust and clamor of *pie poudre*
courts, and there combining reason with authority, reconciled
the discordant, simplified the abstruse, crushed or separated
the intractible, and erred, when he did err, in the endeavor
to prevent general rules from sacrificing individuals; a man,
who taking in, at one view, the end and purpose of the
whole of life, tried to make his actions conform thereto.

But the time has passed when the recognition or denial of
his worth can concern him. His dust will mingle with the
soil from which he sprung; his thoughts and the results
which he achieved will soon be undistinguishably blended
with the common knowledge. Those who reap their benefit
will not know or acknowledge their source. Not a few of
the best and greatest of men have died and left no sign.
Earth is crowded with names kept alive by the fascinations of
the style, or the beauty of the marble that enshrines them.
Other men, like Johnson leaning on Boswell, as on a staff,
and Socrates resting on the shoulders of Plato and of Xeno-
phon, as on the pillars of Hercules, have also solid merits to
sustain them. Others still, like Homer and Shakespeare,
live only in their works. And this at last must be the fate
of all; granite crumbles, triple brass corrodes, memorial tab-
lets and inscriptions overlay and hide each other. Mortality
is inexorable—its law is compensation, its decree is change.
Every life borrows the materials of its organization and the
subjects of its forces, and must restore them to their source.
Decay nourishes; the tiniest moss, the grandest tree, must
pay back its elements to the soil and to the air, to become
the food of other forms. The man must be lost in humanity
—the individual in the race. Names must perish, works become common property; but only in this world. The action,
like the actor, has an immortal soul. " I heard a voice
from Heaven saying unto me, write, * * * *Their works
do follow them.*"

LIFE OF GEORGE ROBERTSON.

CHAPTER I.

As my descendants may desire to know more of me than they might glean from tradition, I commence, this 18th of November, 1858—the 68th anniversary of my birth—to write, for their inspection, a memorial of my life. And, although Autobiography is too much tinged with egotism, yet I will strive to speak of myself as candidly as I ought to speak of any other person, with the eminent advantage of more accuracy, fullness and authenticity in my own case, than in that of another.

My genealogy has not been emblazoned by heraldry, nor illustrated by either statesmanship or arms; and I cannot trace my line of descent further upward, by regular links of concatenation, than to my paternal and maternal stocks of great grand-parents.

My father, Alexander Robertson, born in Augusta county, Virginia, about a mile from Staunton, and northwestwardly of it, on the 22d of November, 1748, was the son of James Robertson, who, with his own father, of the same name, immigrated, about the year 1737, to America from the neighborhood of Coleraine, in the north of Ireland. They were probably a portion of the colony of Scotch-Irish Presbyterians, who settled on Burden's grant, in the then trans Alleghanian wilderness of the colony of Virginia, which had been, a few years before, visited by *Lewis* and *Salling*, the latter of whom was captured by Indians near the forks of James river, and taken, about the year 1725, to Kentucky as its first white visitants, so far as authentic tradition testifies.

My mother's maiden name was Margaret Robinson. Her father, William Robinson, was born early in the 18th century, in the county of Down, Northern Ireland, whence his

father, James Robinson, and himself and six brothers, all
over six feet high, came about the year 1740 to Lancaster
county, Pennsylvania. Not long after his advent he married
Margaret Garrel, a pretty little fair-haired and blue-eyed
Welch girl; his own hair and eyes being dark brown. Shortly after his marriage, he removed to the last crossing of
Roanoke, near Voss' Fort—then in the county of Fincastle,
but when my mother was born the county of Bottetourt, and
now the county of Montgomery, Virginia—and settled on
an improved and large tract of land (called Fotheringay)
which is as fertile and romantic as any in Western Virginia.
He was considered one of the most upright, modest and
handsome men of his day, and my mother's face was said to
be a blooming likeness of his.

My paternal grandfather was tall and spare, but of large
frame. His skin was fair and his eyes blue. His piety was
unquestioned, and his character unsoiled. He married, in
Augusta, Elizabeth Crawford, a handsome girl, of good family. Of her genealogy I know nothing.*

Thus, as early as about 1742, all my grand-parents resided
in Western Virginia, then almost a trackless wilderness.

The *physique*, the *morale*, and the orthography indicate

*Judge Robertson wrote the subjoined notice of his father's sister:—
Rebecca Dunlap, mother of Rev. James Dunlap, the oldest citizen of
Fayette, died at the residence of her son, Col. John R. Dunlap, near Lexington, Kentucky, on the morning of the 7th of November, 1849, in the
99th year of her age
Born in Augusta county, Virginia, on the 23d of July, 1751, she there
intermarried with William Dunlap. In 1784 they emigrated to Kentucky,
and in 1785 settled about four miles from Lexington, where she ever after
resided until her death, within forty feet of the site of her first cabin. Her
husband, William Dunlap, died March 5th, 1816, aged 72 years, 4 months
and 25 days. Her father, James Robertson, about the year 1735, came to
America from the north of Ireland, and in 1739 married Elizabeth Crawford, and settled about one mile from Stanton, then in the backwoods of
Virginia, where Rebecca, his sixth child, and the last survivor of his family,
was born and reared, and where he died in her infancy about the year
1758. He was a plain upright man, of spotless character and exemplary
piety, living and dying a steadfast Presbyterian. She also, at an early
day after her settlement in Kentucky, became a member of the Presbyterian church at Walnut Hill, of which church she continued a beloved and
worthy member as long as she remained on earth. Her long and quiet
life was an admirable model of the grace and humility of genuine Christianity.

that my father's stock was Scotch, and my mother's English, of each of which shoots were transplanted, and probably about the same time, from Scotland and England to the north of Ireland. And this inference is rather fortified by some vague traditions. I am also inclined to believe that Robertson, the historian, and my father were descendants of the same clan. This is nearly authenticated by a genealogical table lately sent to me by Wyndham Robertson, of Richmond, Va., which shows that my father was either a nephew or cousin of Robertson, the historian; and, therefore, as Patrick Henry's father was a nephew of Robertson, the historian, Patrick Henry and myself were of the same stock.*

The descendants of my mother's stock are more numerous in the United States than those of my father; but of the identity or proximity of the individuals of either class, I have only a very partial knowledge. I presume that Genl. James Robertson, who settled Nashville, and Bolling Robertson, who represented Orleans in Congress, were, in some degree, related to my father, and the Reverend Stuart Robinson to my mother.†

One of the purest and almost the last of Kentucky's pioneer band, she lived through three generations, and having outlived the cotemporaries of her children, and sighed over the graves of most of the friends of her meridian sunshine, she stood in her lingering and mellow eventide, a lonely monument of the simple graces and sturdy virtues of a race and age, memorable in the history of American progress and Western civilization. She saw Kentucky in all its phases, from the twinkling light of its struggling dawn to the full radiance of its culminating glory. And when, after an eventful life of rare length and harmony, she had at last gradually descended to the horizon of her probationary day, she sank from the visions of earth as serenely, as noiselessly, and as benignantly, as the setting sun of a mild and cloudless autumnal evening. Blessed in her parting twilight with the consoling presence of a kindred household, and with the long hoped for privilege of dying at a home consecrated by 64 years of buried joys and untold sorrows, she took her eternal leave with a patriarch's blessing on the land she had helped to save and exalt, and with thanks to God for all that she had been permitted to see, to do, and to enjoy on earth. Such a life and such a death are worthy of long and grateful remembrance, and especially by the countless posterity, left by this venerable decedent, to act their parts "for weal or woe" in the trying drama in which the last scene of her long and useful pilgrimage is just closed forever.

*Brougham was a nephew of the same,

†See S. B.

When he was about ten years old my father was left an orphan; and inheriting but a small patrimony, he was bound to James Allin, grandfather of Mrs. Jouett, of Lexington, Ky., to learn the trade of a carpenter and wheelwright, on Middle river, in the county of his birth. He served a faithful apprenticeship, and obtained a good English education, consisting of reading, writing, arithmetic, trigonometry and surveying. I have in my possession a manuscript book containing some of his scholastic exercises in surveying, from which it appears that when a boy he had learned to write neatly and legibly, draw accurate diagrams, and solve difficult problems.

My mother was born April 13th, 1755, on Roanoke, at the "*Hancock Place*," or Fotheringay, so named by her father in honor of Mary Queen of Scots, to whose cause he was a devoted adherent. In the tenth year of her age, her father was drowned in New river, at the crossing of the main western road. The facilities for scholastic education being then very limited, she was at school only six months; but during that short pupilage she learned to read, write and cipher quite well. Children then, and in that country, were trained to moral and industrious principles and habits, and thus, kept from vicious temptations and demoralizing associations, they employed their time usefully, and soon acquired proper education, physical, moral and intellectual. It is to be regretted that it is not so now and here, in this more luxurious and degenerate age.

Liberated from his apprenticeship, my father devoted himself diligently to his trade of making wheels and building houses in his native county, until about the year 1770, when he engaged to build a framed house on Roanoke, for William Madison, father of George Madison, who was elected Governor of Kentucky, and brother of James Madison, father of President Madison. This house I have seen. It is west of the river, and in sight of the house of my grandmother Robinson, which was on a mountain elevation on the east of the

river, and on the site of the brick house afterwards built by
Hancock. While engaged in erecting that edifice my father
became acquainted with and courted my mother, and on the
18th of August, 1773, they were married in Bedford county,
Virginia, whither they and their bridal party had to go to
meet the Episcopal minister, who would not go out of his
own county to solemnize marriage. They were married at
the house of Colonel Howard, the father of Benjamin Howard, once Governor of Missouri. I have a copy of their
license, dated 17th August, 1773. And Mrs. Parker, a sister
of Gov. Howard, said to me about ten years ago, "*Sir, I saw
your father and mother married, and a handsomer couple I never
saw stand on the floor.*" And doubtless she thought so. I
have a vivid recollection of each of them. My mother, when
in her girlhood, must have been beautiful, and, according to
tradition, was generally considered almost peerless in personal comeliness. My father, although only five feet eight
inches high, weighed about 165 pounds, and was of perfect
form His head was large, his forehead capacious, his nose
of large Grecian mold, his complexion fair, his eyes grey,
his hair black and waving, and his countenance benignant
and luminous. I was not quite twelve years old when he
died. When he was forty years old, he had become so cor-
pulent as to weigh 240 pounds. But even as I remember
him he was remarkably handsome. My mother was of me-
dium size, her eyes were dark hazel, her hair black, her complexion bright, her features symmetrical, her countenance
mild and attractive, and altogether she was one of the hand-
somest women of her day and generation.

After their marriage my parents lived with my maternal
grandmother about a year, when they removed to a farm
purchased by my father in "Dunker's Bottom," on New
river, about twenty miles above English's Ferry, where my
grandfather was drowned. There they lived until the fall of
the year 1779, when, resolved to try their fortune in the
wilds of the "Dark and Bloody Ground," they started with a

1

caravan of emigrants for Kentucky; and, after extreme peril
and privation, they arrived, on the 24th of December, at
Gordon's Station, about four miles northeast of Harrodsburg.
Detained for several weeks in Powell's Valley, hunting for
horses lost by some of the company, they were overtaken by
the "hard winter," after which the impracticability of the
wilderness "trace," and the memorable severity of the weather,
prevented them from traveling more than from three to five
miles a day.   They were cordially welcomed by a large party
of friends, among whom were Col. Stephen Trigg and Capt.
John Gordon.   But there was nothing but warm and hopeful
hearts to cheer their advent.   There was neither bread, nor
milk, nor tea, nor coffee, nor salt, nor meat, except scanty
and precarious supplies of the meat of poor buffaloes, so im-
poverished by the winter as to be unable to get out of the
hunter's way.   Nevertheless the occasion was celebrated by
dancing and festivity; but the only refreshment was a little
parched corn.   And I have heard my mother say that she
never saw a convivial party apparently more happy.

   My parents brought with them their only children, all
daughters — Elizabeth, Margaret, and Jane — the youngest
then only two months old, brought in her mother's lap, and
the others carried in baskets swung on a horse fastened to
the tail of the mare ridden by their mother.   The winter,
memorable for the intensity and unremittedness of the cold,
set in about two weeks before Christmas, and this they all
encountered without permanent injury.   Col. Trigg and
Capt. Gordon, intimate Virginian friends of my father and
mother, having preceded them to Kentucky, induced them
to follow and come to their Station, called "Gordon's."   Before his removal, my father had bought from Gordon and
paid him for 400 acres of land, including the Station, and
contemplated it as his home.   But Gordon's Station, continu-
ing to be occupied, my father bought from Silas Harlan a
tract of land called Harlan's Spring, and settled on it during
the year 1780.   Trigg, Gordon and Harlan all fell in the

Blue Lick defeat, August 19th, 1782 Gordon left an infant son his only heir, who could not convey a valid title to the Station tract. My father, not having seen the land when he bought it, had prudently reserved, in the written contract of sale, the privilege of taking some other of Gordon's various tracts of land, if, after inspection, he should prefer any other. He, however, was pleased with the Station tract, and brought a suit in Chancery against Gordon's heir for a title to it; but the Assistant Judges, Stirling and George Thompson, dismissed his bill only because my father had not, before suit, made a formal selection of the tract he preferred! Incredible as this may be, and discreditable, as it certainly was, to the Court, it is certainly true. I have seen the record of the suit. And thus my father neither got the land he bought, nor any compensation whatever.

During the "hard winter" my parents lived in an open cabin, without a chimney, and which had been built for a smoke-house. The cold was so severe as to prevent either chinking the cracks or adding any chimney. I have heard my mother say that her frozen breath often made the hairs on her head stand out as so many icicles, and that the mildest day during that winter was, to her feelings, the coldest she ever felt before or since. And I have heard her also say that their only food was green buffalo meat, without bread or salt. Nevertheless they enjoyed good health, and were happy with the prospect before them.

The spring, near which my father built cabins and settled in 1780, was among the largest and best in Kentucky. It is one of the chief fountains of "Cane Run," and is near the road leading from Harrodsburg to McCoy's Mill, on Dix river, and about two hundred yards from the road from Lexington to Danville, by the mouth of Dix river.

In 1782 my father built a framed house near his cabins. In that house, yet standing, he died and I was born. It was a common plank house, with two brick chimneys, and three rooms on the first floor, and two porches. It was, when

built, the finest house in Kentucky. His homestead tract
contained nearly 1,000 acres, of which he cleared and cultivated about 200 acres. His farm was beautifully situated,
and he was a neat and thrifty farmer. Modest and unambitious, he neither sought nor desired public position or employment. But his exemplary walk and innate integrity and
amenity made him a general favorite, and drew him reluctantly into public life. He was a member of the first County
Court of Lincoln, afterwards Mercer county. He was elected
a delegate to the Virginia Convention of '88, called to ratify
the Federal Constitution, and also a member of the Virginia
Legislature succeeding the session of the Convention. In
those services he was kept from home until about the middle
of February, 1789. He voted, with Patrick Henry and all
the Kentucky delegates, except Humphrey Marshall, against
the adoption of the Constitution. With my present light I
would have voted for the ratification, which was carried by
the small majority of only eight votes. In 1592 my father
was elected the first Sheriff of Mercer; and this was the last
place of public trust he ever held. He died of pneumonia,
August 15th, 1802, when he was not quite 54 years old. I
was then nearly twelve years old, and have even now a vivid
recollection of him. He died unexpectedly and intestate.
My mother administered on his personal estate, and remained
a widow until the fall of the year 1805, when she was married to Job Johnson, of Garrard, a Methodist, honorable and
amiable, but considerably inferior to her in intellect and
knowledge. She survived her last husband about twenty
years. During her last widowhood she lived with her fourth
daughter, Mrs. Martha McKee, widow of Col. Samuel Mc-
Kee, and mother of Col. William Robertson McKee, who
fell at the battle of Buena Vista, 23d February, 1847. Her
residence adjoined Lancaster. Crushed by the death of her
noble son, she survived him only about a year. My mother
having, in the spring of, the year 1846, gone to Frankfort on
a visit to her youngest daughter, Mrs. Charlotte Le her,

wife of ex Gov. Letcher, there accidentally broke a limb near the hip joint, and was confined to her bed until the 13th of June, 1846, when she died of that fracture, in the 92d year of her age, and was buried in the Frankfort cemetery. She retained her mental faculties to the last, and was as colloquial and edifying the day of her death as she had ever been. Her mind was strong and logical, and her memory was accurate and vivid; and in the last scene of her long earthly drama she could recite poetry by the hour. Her native capacity was far above mediocrity, and she was the best living chronicler of the early history of Kentucky I had ever seen. She was the mentor and almost the idol of a large posterity. She was a favorite wherever she was known, and by all who knew her she was considered a woman of exemplary piety and extraordinary moral harmony and power. She was a member of the Methodist church, and left the scenes of earth with placid resignation and cheerful triumph, her mind full-orbed and unobscured. Her whole life and character properly considered, *she was a model woman.**

My father and mother had ten children, five of each sex. Two of the males died in infancy. My sister Charlotte and

*Judge Robertson, in his address on the first settlement of Kentucky, speaks to his mother in the following words:

" But among you here is one—the lonely trunk of four generations—to whom the heart of filial gratitude and love must speak out one emotion to-day. *Venerable* and *beloved* MOTHER! How often have we heard from your maternal lips the story of Kentucky's romantic birth—of "*the hard winter of '79*"—of all the achievements and horrors of those soul-rending days!

" You have known this land in all its phases. You have suffered with those that suffered most, and sympathized with those who have rejoiced in well-doing and the prospect before them. You have long survived the husband, who came with you and stood by you in your gloomiest, as well as your brightest days, and has long slept with buried children of your love. And now, the sole survivor of a large circle of contemporaneous kindred and juvenile friends—a solitary stock of *three hundred shoots*—with a mind scarcely impaired, you yet linger with us on earth only to thank Providence for his bounties and pray for the prosperity of your flock and the welfare of the land you helped to save and to bless. And when it shall, at last, be your lot to exchange this *Canaan* below for the better *Canaan* above, may you, on the great day of days, at the head of your long line of posterity, and in the presence of the assembled universe, be able, myself alone survive — she the youngest and I the next youngest of the ten children.

with holy joy, to announce the glad tidings—'Here, Lord, **are we and all** the children thou hast ever given us.'"

CHAPTER II.

I was born in Mercer county,* Ky., on the 18th of November, 1790. I was named after my father's elder brother, George, who was a tall, spare, blue-eyed man, more like Gen'l John Adair than I ever saw one man like another. The first incident in my early life, which I remember, is my being dressed in calico slips with yellow ground and brown diamonds, when I was not more than two years old; and my recollection of that dress is yet so distinct as to enable me to identify the calico if it could be now seen. The next event in my youthful days, now distinctly remembered by me, is rather ludicrous, though very near being tragical. It occurred in the fall of the year 1793, when I was about three years old. Among other things, bacon and cabbage had been boiled in a large pot for dinner. The kitchen was about forty feet from the dwelling house. My mother, whom I had followed into the kitchen, having assisted the cook in serving up the dinner, had left me alone, standing near the pot nearly full of boiling "pot-liquor," and just as she had reached the vestibule of the mansion, a large dog, rushing to the pot, threw me into it. My mother, hearing the plunge, ran back in time to save me, which she could not have done had I not been clad in thick woollen cloth. But nevertheless I was so much scalded as to leave an indellible scar on my back. I also remember that sometime in the spring of 1794 breeches were first put on me; and I shall never forget that, preparatory to going to bed, my mother having directed a servant to pull off my pantaloons, my pride revolted with the instinct that he who was man enough to wear breeches, ought to have manhood enough to put them on and take them off, without assistance; and that, in my solitary effort to undress I became so hobbled as to fall in

*See Appendix A.

the fire, whereby a wound was made on my forehead, which is yet visible. These facts may not be universally accredited, yet they are chronologically and substantially true.

I was not sent to school until I was seven years old, and I then for the first time learned the English alphabet. I was considered ugly and irascible. My passions were inordinate and rather eruptive. But I was never wild nor untoward, nor fond of juvenile sports. I was inclined, always, to be solitary, contemplative and taciturn. I was pleased with study, learned rapidly at school, was generally at the head of my class, and never was chastised or rebuked with censure or frown by any one of various preceptors. I was, from my early boyhood, peculiarly susceptible of the tender passions.* At every school I ever attended I was in love. And it is rather singular that each of my dulcineas was named Sally— Sally McGinnis, Sally Haggin and Sally Fry.

My tuition in primary schools was continued until July, 1804, during which time I had acquired a good elementary education in all the English branches then taught in such schools, including English grammar, which I had learned with a peculiar advantage.

On the 4th of August, 1804, my mother sent me to Joshua Fry to learn Latin, French and Geography, which, with other branches, he was then teaching on his farm, five miles west of Danville, Ky., once owned and occupied by George Nicholas. He kept a large boarding-school, composed of the *elite* of both sexes. When I went his classes were all in advance of where I was to begin; and therefore he could not take me in unless, with the tutelage of his son, Dr. John Fry, then in his family, I could soon overtake his junior class in Latin, which had been in progress about eight months. Hopeless of any such achievement, I would have returned home, had not some of those who had been associated with me at the other schools, assured me and made a pledge to Mr. Fry that I would overtake the class in three months. On that assurance I commenced in the first Latin Grammar

I had ever seen. Understanding the English Grammar very
well, I had but little difficulty in committing the Latin, which
I accomplished in five days. On the seventh day I was
reading the colloquies of *Corderius*, and after reading also
Eutropius and *Cornelius Nepos*, I was, at the end of two
months, advanced to the class in Cæsar, who had then been
ten months at the Latin. When I joined them they were at
the Bridge across the Rhine. For three weeks I had much
difficulty in keeping up. But after that probation I could
progress with them by studying not more than half my time,
to employ more of which I studied also Geography and
French; and, at the end of thirteen months from the time I
commenced the Latin, I had a good knowledge of geography, and could read Latin and French almost as well as
English. This rapid progress was the result of intense application, facilitated by severe mental discipline and a sort of
mnemonics, which I had excogitated and practiced some time
before. But an habitual concentration, and a peculiar location and association of objects—in acquisitiveness, though
not in retentiveness—had become extraordinary, and in a
good degree, mechanical. By three or four readings I could
commit almost anything I read. But my memory would
soon lose it. As an illustration of this singular fact I state
that the morning before the day of a commencement at
Transylvania, I was requested by the Academic faculty, for a
reason I need not mention, to commit for my speech, in lieu
of one I had prepared, Major Jackson's eulogy on Washington, occupying about twenty octavo pages in print. I did
it, and the next day delivered it *verbatim*, without a baulk or
uneasy pause. But a week afterwards I could not have recited it without reading it over again. It was thus that I
passed Ruddiman's Latin Grammar in five days, and it was
partly thus, but chiefly by instructive docility and intense
and persevering study, I learned Latin, French and Geography, all well, in thirteen months. I derived much more than
ordinary aid also from my preceptor, who, as far as he at-

tempted to teach, was the best tutor I ever knew.   He
taught ideas more than words—things rather than names.
He illustrated the rationale, **and impressed on the pupil's
mind** the principles of whatever he read; and **he** required
him to repeat a recitation until he understood it thoroughly.
His discipline also was rational and wholesome.   After recitation **the** pupil was free to go where he preferred to go, and
to study where and as he chose; and in genial seasons **he**
rambled over and studied in the groves.   All that was **re-**
quired was that he should act prudently and know his lessons
when called to recite.   The mode of living was also congenial with, and essentially promotive of, physical health and
mental vigor and alacrity.   The males slept **on** straw-beds,
ate for breakfast and supper nothing but bread and milk, **in**
a peripatetic style, without table or chair; washed **before**
dawn, **winter** and summer, at a large spring, **two hundred**
yards **from** the house; and recited early in the morning my
Latin class, reciting by candle-light in the winter   But **the**
exercise of dancing every evening was still better for **both**
mind and body.   There were about twenty girls, **all** nearly
grown, and about thirty boys, of whom I was among the
youngest.   Three daughters of George Nicholas, Ann Gist
(step-daughter of Gen'l Charles Scott), Nancy Birney, Nancy
Warren, and Lucy, Martha and Sally Fry, were among the
female pupils; and **R. P.** Letcher, John B. **Bibb,** Samuel
and Nicholas Casey, John Speed Smith, John **C.** and Charles
W. Short, and David C. Cowan, were **among** the males.
Every secular evening we were called into a large saloon to
dance, under the presidency **of** Mr. and **Mrs. Fry,** and con-
tinued to dance until they retired, when we **instantly ad-**
journed.   Thomas W. Fry, negro **Phil,** and myself, were the
musicians.   **When** I was only ten years old, I had learned to
play on the violin well enough to be engaged as chief fiddler
at dancing parties, and in my early manhood performed on
the violin exceedingly well.*   I look back at the season of

*See Note C.

my pupilage under Mr. Fry, as the happiest as well as the
most eventful portion of my life. Having completed my
course with him about the middle of September, 1805, I
went, about the 1st of November following, to Transylvania
University, and boarded on Hill street with old Mr. Samuel
Price, who lived in a large stone house, on the site of Mr.
John G. Allen's present domicil. My messmates were Robert P. Letcher, Robert P. Henry, Alexander Montgomery,
Alexander M. Edmiston, Anthony W. Rollins, Robert A.
Sturges, Joseph Weisiger, Thomas Washington, Andrew
McMillan, John W. Hovey, and —— Denbril—all of whom,
except McMillan, Bibb, and Weisiger, are now (1st August,
1868,) dead. Most of them became distinguished men.
Montgomery, Edmiston, Weisiger, Rollins, and McMillan,
became physicians, and most of them were eminent in their
profession. Montgomery settled in Frankfort, and fell in
the massacre at Raisin, 23d January, 1813. Edmiston settled in Lancaster, Garrard county, Ky., was my family physician, and died there July 2d, 1812 Rollins settled in
Richmond, Ky., and about the year 1830 removed to Boone
county, Missouri, where, some years afterwards, he died.
He was the father of James S. Rollins, now of that county.
Robert P. Henry was a son of Gen'l Henry, of Scott county,
Ky., became a distinguished lawyer and member of Congress
from the Christian District, and died about the year 1827.
Augustus Henry, of Clarksville, Tennessee, was one of his
brothers. Sturges was also a lawyer, and settled in Rich
mond, Ky., where he died about the year 1827. Weisiger
was a son of Daniel Weisiger, who built and for many years
kept the "Weisiger House" in Frankfort. Dr. W. practiced
his profession successively at Danville, Ky., and now resides
in Texas. John Speed Smith practiced law, was a graceful
speaker, succeeded me in Congress in 1821, lived in Richmond, Ky., and died in that neighborhood about the year
1852. Robert P. Letcher was also a successful lawyer, settled in Lancaster, Ky., beat and succeeded Smith in 1823,

continued in Congress until 1835, was elected Governor of
Kentucky in 1840, was appointed Minister to Mexico by
Gen'l Taylor in 1849, and died in Frankfort in 1861.   Washington was a lawyer of high character at Nashville, Tenn.
McMillan practiced medicine, with success, many years in
Harrison county, Ky., and now lives in retirement in the
suburbs of Lexington.   Hovey and Denbril never studied a
profession, and died many years ago in St. Louis, where they
were born.   Of all our mess Weisiger and myself were the
youngest.

Mr Price had five grown daughters, and two beautiful
daughters of his son-in-law, Gen'l William Russell, staid a
large portion of their time at his house.   Such a social nu-
cleus of promising young females and males attracted to our
house, very often, the elite of the young of both sexes of
Lexington and the neighborhood, and we all had joyous
times.   Often we danced, I being general fiddler;* and sometimes the fiddling and dancing were by moonlight on the
velvet lawn in front of the house.   I often revert to that
period also as among the brightest and most pregnant of my
life.

I remained at Transylvania until the fall of 1806, without
graduating.   I would have been entitled to a diploma had I
staid five months longer, which I was importunately urged
to do by the faculty.   But I had a puerile ambition to win
honors at Princeton, whither my friends had promised to
send me.   But they failed to raise the means, and with my
departure from Transylvania my collegiate course ended.

My mother and sisters having removed to Garrard, I went
to Lancaster† in the autumn of 1806, and, soon finding that
I could not go to Princeton, I attended the Academy at Lancaster, as a pupil of the Rev. Samuel Findley, a Presbyterian
preacher and President of that institution, then extensively
patronized.   I continued that pupilage until the spring of the

*See Appendix D.

†See Appendix B.

year 1807, when I was appointed assistant teacher, in which
situation I continued until the close of that year. The winter of 1808 I devoted to historical and miscellaneous reading.
In April, 1808, I went to Frankfort to read law with Gen'l
Martin D. Hardin; but not being able to engage eligible
boarding, I returned to Lancaster, and there studied law in
the family of my brother-in-law, Samuel McKee, who was
then a member of Congress. My studies were solitary and
unassisted by the instruction or examination of any preceptor. Frequent conversations with Chief-Justice Boyle,
then living near Lancaster, were serviceable to me; and this
was the chief assistance I had in my probationary studies.
In September, 1809, Chief-Justice Boyle, after a thorough
examination, signed my license. The signature of another
Appellate Judge being necessary, I went to Judge Wallace,
of Woodford, who was one of Boyle's associates. The accidental lameness of my horse prevented me from reaching his
house until Sunday morning. He was a Presbyterian. His
family were at breakfast when I arrived and handed him an
introductory letter from Judge Boyle, explaining my object.
Without inviting me to eat or sit down, Judge Wallace, with
morose countenance, reprimanded me for a visit so inoppor-
tune on secular business, in desecration of the Sabbath.
Almost petrified, in such a presence, by such rebuke, I stood
like a statue. Mrs. Wallace, compassionating my condition,
tried to relieve me. She urged me to eat and to go with the
family to church both of which invitations I declined. The
September Term of the Garrard Circuit Court was to commence the next day, and I desired then and there to make
my debut by an address to the grand jury. I therefore resolved to return at once without Judge Wallace's endorse-
ment. The family started to church, leaving me in the yard,
and my horse unfed at the fence. Judge Wallace, after putting a foot in his stirrup, returned, and walking past me to
his office in quest of an overcoat (as *he* said), said to me as
he was passing me, "*Where's your license?*" I handed it to

him, and, after going again to his office, he handed it back to me folded up, and, without uttering a word, passed on to his horse and rode off, leaving me alone. I instantly opened the paper and found his signature! I then thought that in certifying, as he did, that he had carefully examined me and found me well qualified, when he had refused to ask one question on law, he had committed a greater blunder than he could have done by first examining me on the Sabbath.

CHAPTER III.

When I was licensed to practice law I was not quite nine-teen years old ; and I was certainly crud and immature as a lawyer. But feeling a strong desire to assume the responsi-bilities and act on the arena of manhood, I determined to anticipate the growth of a few years, and try my fortune, however premature and perilous my lonely start. I had become acquainted with and engaged to marry my present wife, Eleanor James Bainbridge, a daughter of Dr. Peter Bainbridge, of Lancaster (who was a cousin of Commodore Bainbridge), and of Eleanor James McIntosh, the only daughter of Gen'l Alexander McIntosh, a wealthy planter of South Carolina. My wife had no patrimony, not a dollar. But she was very beautiful. My father's estate was ample enough to have made all his children rich ; but the most of it had been lost by neglect and improvidence before I was old enough to attend to it. I had received none of it. And although my brothers and sisters, older than myself, had distributed among themselves considerable portions of it, and owed me as much as would have made me comfortable and independent, yet I was too proud to ask for, and they were too tenacious to offer me, anything. All I ever received of my father's estate was a horse and an old negro woman, while my oldest brother, although my father died intestate, received the homestead farm of about 750 acres, and some other property.

Yet, thus juvenile, poor, and proud, I ventured not only on the rather hopeless prospects of professional life, but, on the 28th of November, 1809, when I was only ten days over nineteen years of age, I ventured on the far more momentous contingencies of marriage. and, linking my destinies with a wife only fifteen years and seven months old, we embarked,

without freight or pilotage, on the untried sea of early marriage. I had never made a cent, and had nothing but ordi
nary clothes, a horse, an old servant, a few books, and the
humble talents with which God had blessed me. I borrowed
thirteen dollars as an outfit, and out of that fund I paid for
my license and handed to my groomsman, R. P. Letcher,
five dollars for paying the parson, Randolph Hall, father of
Rev. Nathan H. Hall. Some days afterwards Letcher rather
slyly put into my hand a dollar, suggesting that he had saved
that much for me by paying the preacher only four dollars.
This looked to me as such minute parsimony as to excite my
indignation, important as was only one dollar then to me.
And I manifested that feeling in a manner both emphatic
and censorious; to which Letcher replied that four dollars
was more than was then customary, and that Mr. Hall, when
he received it, expressed the warmest gratitude, and said that,
old as he was, he had never received so large a fee for sol-
emnizing the matrimonial rite! This reconciled me to the
return of the dollar.

My wife and myself lived with her mother until the 9th of
September, 1810, when we set up for ourselves in a small
buckeye house with only two rooms, built and first occupied
by Judge Boyle, and respecting which I may here suggest
this remarkable coincidence of successive events:—That Boyle
commenced housekeeping in that house, and, while he occupied it, was elected to Congress; that Samuel McKee commenced housekeeping in the same house, and succeeded
Boyle in Congress; that I commenced housekeeping in the
same house, and succeeded McKee in Congress; and that R.
P. Letcher commenced housekeeping in the same house, and,
after an interval of two years, succeeded me in Congress. I
was unable to furnish it with a carpet, and our only furniture
consisted of two beds, one table, one bureau, six split-bot-
tomed chairs, and a small supply of table and kitchen furniture, which I bought with a small gold watch. I had bought
a bag of flour, a bag of corn meal, a half barrel of salt, and

two hams and two middlings of bacon; and these, together
with the milk of a small cow given to my wife by her mother,
and a few chickens and some butter, constituted our entire
outfit of provisions. But all our supplies were stolen the
night we commenced housekeeping. This was, at that time,
a heavy blow. I had no money; and, though I had good
credit, I resolved not to buy anything on credit. And that
was one of the best resolutions I ever made. It stimulated
my industry and economy, and soon secured to me peace
and a comfortable sense of independence. In adhering to
my privative, but conservative resolve, I often cut and carried on my shoulders wood from a neighboring forest. For
two years I did but little business in my profession. I was
not only too young and crude to expect much, but I was too
proud to seek it and too diffident to manage it in Court without agonizing trepidation. If I expected to make an argument, I could scarcely eat or sleep for days preceding the
appointed time. And I am satisfied that, had I not been a
husband lashed on by necessity, I never would have practiced the law for a livelihood. My experience has convinced
me that, to assure eminence in that profession, both *"poverty
and parts"* are indispensable; and I believe that my poverty
did quite as much for me as my parts. In addition to these
drawbacks, Mr Gallatin, Secretary of the Treasury of the
United States, offered me the appointment of Register of
the Land Office, which the General Government contemplated establishing at St. Louis, for the first sales of public
lands in Missouri. Pleased with the prospects of such a
position, I expected to remove to St. Louis during the year
1811. But the prospect of a war with England, deferred,
from time to time, the opening of the office; and, apprehensive that it would not be opened soon enough for my exigen-
cies, I determined, in the winter of 1812, to renounce the
prospective appointment, and rely altogether on my profession, on which all reliance had been temporarily suspended
by my temporary purpose of removal and devotion to a

2

different avocation.   **When** necessity impelled me to that
resolution, although I had never thought Lancaster the most
eligible location, nor intended to make it my permanent resi-
dence, I was too poor to remove from my kindred and **the**
friends of my youth; **and therefore I** resolved **to** try my
fortune there.   The Garrard Bar was then **very able.**   Mc-
Kee, **Owsley,** and **R.** P. Letcher, were among **its** resident
members; and John Green, Thomas Montgomery, Paul I.
Booker, George Walker, Samuel H. Woodson, and occasionally John Rowan and James Haggin, were among its non-
residents.

Had I gone to St. Louis, under **the** promised auspices, I
think it probable that **I** would have become one of the rich-
est men in America; for, although that **town was** then a
small village, yet I had such prophetic vision **of** its destiny
as to make me resolve, in the event of going there, to apply
every dollar I could spare to **the purchase of land and lots,**
and **to** hold on to the property as long as **the city** might
grow.   But I am well satisfied with my reluctant choice.   I
have always lived comfortably and independent, and have
acquired not only a rational competency of estate, **but as**
much honest fame as I desired or could have earned in **Mis-**
souri.   I never craved more of property than enough to
secure to me and mine independence; and, with prudent
limitation of our wants, **a** comfortable mediocrity will be as
much as needful.   He that cannot be contented with this
would be less tranquil with more, because his appetite is
morbid and becomes more voracious the more it feeds on.
Nor did I **ever** seek **for** fortune to transmit to **my** children.
Hereditary fortune is oftener a curse than a blessing to its
recipients.   **The** best **and only** reliable capital to start **the**
business of **life** on, is good education, moral and physical as
well as intellectual, and domestic as well as academic.   A
young man thus armed will be almost sure to cut his way,
and make and save fortune enough.   But one without such
panoply would scarcely ever make his own, or take care of
patrimonial fortune.

How I sustained my family until the year 1812 I cannot well explain. Often how, without going in debt, which I would not do, I would be able to procure some necessary supply, I could not foresee; but always, at the proper time, Providence provided the means and pointed out the way; and I lived well and happily. And here candor requires that I should state that I indulged, more from necessity than taste, some associations and habits, the memory of which, even yet, subjects me to self humiliation. Most of my associates frequently spent considerable portions of their time in various games of cards. Not having much business to do, I often played with them, sometimes for amusement, but generally for money, *honorably* to be won or lost by fair play and skill alone. I soon acquired extraordinary skill, and, with reasonable luck, I was considered invincible by fair means. I never employed any other means, and had, by observation and association at the card table, become so thoroughly acquainted with human nature in all its multiform phases, as to be able to prevent my adversaries from the successful employment of dishonorable artifice or other false means. While I was in the habit of playing, I do not remember that, in any one instance, I ever lost anything. Our games were generally loo and whist, and the betting was on a moderate scale. I almost always won from five to fifty dollars—sometimes more than fifty, not often less than five dollars. I have alluded to this occasional deflection in my early life to explain how, for the first three years of my marriage, I maintained my family without going in debt. But while I regret the aberration on account of its pestilent example, I feel no other cause for self-reproach. I never cheated, or dissembled, or did any other act dishonorable or reprehensible in all my card playing; and it not only kept me from starvation or servile dependence, but made me practically acquainted with the wiles and ways of men, to an extent which I could not otherwise have attained.

In 1812, having abandoned my Missouri purpose, and de-

termined to rely on my profession alone, and not being able
to remove from Lancaster,* where I had neither expected
nor desired to remain long, I accepted from the Circuit Judge
(Kelly), the office of Prosecuting Attorney for Garrard, and,
devoting myself sedulously to the law, I soon received encouraging patronage, and was cheered with assuring proph-
ecies of success.   I did succeed.   And it was not long before
I was engaged in nearly all the litigated causes near me,
without ever soliciting employment.   I never encouraged a
litigous. spirit, often induced antagonist parties to compromise, and oftener induced forbearance in frivolous and vin-
dictive cases, in which the least professional countenance
would have bred vexatious litigation.

     I had more success in argument before a court than a jury.
I never had much of the ad captandum.   I was quite fluent,
and was accurate in style and pronunciation.   I relied on
lucid order and the logic of ideas on the law and the facts.
I never wrote out or committed any portion of a speech at
the bar.   Nor was I accustomed to take notes of the testimony; finding that they confused and diluted my argument,
I generally relied altogether on my memory, which, whenever it was my sole reliance, never failed as to any material
fact or witness.   And thus retaining all that was essential,
and unembarrassed by non-essentials, my memory was more
vivid, my ideas more consecutive and clear, and my argu
ment more vigorous, concentrated and impressive.   I was a
clear, chaste and ingenious debater, but was never what is
generally considered an orator.   I succeeded in many hopeless cases, and but seldom lost a good one.   I charged low
fees, and was so indulgent in the collection of them as to lose
about half of my earnings.   I never deceived a client, nor
played on his ignorance or fear or confidence in me, to extort an exorbitant fee.   And invariably, when I had done a
client's business without a special contract, I charged the
minimum fee for the like services.   As early as 1815, I had,

*See Note B, Appendix.

by study and practice, become a good lawyer, and when only 25 years old, I thought I knew more law than I think I do now at the mellow age of 68. This was not the effect of juvenile vanity, so much as of comparative ignorance; and my case, in that respect, is every man's case who progresses in knowledge. The sciolist is dogmatic and vain, because he is ignorant of the vast field of knowledge unseen by his circumscribed vision. The higher he rises the more extended becomes his horizon of unexplored knowledge; and the more he learns the more he feels the insignificance and uncertainty of all human knowledge, compared with a philosophical cyclopedia of universal truth; consequently the more he knows, the more he sees which he does not know, and his humility increases, *pari passau*, with his progress in *true science*.

I remember many forensic incidents which occurred in my junior practice—some of them didactic, some intensely dramatic, and some ridiculously ludicrous—and, for the amusement of those who shall come after me in a more. polished age, I will here recite three of the latter character.

1. * * * * "Sheriff," said the Judge, "take that man to the stocks and keep him there till the further order of the Court." "There's no stocks," replied the Sheriff. "Then," rejoined the Judge, "I see a new fence near the door; take him there, raise some of the rails and put his neck between them." The Sheriff executed the last order; and the rails, being new and large, choked the man until the Sheriff, thinking he was dying, ran into Court, and, acquainting the Court with the alarming fact, was directed to take the man out. When the Sheriff extricated him he was breathless and blue, and was not revived for some time, but, as soon as he could speak, swore that it was the last time he would be guilty of contempt. Of that scene I was not a spectator, but the facts are well authenticated.

2. I was at the first Circuit Court holden in Mount Vernon, Rockcastle county. There was no court-house. A

large log-house (Langford's), without any opening, for ven-
tilation, except a door and a small window on the same side,
was fitted for the temporary use of the Court, by a high
bench for the Judge to sit on, and a lower one to rest his
feet on, each made of the 'half of a green poplar tree, split
for the occasion. The first day of the term was an exceedingly hot one in August; and a large crowd of men, women
and children having come, in their mountain habiliments, to
see the first Court ever opened in that quarter of the State,
the court-room was full of humanity and human odor, with
scarcely more vital atmosphere than the "black hole of Cal-
cutta." Judge Kelly had taken some mint punch, and was
very much annoyed by heat, stench and noise. Henry Buford, the Clerk, was fond of a dram, and had taken a little
too much. He sat at a square table in front of the Judge.
In the evening, when the Judge had become impatient and
irascible, a large fat man, named Spencer, dressed in leather
hunting shirt, breeches and moccasins, with a butcher's knife
at his side, disturbed the Court by obstreperous cursing near
the door. The Sheriff, having brought him into Court
drunk, the Judge fined him five shillings for being drunk.
He pulled out a long and greasy leather purse, full of silver
dollars. The attention of the entire crowd was attracted by
the novel scene, and perfect silence prevailed during the
whole drama. After repeated efforts to untie the purse,
Spencer carefully picked out a dollar and tendered it to the
Clerk, saying, "There, Harry, give me my change." The
Clerk having refused to take the money, Spencer, drunk as
he was, crawled up to the Judge, and, holding the dollar
between his fingers, said, "Here, Mr. Kelly, is your money;
take your pay and give me my change." The Judge, re-
buking him, told him that it was not his money, and he
would not change his dollar. Thereupon Spencer deliber-
ately replaced his dollar in his purse, which having slowly
tied, he marched out through the crowd with a triumphant
and defiant port, ejaculating, "The *poorest* Court *I ever* seed
—can't change a dollar!"

3. Many years after the foregoing scene, another Judge of the same Court, arriving through mud and rain the first day of a term, took the bench wet and chilled, and in a mood not altogether pleasant. The crowd in and out of the court house was large, and disturbed the Court by noise. A jack led around the court-house aggravated the disturbance, and the Judge had ordered it to be removed. The order not being promptly obeyed, the jack continued for sometime to bray near the court-house. Just at that time a man was heard cursing loud at the door, who, being brought in for contempt, was fined. He then, in a suppliant tone, assured the Court that he had intended no contempt, and in response to the question, "Why were you swearing so loud at the door?" said, "Judge, a man was showing a little jackass around the court-house, and the jack was braying so that nobody could hear nothing else, and the Court couldn't do no business, and I jest said, *God damn that jack*." The Judge, rising with sympathetic indignation, said to the Clerk, "Remit that fine; *I say damn the jack too*."

When I was engaged as prosecuting attorney, an unusual quantity of indictments were filed for misdemeanors and crimes, principally in the county of Knox, one of which I may be permitted to mention with emphasis, on the last day of the Knox February term, and after the Grand Jury had been adjourned, two twin brothers from North Carolina, passing through to Indiana, and genteelly clad, were brought into Court on the charge of larceny at Cheek's public house, on the high road, a special Grand Jury was summoned and found true bills against both of them, each of whom was thereupon tried, convicted and sentenced to confinement in the Penitentiary, and before sundown that same day they were both on their way to the place of punishment. This remarkable case may illustrate the dispatch and fidelity of the public functionaries of that day in the mountains of Kentucky.

I resided in the house I first occupied only three months.

I removed to a framed house with two rooms, called the tanyard place, improved by Col. Yantis. There my oldest child, Margaret Eliza, was born January 25th, 1811. She was born apparently dead. We named her after my mother and my wife's sister, Shackleford. She was married to William S. Buford, when she was only about three months over seventeen years of age. She is still living, the mother of nine children, is also a grandmother, and is only about twenty years younger than her father.

In the summer of the year 1811 I removed to a log house on the Danville street, adjoining a framed house on the southwest corner of the public square. There my daughter, Eleanor McIntosh, was born January 28th, 1813, and was named after her maternal grandmother. She was married to Dr. Samuel M. Letcher, is the mother of seven children, and now lives near me in Lexington.

About a year before her birth, finding that I wasted small sums of money which I thought I might prudently save, I cut a hole in the top of a closed cigar box, and determined to put into it every piece of silver I could from time to time spare, for one year, for the purpose of saving all I could without mean self-denial. At the end of the experimental year, supposing that I had not saved more than about fifty dollars, I opened the box and was agreeably surprised when I found four hundred and fifty dollars, not one cent of which would I have saved had I not resorted to that expedient. With this discovery I felt quite rich; and, to avoid a waste, I immediately invested the fund in a new brick house on the north side of Danville street, to which I removed in April, 1813, and where I lived nine years. There my daughters, Mary Oden Eppes and Charlotte Corday, and my son, Alexander Hamilton, were born—the first, May the 5th, 1815; the second, June the 14th, 1817; and the last, March the 17th, ——.

Not long after I became a freeholder I abstained more and more from card playing for money, until about the year

1821, when I quit it altogether. As long as I continued to play, I was inflexibly abstemious, and acquired no other bad habit or taste from improper associations. When I was not more than eight years old I had been so much tempted with intoxicating liquors used almost daily by company at my father's, as to fear that my appetite had become morbid; and convinced that if I persisted much longer in the indulgence of it I could never be a proper man, I resolved to try the experiment of total abstinence. But fearing that I could not adhere to a resolution *never* to drink, and even then feeling that to break a mental pledge would impair the efficacy of a re-resolve, I determined not to taste for one month. This, through great temptation and tribulation, I completely fulfilled. But it was a sort of *experimentum crucis*. My self-complacency at my triumph more than compensated for all the privation and agony of the fearful ordeal. When my month was out I did not, as most boys and even men would have done, drink a drop, but, concluding that as I succeeded once, I could more easily and certainly succeed again. I continued tetotalism from month to month for more than a year before my appetite was entirely subdued. For several years afterwards I tasted no intoxicating drink, and can truly say that, although in my public life I have been in many convivial parties where others became inebriated, yet I was never drunk in my whole life. I never allowed myself to pass the limit of pleasant exhilaration and perfect self-possession.

In 1814 I was appointed principal assessor of the Federal direct tax for my Congressional district. The duties of that office engaged a large portion of my time for about a year, and enabled me to make nearly twelve hundred dollars, and extend my acquaintance with the people of the district. The manner in which I fulfilled the trust and mixed with the people in a candid, upright and affable spirit, commended me to their approval and favorable consideration. I also argued causes at the bar. In 1815 I appeared in the Mercer Circuit

Court for the first time as sole counsel for Gen'l **Thomas** Kennedy, in an action of detinue brought against **him by Edward** Worthington, for about fifty **valuable slaves.** Rowan, James **Haggin, and several** other distinguished counsel, appeared for **Worthington.** I **had** confidence in **my** case, which **turned, as I** thought, **on the legal question** whether **an** oral gift to Mrs. Worthington in Virginia since 1758, and **when** she was **an** infant in the family of her father, under **whose** transfer Gen'l Kennedy claimed the descendants of a female slave so given to the child, was valid against *bone fide* purchasers from her father. Being comparatively young, at a strange and celebrated bar, and standing alone against such an array of the most distinguished lawyers in Kentucky, **and** in a cause so important, I advised my wealthy client to employ some assistant counsel. But having been successful for him in other cases, he ignorantly thought **that** I could not fail in **a** good cause, and *would* stake his fifty slaves on me alone. When the Plaintiff closed his evidence I moved for a non-suit, which motion, after elaborate argument, was sustained **by** Judge Kelly, who, although a brother-in-law and admirer of Rowan, was also my friend, and firm **and impartial** in his judgments. My argument and success in that **case** gave me **great eclat** and more reputation than I deserved.

CHAPTER IV.

As early as the close of the year 1815, when I was only about 25 years of age, I had, through my little office and my profession, become a rather conspicuous favorite in my Congressional district. In the spring of 1816, the only newspaper in the district—the Luminary—announced that McKee would not be a candidate for re-election, and that I was a candidate to succeed him. I never could ascertain why or at whose instance that announcement had been made. McKee, who was my brother-in-law, had not declined, though he had been talking about a purpose to do so, and I had never thought of being a candidate. Having just then obtained an extensive practice, and being poor and the father of three children, I had no political aspirations, and felt that to quit my practice, just become profitable and promising, and embark on the sea of political life, would be premature and inexcusably unjust to my dependent and growing family. Under the influence of that sentiment, strengthened by surprise and mortification at a publication so unauthorized, so unexpected, and so unwelcome, I resolved to contradict the announcement; but McKee and other friends advised me to await some spontaneous development of public opinion. I soon discovered that my supposed candidacy was favorably received, and that I could probably be elected. I then concluded to let the people use me as a candidate, resolving, as I thought I did inflexibly, that, if elected, I would serve only one term, and employ no electioneering means of conciliating popular favor.

In a short time Gen. Robert B. McAfee, Governor Slaughter, Col. George C. Thompson, all of Mercer, and Gen. Samuel South, Major Robert Caldwell, and John Speed Smith, all of Madison, were also announced as candidates. After feeling the popular pulse, all of these competitors, except Caldwell and Smith, declined; and Smith also declined about two months before the election, leaving the track to Caldwell and myself, who ran the race alone, and which resulted in my election by a majority of 1,036 votes. At Harrodsburg alone I received, on the first of the three days election, about 1,000 votes, which was the best vote ever given there for any candidate before or since. And in my own county of Garrard I lost only 62 votes during the entire election.

During the whole canvass I drank nothing intoxicating myself, and was opposed in principle to the use of any such prostituting argument for aiding my election. I told the people so in my public addresses, in which I was, in all respects, perfectly candid. I did not desire success otherwise than by a spontaneous preference of me, after as full an exhibition of my principles and character as I could afford to the electors. To have succeeded on any other ground would have been to me not an honorable, but humiliating, triumph. Consequently, although the political obligation of popular instructions was the current and apparently universal doctrine, and no inquiry was made of me concerning it, nevertheless I felt it my duty to tell the people that I did not recognize that doctrine, and that, if elected, I would, with proper respect for public opinion, always act on my own judgment of my duty to my whole country, and on my whole responsibility, representative, personal, and constitutional. And while my prudent and more diplomatic friends expostulated and argued that I would gratuitously commit suicide by advocating an unpopular doctrine, which no other person agitated, I continued to discuss it, because I was unwilling to be elected without showing a full hand. And the result proved that the truth, *properly defended*, will, sooner or later, be indorsed by the people, and will never long injure its firm, candid, and competent champion. In all my elections to Congress and the State Legislature I never used money or liquor to procure votes; nor did I ever conceal or dissemble an opinion to conciliate opposition. I never resorted to any species of artifice or electioneering otherwise than by what little intrinsic strength I possessed and the power of my principles. I never, at the polls or in a deliberate assembly, gave a vote on any other ground than principle; therefore, had I the power, I would not change a vote I ever gave. Consequently I never felt any embarrassment or perturbation in the discharge of my public duties, and was never disturbed by any fear of, responsibility. My controlling maxim was "better to be right even at the cost of temporary ostracism, than to be President at the expense of hypocrisy, felt error, or remorse of conscience." And now, for the encouragement of others, I am pleased to say that I never suffered in public opinion or incurred reproach for any vote I ever gave.

In my first canvass for Congress an incident occurred, both ludicrous and memorable, which I may, without impropriety, here record. Clay county, on the frontier of my district, included all the Cumberland mountain territory now in that county and the counties of Harlan, Letcher, Perry, Owsley, and Breathitt. My first visit to that county was in June, about six weeks before the election. I reached Manchester late in the afternoon of the first day of a Circuit Court. I was surprised to see a crowd of nearly two thousand men, women and children, who had congregated from all parts of the county to see Court, which many of them had never seen before. I had never before seen more than a dozen of the voters of the county. Caldwell and Smith were both well acquainted there, and were popular; and each of them used money and whisky without stint. Finding the vast crowd clamorously shouting, some for Caldwell, some for Smith,

and none for me, I regretted that I was there. Without
speaking to any person, I retired to a shed of the cabin
tavern, and there remained sleepless all night.   Ruminating
on what I should do to initiate an acquaintance with the sov-
ereigns of the mountains, I concluded to make a public address to them; but I was perplexed as to the character of
the speech best adapted to such an auditory.   Before I left
my room next morning I had moulded the substance of my
speech, and when Court was about to sit I was politely tendered by the Judge the use of the court-yard, and the Sheriff
having made proclamation of my purpose, a vast crowd soon
surrounded me and listened with great respect and interest
to my speech, which happened to hit the nail right on the
head.   I never made a speech so universally satisfactory and
effectual.   I was greeted with obstreperous applause, and
the people of all ages and both sexes sought introductions to
me, and followed me with shouts and pledges of their support.   This result was so unexpected as to make me feel
much self-complacency.   But, apprehending that the favorable impression I had made would be transient and be soon
overcome by other influences, I had no expectation that,
without organization or money, I would receive many votes.
I intended instantly to leave for home not to return; and,
full of gratification for the first fruits of my hopeless visit as
a stranger, I started for the tavern to pay my bill and order
my horse, but, attracted by an immense circle of men and
women, I paused, on my way, to see what they were doing;
and, finding that persons were dancing within the ring, I
I pressed through to the inner edge of the circle, and saw a
man dancing a solo to the fiddle of a small man, half Indian,
named *Sisemore*, who had come from Lee county, in Virginia, to play for the occasion.   I observed that the dancer
had on an old iron spur, and that when he had finished his
part in the novel drama, his successor put on the same spur.
The reason of this I did not inquire, but presumed that it
was to show the superior skill of the dancer.   While I was

thus enjoying the strange scene as a spectator, I observed
men on the opposite side of the circle engaged in conversation and looking toward and pointing at me. I at once
thought that some person had told them that I performed
admirably on the violin, and that they were consulting about
inviting me to give them a sample of my music. I was not
mistaken. They approached me, and, bowing, said that
having heard that I was the greatest fiddler in the world,
they requested me to play a tune. Anticipating their object
before they saluted me, I had resolved to comply with their
request with apparent alacrity; for, although it was almost
crucifixion to be placed in such a position—a candidate for
Congress fiddling in the street for such a multitude—yet I
knew that refusal would be ascribed by them to aristocratic
pride, and seal my destiny in the mountains; and, feeling
that reluctant compliance would be unsatisfactory, I determined to make the effort without hesitancy and with all
possible grace. I therefore instantly responded that I could
not equal their Virginia musician, but that I would, with
pleasure, do the best I could. Sisemore played unusually
well for such an occasion; and, although with a good violin
and at a suitable place, I could then play exceedingly well, I
apprehended that, there in the open air, on a cracked fiddle
I had never touched, and in such a presence, I would not
please the expectant crowd as well as Sisemore; consequently, knowing how much depended on my performance,
I took his backwoods fiddle and tuned it with as much
tremulous anxiety as Wellington when he commenced the
battle of Waterloo. They requested an old Virginia reel,
which was one of my favorites. I did my best, and played
the tune with variations in such a style as to transport, with
obstreperous joy, the whole crowd. Sisemore was kicked
out, and told that he was no fiddler. The people were so
spell-bound as to detain me, *vi et armis*, for two days and
nights. They all declared that I *should* be elected, and some
of the men swore that they would go with me to Washington just to hear and dance after my music on the way.

Knowing the popularity and appliances of my competitors, I expected that the good impressions my speech and music had made would be fugitive, and soon give way to other influences. This was my first and last visit to Clay. I left not a dollar, and made no arrangements for organizing and bringing voters to the polls. Smith declined, and Major Caldwell and myself ran the race out alone. I received about 800 votes, and Caldwell only about 70.

In the canvass and election, I did not spend a dollar, except for a printed circular and traveling expenses, which altogether did not amount to fifty dollars! I had no money to waste, and, if I had been as rich as Astor or Girard, opposed in principle to the prostitution of the elective franchise, I would not, to save my election, have applied, directly or indirectly, one cent to bribery. In all my addresses I told the people so. And this, in my judgment, helped much more than it hurt me.

When I received the certificate of my election I was not twenty-six years old; but I did not take my seat until I was about ten days over twenty-seven. The best mode of traveling then was on horseback; and I thus went to Washington in November, 1817, and also in 1818, and consumed nineteen days in the first, and seventeen days in the latter trip. Members of Congress then earned their allowance of three dollars for every twenty miles of a travel, which was comparitively tedious, toilsome, and expensive. And I will here mention an incident in my first trip to Washington, which may be as useful as it is incredible: I bought a blooded three-year old horse for my first journey to the National Capital. He had never been shod. An old friend in Garrard (Elijah Hyatt), who was famous for both skill and care in the management of horses, took my young horse and prepared him for the work before him. The day before I started for my destination, he selected the iron and the shoes, saw the shoes put on and every nail made and driven; and when he brought the horse to me, he said, "Now,

George, *all's right;* your horse will carry you over the long and rocky road to Washington without breaking a shoe or loosening a nail." And so it turned out. Several gentlemen who accompanied me frequently had their horses' shoes removed or repaired, and mine reached Washington with his shoes apparently as sound and firm as when I started. I sent him to the country to be kept during the session, which continued about seven months. He was brought in to me the day I left for home, and the keeper told me he had used him as his saddle horse, and never had touched his shoes, which appeared as good as ever Being impatient to start, I did not have them examined, but rode him as he was to Wheeling, brought him to Maysville on a flatboat or ark, and rode him thence to Lancaster; and when I reached home his hoofs and shoes seemed to be in good condition!

During the session of the Kentucky Legislature, commencing the first Monday in December, 1816, a resolution passed the House of Representatives for a new election of Governor over the head of the Lieutenant Governor, whose term of four years had just commenced. This led to a popular excitement which agitated the State almost to revolution for more than a year. In the summer of 1817 I wrote an argument against a new election, over the signature of "*A Kentuckian,*" which the sympathizing party had published and extensively circulated in pamphlet form. It turned the tide, and gave me a very high character, much beyond my deserts. Thus I took my seat the first Monday in December, 1817, under auspices peculiarly encouraging. I was put on the Committee of Internal Improvement, then one of the most important, especially as the President (Monroe) had, in his first message, attempted to forestall Congress by an argument against the constitutionality of congressional appropriations for national improvements. Gen'l Tucker, of Virginia, was chairman, and Henry Storrs and Gen'l Talmadge, of New York, were associate members of the committee. We were unanimously of the opinion that the

3

President was wrong, and so reported. But, as strict con-
structionism prevailed in Virginia, our chairman, who wrote
an elaborate report, argued only to prove the power *with
the consent of the States!* The other members of the committee thought that, if the Constitution did not confer the
power, the States could not. But, to go with their chairman, they consented to his report as far as it went, reserv-
ing the right to urge, in oral argument, the *unconditional*
power. The chairman opened the debate on the report.
It was expected that P. P. Barbour, of Virginia, would re-
ply, and, by the arrangement of the committee, I was to
answer *him.* As I was the youngest member in the House,
and had this herculean duty devolved on me before I had
made my *debut,* I prepared a written speech, moulded for
such additions as the occasion might suggest   Mr. Clay
read and extolled it. It contained all the substantial arguments ever since made in favor of the power. But it was
never delivered. When Gen'l Tucker closed his opening
speech, and Barbour, as expected, was taking the floor,
Mr. Clay rose and challenged him to a single combat; and
consequently when Barbour closed, the committee yielded the
immediate rejoinder to Mr. Clay, who, therefore, followed
him and anticipated so many of my arguments as to preclude
me from then speaking with proper respect for the House or
myself. A protracted debate ensued. While it continued
I was frequently urged to speak, and every day took the floor
for that purpose; but some bolder and more practical debater always got the start of me, until I felt that it was too
late for me to speak to reluctant ears. I retained the draft
of that projected speech until lately, and, by comparing it
with all that has since been urged by others, can truly say
that it presented every good argument that has ever been
made in favor of the power.

My first speech was made on a commutation bill, which,
on my argument, was radically changed by an unanimous
vote.

During the session, which closed in May, I acquired a character better than I had any right to expect. In April I went with my friend and colleague, R. C. Anderson, to Philadelphia, where we remained a week, seeing and enjoying much. Our *fille de chambre* was a beautiful girl, the daughter of a lady of broken fortunes, who resided in a fine house opposite to the "Mansion House" on Third street, where we sojourned. The only compensation the servants expected was from the voluntary contributions from the patrons of the hotel. When I left I handed her five dollars. She thanked me graciously, and said that some dog who had been occupying my room not long before had given her only a lottery ticket, which she considered worthless. But I was gratified by reading in a Philadelphia paper, shortly after my return to Washington, that her ticket drew the highest prize of $100,000!

At the first dinner after our arrival in Philadelphia, an incident occurred which was rather embarrassing to me. A few minutes after our names had been registered, dinner was announced. On entering the dining saloon I discovered a brilliant party, consisting chiefly of foreign diplomats and naval officers, and I saw that every plate except Anderson's and mine was served with bottles of various wines. This was what I had never seen before. Without inquiry or reflection, I supposed that wine was a part of the dinner, and was, for convenient use, placed at each plate; and that the only reason why our two plates were not supplied like all the others, was that the dinner service had been completed before we arrived. With that impression, I bowed to a naval officer to my left (Commodore Chauncey, I think,) and asked him to join me in a glass of wine, he having three bottles and I none. After a momentary pause of evident surprise, in which the other guests seemed to sympathize, he courteously assented, and requested me to choose my wine. I shortly afterwards proposed a glass to Anderson, which he significantly declined, having, as I also had, discovered, by

the impression my blunder had made, that all was not *a la*
Chesterfield.   As soon as I had dined I reprimanded the
major domo for not furnishing me with wine.   He, instead of
replying that I had ordered none, apologized, and promised
that, if I would excuse him, I should have no further cause
to complain, and, inquiring what kind of wine I would have
for dinner next day, I ordered a bottle of Maderia and
another of Sherry, intending to redeem my character next
day.   But, to my regret, my neighbor was gone.   And I
have no doubt that he often told the ludicrous anecdote about
the young member of Congress from the backwoods of Kentucky.

I returned home about the 22d of May, 1818.   Col. R.
M. Johnson, J. J. Crittenden, and myself travelled home-
ward together—Col. J. in a Jersey wagon, and Mr. C. and I
on horseback to Wheeling, whence we descended to Maysville in an ark, with much privation and discomfort.   When
I beheld my native Kentucky,* at the mouth of the Big
Sandy, I could not refrain from tears; my long absence and
instinctive attachments overwhelmed me with the memories
and the hopes of young wife and children and "*Sweet
Home.*"

On reaching home I found John Speed Smith a candidate
for my seat; and, although I did not desire a re-election,
and had so announced, yet unwilling to be apparently shoved
out, I felt it due to honor to become a candidate again.   But
after canvassing the district a few days, Smith again declined,
and I was re-elected without any opposition.   During the
next session, without consulting any person, even my friend
John Scott, then the delegate from Missouri, I introduced a
bill for the organization of the Territory of Arkansas.   When,
on discussion, the House became reconciled to the bill, and
it was ready for the question on the third reading, John W.
Taylor, of New York, moved an amendment interdicting
slavery.   After an exciting debate, the amendment for pro-

*See Appendix C.

spective interdiction prevailed by a vote of 72 against 70.
On my motion, the bill was then recommitted to a large and
conservative committee, who struck out the anti-slavery
clause, and recommended the passage of the bill in the original form in which I had first presented it. On the question
of concurring with the committee, two of my Northern
friends, who had voted for Taylor's amendment, being pur-
posely absent, the vote was 70—70, and Mr. Clay (then
Speaker) gave the casting vote against Congressional intervention. My speech against intervention was published, and
is yet preserved in my "Scrap-Book." In that speech I conceded the mere power of Congress, but endeavored to show
that policy forbade the exercise of it; and *I predicted the
consequences which would result, and have resulted, from the
national agitation of slavery.*

President Monroe offered me the appointment of Governor
of the new Territory, which I first declined; but, being
urged by his Cabinet, I agreed to accept, with the understanding that I would take my family to the Territory, and,
if we should be unwilling to make it our permanent home, I
might resign. There were several applicants for the office,
all of whom withdrew because they were told by the President that I would be appointed. But in the meantime I
voted for Mr. Clay's Seminole resolutions, which offended
Mr. Monroe, who then revoked his invitation on pretence of
ineligibility on the ground that I voted to create the office,
although the law was postponed in its operation until the
4th of July, 1819, four months after the expiration of my
Congressional term, and although many precedents recognized my constitutional eligibility; and even though the
Cabinet unanimously decided that the President's objection
was indefensible. These facts being known, nearly every
Senator, and multitudes of others in high position, voluntarily, without my agency, urged my appointment. I was
then a favorite in Kentucky, and popular in Congress, and a
knowledge of this fact, and the unusual importunity and

unanimity of disinterested men in my favor, impressed the
President with the perilous responsibility of his conduct.
And, to help rescue him in Kentucky, he, without solicitation, nominated my brother-in-law, R. P. Letcher, a Judge,
and R. Crittenden, brother of J. J. Crittenden, Secretary of
Arkansas.   On the third of March, a Cabinet council was
held on the subject of my appointment, at the close of which
John Quincy Adams, Secretary of State, requested me not
to leave, as I intended, that day for home, as the President
would send my nomination to the Senate in an hour, and desired me to remain a few days to receive some instructions.
But in less than an hour, Col. Miller, of the army, who had
never before been suggested for the office, was nominated!
This surprised Cabinet, Senate, and all applicants for territorial appointments, and, as much as any other person, Miller,
Letcher, and Crittenden themselves.

This case illustrates one of Mr. Monroe's infirmities—unreasonable and invincible obstinacy when egotism or passion
operated on his opinions.

Having promised to accept the appointment on the condition that if, on a visit with my family to the Territory, I
should prefer not to settle there, I might resign, I bought a
traveling carriage at $1,000, for which I had no use in Ken-
tucky, and the purchase of which absorbed one-fourth of
my estate; and I did think that the President ought to have
taken this unbefitting incumbrance off my hands.   But all
he ever did for reparation was to offer me, as he afterwards
did, several more attractive offices than the proconsulship of
Arkansas—all of which I declined on an inflexible resolve
to accept no favor from him.   In the summer of 1819 he
visited Kentucky and sojourned for some weeks at the Green-
ville Springs, in my district, where I attended him during his
stay and treated him with all proper courtesy and hospitality;
and when he left, I accompanied him to a ball given to him
at Danville, and introduced him to my constituents there
assembled to see and to honor him.   Had I received the

appointment provisionally, as alone I had agreed, I am satisfied that I would not have retained it long, or settled in Arkansas.

In 1820 I initiated the present system of selling the public lands, which, as a substitute for the former mode of selling on credit at a minimum of two dollars an acre, requires payment without credit, reduced to the minimum of price to one dollar and twenty-five cents, and of quantity to eighty acres, whereby any poor man who could command one hundred dollars might purchase a home, and non resident speculations were in a great degree prevented, heavy and hopeless indebtedness to the General Government avoided, and the population of the vacant territories facilitated and encouraged. I now, as I then anticipated and argued, look on this as one of the most beneficent measures ever enacted by Congress. The Western members, with the exception of R. C. Anderson, Ben Hardin, and myself, opposed it as anti-western, and I was warned that my support of it would seal my political ostracism. But, sure that I was right, I urged it in defiance of the prospect of personal proscription. *Henry Clay* opposed it with great zeal, and his argument against it occupied the session of one day. I replied to him in a speech of three hours length, the substance of which was published in the "National Intelligencer," and is preserved in my "Scrap-Book."

To my surprise, no one of my constituents complained of my conduct, and the act soon became universally popular. The discussion was confined almost exclusively to Mr. Clay and myself, and the bill was passed by a majority of about four-fifths of the votes in the House of Representatives. When General Harrison was a candidate for President, his popularity was greatly increased in the West and Northwest by the ascription to *him* of the authorship of that enactment. I was silent, and he then got the credit of it, though he was not even a member of Congress when it was introduced and passed.

During a service of four years, I was a member of the committee on internal improvement, and also of the judiciary, and chairman of the committee on private land claims. In the latter capacity I saved to the Government the whole of the land called the Washita grant. Reports had been successively made in favor of the claimants by Richard Rush as Attorney General, and by Albert Gallatin and A. J Dallas, Secretaries of the Treasury. Robert Walsh, as agent of the claimants, presented their claims to my committee. The original grantee undertook to bring to that country four hundred families and settle them within a definite boundary. He and his assignees constituting the petitioning company, claimed all the land within the prescribed limits, on the ground that he had partially performed his contract, and would have fulfilled his entire undertaking had the Government complied with its obligations, and that his failure was produced by conduct of the Government. The committee, excepting myself, were for some time unanimous for a report in favor of the claim. I deferred a report until I ascertained, and convinced the other members, that had the grantee fulfilled his whole contract he would have been entitled only to certain water power for flouring and other manufacturing purposes, and could have had, in no event, a right to any land. And finally we so reported, and Mr. Walsh retired greatly disappointed, and the claim has never been renewed.

I had been elected for a third term, the elections then being the year before the commencement of the term. But, on my return home after the close of my second term, I resigned my third term. I was pleased with political life, and my prospects were encouraging. Had I been affluent, or without a family, I would have preferred to continue in public life. But, poor, and having a growing family, I felt a a paramount and sacred obligation to give up my political prospects, and devote myself to my profession and my wife and children.

CHAPTER V.

In the spring of the year 1821, I resumed the practice of law, and soon had as much employment as I could well attend to. Gov. Adair, though a political opponent, spontaneously offered me the Attorney Generalship of Kentucky, which I declined; after which he, in like manner, tendered me the Judgeship of the Fayette Circuit, backed by an offer of the Trustees of Transylvania of the professorship of law in that institution, both of which I also declined, because I desired no office, and felt resolved to prosecute my profession vigorously for some years, until I could thereby procure a competency for independence, which I might have done in ten years or less.

But the professional purpose of my resignation of a seat in Congress was, in a great degree, frustrated by my Garrard constituents, who, in 1823, *nolens volens*, sent me to the House of Representatives of the Kentucky Legislature, to help to guide the ship of State through the *"relief and anti-relief"* and *"new and old court"* storm which had then commenced to rage, and which, having reluctantly embarked, I rode out until 1827, when it was lulled by the final triumph of the Constitution. During three years of that service I was Speaker of the House of Representatives, and during the whole of it was almost incessantly engaged, on the stump, through the press, and in the Legislature, in debating the constitutional questions which agitated the State more than it was ever convulsed before or since. Some of those addresses are preserved in my "Scrap Book," and may speak for themselves and for me.

During that convulsive period I had to neglect my forensic practice to such an extent as to leave me but little profit from it. But, in the spring of the year 1827, I resumed it with energy, and encouraging prospects of soon obtaining all I ever coveted of earth's trash—a competency for rational comfort and independence. And this I might have soon secured had I been able to persist in my resolution of self-denial of all political and official allurements, and, comformably with which resolution, I declined the offer of nomination by my party for the office of Governor in the year 1828. Gen'l Metcalfe, having been substituted and elected, urged me to accept the post of Secretary of State, which I declined; but, my party requiring my acceptance, I finally accepted, and was preparing to settle in Frankfort, where the changed condition of the bar and augmented business of the courts and my favorable position in the public eye would have in sured me affluence in a few years. But again my party, treating me as a leader whose services they claimed the right to call into any field of labor, controlled my will, and called me to the Appellate bench, then by far the most onerous and irksome, and, to me, the least welcome of all important and honorable public trusts. I had no taste for judicial service. The labors of an Appellate Judge were then herculean. The salary ($1,500 in the depreciated currency, worth less than $1,000 in cash,) was grossly inadequate, and about equal to my salary as Secretary of State—to me a place of pastime—and, by going on the bench I knew that I would not only make an immense pecuniary sacrifice, but be doomed to ostracism from popular favor, and subjected to an unwelcome privation of social and personal liberty. I therefore revolted at the prospect of such crucifixion on the bench. But the defeated party had a small majority. Some of them preferred me, urged me to accept, and would vote for no other person in the victorious party. My party therefore demanded my nomination and acceptance, and left me no other honorable alternative; and assuring me that I might resign at any time after one year's incum. bency, I was constrained to yield, and felt that I was going to the altar as a self-sacrificed victim to party policy.

Upon my appointment, Chief-Justice Bibb, who had been leader of the antipodal party, resigned. His place was not filed till the 16th of December, 1829, when I was commissioned Chief-Justice of Kentucky. My commission as Judge was dated December 24th, 1828. During the interval of nearly a year between these commissions, all the heavy duties of the court devolved on my associate (Judge Underwood) and myself, and we had not one day of relaxation; and, for about seven succeeding years, I was not permitted to enjoy the undisturbed leisure of a "Cotter's Saturday Night," and consumed *many entire nights by the judicial lamp without a moment of repose*. I often tried to abdicate, but was always overruled, until the 1st of April, 1843, when the Governor again declining to accept my tendered resignation, I filed it myself in his office, and left the bench. I thus unexpectedly and unwillingly devoted nearly fifteen years of the prime of my life to incessant and self-sacrificing labor on the Appellate bench, and resumed my mental and locomotive liberty, poor and fifty-two years old. All I am now worth, and much more given to my children and paid for friends, I have made by a voluntarily limited practice of the law for about twelve years since 1843, having chosen almost total retirement for the last six years.

How I discharged my judicial duties, my reported opinions may partially serve to show; and how my professional functions, the public verdict will decide. All I can say is that, in these, as well as in all my other relations of public and private life, I have studied only my duty, and faithfully tried to do it to the full measure of my abilities.

During my service on the Bench I could have been elected to the United States Senate twice beyond question, if I had consented; and on another occasion I would have been elected without my knowledge had not my brother-in law (Letcher) withdrawn my name from the balloting, after which J. T. Morehead was elected.   At another time, in 1846, Ex-Gov. Letcher and Judge Underwood being rival candidates, I was urged by many prominent members of the Legislature to allow my name to be put in as a *pis aller*, after many unsuccessful ballotings between the two principal candidates. And some of the friends of both of them visited me and assured me that Underwood, desiring me to be nominated, would withdraw and secure my election if I would only consent to a nomination.   I refused, however, unless Letcher also would withdraw.   This he refused to do, and thereby weakened himself and strengthed Underwood, who was therefore finally elected.   I had no reason to doubt that, if Letcher had acceded to the proposed compromise, I would have been elected *una voce*.

In 1848 I was elected to the State Legislature by the people of Fayette, without solicitation and against my will. During the succeeding session the non-importation act of 1733 was substantially repealed.   I spoke and voted against the repeal.   In that speech I uttered my sentiments on the policy of non-importation of slaves into Kentucky, on abolition and emancipation, and also on slavery itself, and the proper mode of treating it.   And to prevent injurious agitation and secure peace and stability, I suggested the propriety of embodying in the Constitution the principle and policy of non-importation.

On my return home after the close of the session, I was urged by all parties to be a candidate for the Convention which had been called by the popular vote against my counsel and vote.   Knowing from the temper of the times that the new would be worse than the old Constitution, I preferred to be no actor in the body that would be responsible for the deterioration.   But, submitting to the *then* manifest choice of my fellow citizens, I consented to be announced as a candidate. Not long afterwards, and before there was any other candidate, Mr. Clay's letter in favor of emancipation was published, and Robt. J. Breckinridge and many others in Fayette, presuming on Mr. Clay's co-operation, stirred the question of emancipation as the controlling consideration in the election of delegates to the Convention. The agitation became intense and pervading until, degenerating into a stultifying mania, it produced fanatical coalitions between pro-slavery Whigs and Democrats and emancipation Whigs and Democrats, who assembled in separate and stormy conventions, each of which, in a whirlwind of passion, nominated a Whig and a Democrat as their antagonistic candidates for the Convention. The leaders of the pro-slavery party urged me to be one of their candidates, and offered me the nomination on condition that I would waive my policy as to non-importation being imbedded in the Constitution. This I peremptorily declined, as I did also overtures from the other combination to consent to be placed on their ticket. Thus threatened to be overwhelmed by two mountain waves, between which I stood alone as a committed candidate, my personal interest and comfort would have induced my indignant withdrawal, had I felt free to consult my own ease and inclination. But, assured that I was right, and that a large majority of the people of Fayette had stood, and, when rational and deliberate, would again stand on my platform as to slavery and the principles of a new Constitution, I felt it my public duty, on an occasion so eventful, to meet the issue and try to quell the storm and save the country from political revolution and from the curse of such a Constitution as I foreboded from that agitation, and as it has imposed on us and our children. The programme I advocated may be seen in a handbill preserved among my papers. During the discussions on the stump I became reassured that a large majority of the people of Fayette concurred with me, and that, if many of those committed in their coalition conventions could emancipate themselves, I would be elected.

Robert J. Breckinridge as a Whig, and Samuel Shy as a Democrat were the caucus candidates for the emancipation party, and A. K. Woolley, Whig, and R. N. Wickliffe, Democrat, were the nominees of the ultra-pro-slavery junto. Most, probably all, of the Whig emancipationists preferred me to Shy, and all the pro-slavery Whigs preferred me to Wickliffe; but many of these felt handcuffed by their hasty agency in the adulterous nominations, and not a few who were anxious to assert their independence, were prevented by importunity and indifference. I heard it often asserted that Breckinridge urged Whig emancipationists to vote for Shy, and told them not to vote for him, if they *would* vote for me. And by this clerical indoctrination, some of my warmest personal and political friends were induced to vote against me. Similar means had the like effect on pro-slavery Whigs. In addition to all these unpropitious embarrassments, the fact that I had no associate in the canvass operated powerfully against me by necessitating a division of my votes among my adversaries, and thus requiring for my success nearly double as much strength as that of either of the opposing candidates.

Had I been before either of the caucus candidates when the polls were announced at one o'clock the first day of the election, my election would have been sure; but at that critical time the two belligerent tickets were side by side, and I was a little behind. This accident I considered as decisive of my fate, and, having told my friends so, most of them afterwards voted for one of the other tickets. Had not Samuel Bullock, who had agreed to be an associate candidate on my platform, died before the election, I would have been elected, or, with all the disadvantage of running alone, Breckinridge and myself would have been elected, if he had conducted the canvass impartially. But his misdirected course against me, which I will not here theorise, expose, or describe, defeated himself and helped to beat me.

In the canvass I told the people that no emancipationist,

unless possibly Breckinridge, would be elected, and also that
even if every emancipation candidate in the State should be
elected, that party would be in so small a minority in the
Convention as to be unable to do anything for emancipation.
And after elaborate discussion on emancipation, all over the
county, between Breckinridge and myself, in which I endeavored to prove, and thought that I had proved, the
impolicy of agitating the question before the people, or in
the Convention, seeming to be persuaded of its impolicy, he
declared publicly at Elkhorn precinct, just before the election, that if elected he would not only *not move* emancipation,
but would vote against it, if moved in the Convention by any
other member. And I predicted that the indiscreet and
premature agitation of an enterprise so impracticable and
disquieting would aggravate and prolong slavery, and throw
into the Convention a crude and effervescing material which
would curse us with the worst constitution in the Union; and
such already is felt to be the result; but popular ebullition
was too strong for reason or sober deliberation. And my
course in the canvass, and the causes of my defeat not being
understood out of Fayette, my unexpected failure made
many persons elsewhere suspect that I was unpopular at
home, or was unsound on the subject of slavery. I have
ever since suffered greatly from this ignorant and unjust prej-
udice. Never soliciting office, and long preferring the pursuits
of private life, I have had neither suitable occasion nor actu-
ating motive for altogether rectifying that unreasonable
misconception, for which nothing in my history or in my
many speeches and writings on slavery in all its phases,
affords any semblance of excuse.

Had I been in the Convention, the Constitution as it is
might never have been adopted; and had my warnings been
heeded, or my uniform policy observed, abolitionists, free-
soilers, and secessionists would never have disturbed the
fraternity of the State, or jeoparded the Union.

In December, 1834, I accepted the professorship of Constitutional Law, Equity, and International Law, public and private, and, on the 4th of July, 1835, I settled in Lexington, where I still reside. The professorship I retained until 1858, where I helped to make more than twelve hundred lawyers, scattered over the United States, but principally over the Western, Southern, and Northwestern States and Territories. They left me all right in fundamental politics; and many of them have become distinguished jurists and statesmen, occupying high places at the bar, on the bench, and in the Legislative councils, State and National. For the labor and privation encountered in their tutelage I feel more than compensated by the assuring hope that the seed I sowed will, by its wholesome fructification, help to save our institutions and bless our posterity.

Poverty and domestic obligations having compelled me to resign my seat in Congress, and my reluctant and gainless devotion to the bench afterwards for nearly fifteen years of the prime of my manhood, having left me poor, I had, when I resigned the Chief Justiceship of Kentucky, no other consistent option than to try, by the practice of the law, to acquire an humble competence for the independence and comfort of my family; and this I had not attained before about the year 1851. Consequently, whatever my personal preference may have been, I could not have consistently quit my profession for any political post, even the National Senate, which I would have preferred to any other.

This sense of paramount duty to my family induced me to decline the offer of an election to the United States Senate and of other preferment more than once. But when I had reached a condition of life which would have made the Senate eligible to me, I was voted for on two occasions in 1851, without my solicitation and without my interference in any way, and would, nevertheless, have been elected either time had not untoward accidents prevented. I was then a member of the Kentucky Legislature. I was urged to be Speaker, which I declined. My nephew, G. R. McKee, then became a candidate, with some other friends, who preferred me for the Senate. After many exciting ballots the House adjourned without an election. Fearful of a disruption by this hopeless antagonism of friends, our party nominated and elected me against my will, as a peace-offering, and the effect on me was to make all the aspirants to the chair, except my nephew, violently adverse to my election to the Senate. In addition to this Mr. Crittenden, then a member of Mr. Fillmore's cabinet, and not believed to be a candidate for the Senate, was urged for an election by a few of his admirers. His friends were generally mine, and, had not his name been thus unfortunately used without his known sanction, my election was sure, notwithstanding the loss resulting from the Speakership. I was not, and refused to be, a candidate, but had said that if spontaneously chosen, I would not decline the call. I was opposed to the use of his name, which was persistently made against the judgment of all his discreet friends, and I announced, at once, that I could not co-operate in any such unauthorized effort, which I considered, as it turned out, injurious to him, and unjust, as it certainly was, to other citizens who had been fighting for him and for conservatism for many years, without any preferment. And, accordingly, I did not vote for him. This alienated his friends from me, and made most of them, even my own Senator, zealous and active against me during the entire session of that Legislature.

Mr. Crittenden, Mr. Dixon, and myself were voted for. After several ballots, in which I was well sustained, seeing that the contest was degenerating into a fatal split of our party, I had my name withdrawn in defiance of earnest remonstrances by many of my friends. Between Crittenden and Dixon the balloting was continued for many days, some members, who were opposed to both of them, putting up a third man on each successive ballot. At last, our party being in imminent danger of dissolution, Mr. C. and Mr. D. were both withdrawn, and a caucus assembled to select a

4

candidate.   Some of the members who were excited against me arranged a platform which would be most likely to defeat the strongest man—which was, that every member might nominate whom he desired, and that no nominee should be preferred until he had, *successively*, beaten **every other.**   To illustrate the effect of that programme, we may suppose that every letter in the alphabet was in nomination **(and** it was in this case nearly so).   A would be ahead at **the first** ballot; then he would have to run against B, for whom all **or nearly** all the friends of the other nominees would vote for the purpose of breaking A down; then B would have to run against C, who would, in the same way, **beat** him; and so on, the same result would follow until Z would beat Y; **then** Z **would** run against A, who, of course, would in like manner beat him; and so the same farce would be repeated.   And just so it was in this instance.   On **the** first ballot I was foremost; **C. S.** Morehead was next; he then beat me, and himself was beaten, as others were successively until John B. Thompson, who was the lowest on the first ballot, was ahead; I then beat *him;* and the same round was run again, with the same results, until eight of my friends, despairing of any conclusion of **such** a farce, left **the scene.**   After they had gone **a** third round was commenced between Thompson and me, when, as I believe from **various** information, I beat him again.   But the chairman (my Senator) declared him nominated.   Many members remonstrated, and denied, moreover, that he could, even had **he** beaten me, be nominated until he had beaten every other **competitor.**   But the chairman persisted, and adjourned the meeting in **a stórm** of clamor, declaring that Thompson **was nominated.**   This having gotten out, it was thought best not **to attempt to correct** the blunder; and, **in this** way, Thompson, **who was** the weakest in the race, was made the Senator. **There was no** doubt that I, **in a fair** trial, would have been **nominated and** elected.

    After that abortion, Mr. **Clay** having resigned, Dixon,

Morehead, and myself were put up for the succession; and the members, sick of the first ridiculous programme, resolved to have no caucus, but vote in the Legislature as between those who should be nominated there. The opposing minority being strong enough to prevent the election of a Whig as long as more than one Whig was running, our party resolved secretly to begin to drop the hindmost on the fifth ballot. The Democrats ran James Guthrie to embarrass the election and insure the election of a Whig whom they preferred. With the exception of about one-fifth of them, they preferred me ; and, understanding that on some ballot unknown to them, the hindmost would be dropped, they intended to vote for me on that ballot. But my friend who was chosen to give them notice when the ballot had come, was accidentally out when it arrived, and the Democrats still voted for Guthrie, but Morehead's friends of the Democratic party (about seven), understanding when the trial ballot came, voted for *him;* and two of my Whig voters being accidentally out on that ballot, I was dropped by one vote! My election was considered certain by all who knew the determination of a large majority of the Democrats, and my failure was almost miraculous. The following letter, published in a Maysville paper, and which was evidently written by some friend who knew the facts, will explain this affair correctly:

JUDGE ROBERTSON AND THE SENATORIAL ELECTION.

We have been furnished by a citizen of Maysville. the following extract from a letter from his correspondent at Frankfort, explaining the influences and accidents, according to the view of the writer, by which the election of Judge Robertson as a Senator of the United States to succeed Henry Clay, resigned, was prevented. We comply with the request for its publication, because, notwithstanding the election resulted in favor of another, the facts stated are interesting in themselves.

Judge Robertson is, unquestionably, a citizen whose peculiar qualities eminently fit him for the grave and dignified post of Senator in Congress. His intellect, giant-like in proportions and powers; a statesman, liberal, comprehensive and national in his views; a jurist, learned, able and profound; a citizen of ripe experience in all the diversified walks of public service; ever pure and self-sacrificing in his patriotism; a scholar and a gentleman of spotless private life; with such qualifications, Judge Robert-

son, had he been chosen a Senator of the United States, would have
discharged the duties of the high station with credit to himself, with honor
to Kentucky, and with eminent advantage to the Union. On entering
that illustrious body, he would, by the force of his character and intellect,
have immediately taken rank in the very first line of American statesmen.
The cast and mould of his mind are peculiarly Judicial and Senatorial;
and we should deem the country fortunate yet should it secure his services
in the Supreme Court or in the Senate of the United States.

But to the letter—here is the extract:

"You expressed a hope that Judge Robertson's 'luck' would be better on
the late than it was on the former occasion. It was not much better.
Your members did not vote for Robertson—*not one of them.* Had they,
or any of them, voted for him, he would have been elected. The *hot*
Crittenden men—the most of them—(including Robertson's own Senator,
and some others who had, at the beginning of the session, avowed themselves for him against Crittenden himself) all proscribed him *only because
he voted for Dixon!* Still he would have been elected had not a singular
accident occurred. Morehead had no chance, because all Robertson's
votes except three were for Dixon next; so that, out of seventy-five Whig
votes, Morehead could not get more than twenty-two against Dixon.
The *secret* agreement among the Whigs was to begin on the fifth ballot to
drop the hindmost. Robertson ran ahead of Morehead on the first four
ballots, and would have done it also on the fifth by an increased majority,
but on the decisive fifth, Morehead got five Democratic votes, and was *thus*
thrown one vote ahead of Robertson, who, notwithstanding the five Democratic votes, would have been several votes ahead of Morehead, had not
Dr. Burnet and several other Democrats, all anxiously awaiting to cast the
test-vote, which they were determined to do for Robertson, been accidentally misinformed as to the proper time, and in that way held to Guthrie
until Robertson was unexpectedly dropped by one vote. · Had Robertson
beaten Morehead on that ballot, as he could have done easily, his election
was considered certain by his own friends, as well as by the best informed
of Dixon's. He would, on the next ballot, have received, as against Dixon,
all of Morehead's votes except about three, which would have made his
Whig vote equal or perhaps about two more than Dixon's; *and there is no
doubt that he would have received a large majority of the Democratic
votes.*"

I never, either before or since, sought the place, pleasant
and eligible as it might have been to me; and although I
have more than once been voted for, I was never a candidate
for it or uttered a word or did an act to obtain it. Nor,
while I have resigned high public posts and declined the acceptance of many others spontaneously tendered to me, did I
ever apply for or in any way seek official promotion. I
would not feel honored by the highest station unless it seeks
me and comes *sua sponte*.

My retirement from political life has been both voluntary

and cheerful; and I have enjoyed it without envy or regret.
No disappointment has corroded my peace; no sense of unjust pretermission or neglect has made me either cynical or
resentful. Whatever may have been my position or personal
fortune, I have, without the slightest deflection, been always
true to the same principles, and have never faltered in
humble efforts in my sphere to rectify the popular mind,
regulate the popular will, and promote the welfare of my
country. And I hope to die in the assurance that, whilst
my position in the public eye, and my unpatronized personal
power have not enabled me to do or to be all I wished, I
have nevertheless done the State some service, and my countrymen some good, that will last and fructify long after my
name may be forgotten.

CHAPTER VI.

Concerning my personal character and habits I will add only a few words.

When I married I was five feet ten inches high, and weighed only 126 pounds; at 30 years of age my weight was 200 pounds, at which it continued nearly stationary until lately; it is now (16th November, 1863) 240 pounds. Organically sound and temperate in all things, I have, ever since my 17th year, enjoyed unsurpassed health of body and mind. During the last 56 years of my life I have abstained from medicine, and relied on the *vis medicatrix naturae*. When out of order my remedy has been abstinence and quiescence. Since my marriage I have never felt a symptom of headache or any cerebral excitement. My only maladies have been a chronic inflammation of the schnyderian membrane degenerating into nasal polypus, and a local eruption on the skin, which I have considered an efflorescence of a scrofulous taint. With these exceptions my physical health is robust and perfect. And I have the comforting conviction that, with a sound body, I am still blessed with a sound mind—*mens sana in corpore sano*. In my own judgment, my intellectual faculties, though sobered and mellowed by the autumn of age, are as strong and as clear as ever, with the exception only of a slight decay or absence of memory; and this impairment I ascribe more to tobacco than to senility. Since my early manhood I have used this narcotic in the double form of chewing and smoking. Conscious that the habit was vulgar, inconvenient, and often hurtful, I frequently

denied myself for months, and without much sense of privation; but finding that I increased in fat, I as often resumed
the use of the stimulant.   And I yet persist in the prudent
and temperate use of it, not so much as an exhilerant or sed-
ative, as a medicine to prevent nausea, neutralize malaria,
and restrain a constitutional tendency to oppressive corpu-
lence.

My passions were strong and vehement; but I soon acquired habitual control over all of them.   My temperament
was bilious, but was generally considered rather phlegmatic,
because a supreme will of self-denial restrained and generally
subjugated feelings that were sometimes almost volcanic, and,
without extraordinary power of self control and constant
vigilance and discipline, would often have exploded with
eruptive violence.

I never fell from self-poised uprightness, and I was never
guilty of an act of incontinence.   And, while ambitious of
the fame that follows worth, I never sought it by the vulgar
means by which meretricious notoriety has, in all time, been
easily acquired by selfish mediocrity, impudent upstartism,
and suppliant prostitution.   I never had any prurience for
office or place, and never held one with self-satisfaction.   My
sentiment has ever been, that he who deserves an office
would do better without it; and that every one who seeks
or accepts a trust for which he is not qualified, is guilty of
incivism and makes himself ridiculous.   And I have always
admired the maxim illustrated by Epaminondas and Washington, that place does not honor the incumbent, but the
incumbent the place; and that the place should seek the
man, and not the man the place.   And my practice of this
doctrine is the only reason why retirement has so long blessed
my domestic peace.   I have more than once declined a seat
on the bench of the Supreme Court of the United States,
seat in the cabinet, and foreign missions, tendered to me
without solicitation.

I know all the highways and byways which successful aspirants travel to spurious honor.   But rather than tread those crooked paths, I feel with Pope, that "the post of honor is a private station."   And this, therefore, has been my fortune for years, and must continue with my life, unless unexpectedly I shall be called to some public service neither solicited nor desired.

Since my advent to the bar, forensic, political, and judicial intrusions on my time have not allowed me secure and settled relaxation sufficient for methodical study.   My reading, though varied and extensive, has necessarily been rather miscellaneous and scattered.   My political principles, matured and settled before I was elected to Congress, are national and conservative.   They have never been changed in any essential particular, and have, under all circumstances and in every instance, guided my political conduct.

For the last seven years I have studied Theology more than all other subjects.   The Bible has been my *vade mecum*, aided by collateral illustrations,—geological, metaphysical, and historical,—and by exegetical speculations—didactic and polemical.   I have not studied as a rationalist in either the dogmatic or scholastic sense.   But, within the limited sphere of human power, reason has guided me to my conclusions, so as to make the Bible harmonize in all its parts and exhibit a simple, rational, and God-like system, free from the mysticism and incongruities of the sects and the schools, and relieved of most of its imputed mysteries.   Still God is a mystery; life, both animal and vegetable, is a mystery; mind is a mystery; even matter and its laws are mysteries.   Here philosophy, guided by intuition and confirmed by faith consistent with reason, though beyond its range, is our only guide.   And on this foundation I build my theory as to Ontology, Theosophy, and the connection between an omnipresent, omniscient, and omnipotent Spirit, and the subordinate and illimitable universe of matter and mind.   My process results in the explosion of hylozoic or material pantheism, of the scholastic doctrines of the fall, of original

sin, imputed righteousness and imputed sin, of the incarna-
tion and crucifixion of God as *expiatory* instead of *propitiatory*,
the garden of Eden, the serpent, and the trees of life and
of the knowledge of good and evil, and predestination, election, and necessitarianism.   This is not the proper place for
a full discussion of these topics, or even for a statement of
my views in respect to any of them.   If time be allowed to
me I may hereafter write something more explicit and satisfactory.   I will only say now that my theories, if generally
known and adopted, would rectify many errors in dogmatic
orthodoxy, exalt our conceptions of God and man, commend
the pure Christianity of *Love*, remove its many stumbling-
blocks, and soon renovate society and evangelize the world.
And I presume to add, that my interpretation of the Bible is
not only consistent with, but is required by, its context and
pervading spirit as an inspired whole.

My habits have always been self-denying, and my tastes
domestic.   Prudence and a supreme love for a comfortable
and independent mediocrity of fortune constrained me to for-
bear habitually the gratification of incompatible personal and
social tastes.   I have been careful to apply my personal
means to objects the most essential.   I would even wear old
clothes when I had not the money in hand to buy new ones
without neglecting more essential uses of it.   But whenever
I had money not needed for more useful and important objects, I used it freely for the gratification of my own taste or
that of my family and friends.   Ever since I was 25 years
old I took care to have always some money on hand, so as
to feel free and independent.   I was always punctual in
fulfilling my contracts, and all my engagements and appointments.   And my systematic and self-denying economy—
never degenerating into parsimony—enabled me to live as
well as any rational man would ever desire, and to appropriate to public and private charities and social benefactions
often more, but never less, than five hundred dollars a year.
My wife, very domestic and excellent in household manage-

ment, was also prudently economical, but far from being
selfish or sordid.   Her domestic cares and housewifery were
never directed or intruded on by me.   She was enthroned as
queen of the house,—kitchen, parlor, and all—and in that
sphere her will was my law.   I never either dictated or complained of her household administration, or directed or
objected to any expenditure she ever made for her person,
her house, or her table. |

When business did not call me away, I staid at home
habitually and with but few exceptions, and was seldom absent at night.

My habit of writing, like that of reading, was rapid and
irregular.   Whatever I wrote was accomplished *per saltem*,
and without copying or much revision.   I wrote with too
much celerity.   Even my judicial opinions, though well
considered and matured before I put pen to paper, were
written *currente calamo*, so as to finish in an hour what might
prudently have occupied a whole day.   As an illustration, I
will only say that the opinion in the perpresture case of L.
and O. R. R. vs. Applegate, &c., covering twenty-two pages
in 8th Dana's Reports, was written out from beginning to
end in six hours.   The duties of the Appellate bench, when
I was upon it, were exceedingly onerous, and required extraordinary dispatch to avoid vexatious delays.   Anxious to
keep up with the docket, I have often labored at the oar all
night; and, whether at home or at court, I seldom enjoyed
even the rest of one Sabbath day for nearly fifteen years.
My labors were constant and herculean.   And I regret that
I permitted my anxiety for the dispatch of justice to jeopard
my health, disturb my comfort, and subject my judicial reputation to unnecessary criticism.

And now, on my 73d anniversary, I would close this meager sketch.   It is possible, if I live much longer, that I may
not only revise and correct, but enlarge it.   However this
may be, I desire that some surviving friend, who knows me
well, will, after I take my leave of earth, fill up the outline I

leave behind, and furnish a fuller and more complete biography than I ought to, if I could, write of myself. And such a memoir I wish published, together with the revised contents of my "Scrap Book," and with the addition of all other documents I may leave marked for that end in my portfolio. And the entire work, cost what it may, I require to be done in the best typographical style of the very best American publisher, with the best style of paper, and my autograph and photograph prefixed. All this I desire, not in a vain hope of posthumous fame, but in the belief that it may be my best legacy to my descendants, useful to surviving friends, and of some service to my succeeding countrymen.

CHAPTER VII.

AUGUST 30th, 1865.

On the 13th of January, 1865, my admirable and devoted wife died of pneumonia, and on the 25th of the same month she was removed from the home she had so long graced, and was laid side by side with our darling son George, in our vault in the Lexington cemetery, where I expect soon to join them and repose, dust to dust, until the eventful day of the restitution of all things, when I hope we shall all, with other kindred, once more and forever live together in the brighter and happier *home* of all those most sorely tried on Earth to be blessed in Heaven. After a most happy and endearing cohabitation for more than fifty-five years, which had cemented us as one, this last and severest of all my many afflictive bereavements, like the separation of the soul and the body, has overwhelmed my manhood and left me, in old age, desolate, cheerless, and hopeless of earthly happiness. Uncommonly beautiful in early life, and always modest, neat, and truthful, devoted to home and fond of domestic cares and employments, my lost partner was a model wife, mother, mistress, and friend—conspicuous in all the virtues and feminine graces which most adorn and dignify womanhood. The memory of a woman so admirable and true, deserves the first place in this brief memorial of her husband, begun and nearly finished when he hoped that she would survive to close his eyes and embalm him with her affectionate tears. Therefore, in the discharge of this sacred duty, mournfully left peculiarly and impressively for him, he cannot do less than to place her by his side by transcribing herein the following short and imperfect, but, as far as it goes, true and faithful obituary by her oldest son:—

OBITUARY.

Affection and justice alike prompt this brief memorial of a more than friend by one who knew and loved her long and well.

ELEANOR J. BAINBRIDGE—born on lake Seneca, New York, April the 27th, 1794—was the daughter of DR. PETER BAINBRIDGE, an eloquent Baptist minister and eminent physician, and of ELEANOR JAMES McINTOSH, only daughter of Gen. ALEXANDER McINTOSH, of the Revolution, a wealthy planter of South Carolina. Both parents were of Scotch descent.

Dr. Bainbridge settled in Lancaster, Ky., in the year 1799, where, on the 28th day of November, 1809, Eleanor, then only fifteen years and five months old, was married to GEORGE ROBERTSON, whose age was nineteen years and ten days. They commenced their married life with no other fortune than the natural gifts with which God had blessed them. By habits of rare industry, prudence, and self-denial, they lived prosperously and happily together for fifty-five years, one month, and sixteen days; when, on the 13th of January, 1865, after an illness of nine days, she died of Pneumonia, at their residence in Lexington, Ky., whither they had removed on the 4th of July, 1835.

They had ten children, five of each sex; only one-half of them survived their mother, who left them and a large number of grandchildren and great-grand children, to mourn their irreparable loss, and imitate her precious example as wife, mother, Christian, friend.

Her neatness, modesty, justice, and high regard for truth, won the esteem and love of all who knew her well. Whatever her husband has accomplished is due as much to her untiring energy and faithful co-operation as to his own exertions.

In early life, the beauty of her face and form was of the highest order; and she retained her fine mold, and expression, her activity and maiden erectness to the last. She was resigned to death, only wishing to live longer for her husband, whom she grieved to leave alone, in his old age, hopeless of earthly comfort. In the year 1826 she became a member of the Presbyterian Church, and a perfect knowledge of her meek and steady faith and consistent life, gives full assurance to her family that she has entered upon that eternal rest which remains for the people of God.

It is but a just tribute to her memory to publish herewith the following extract from a letter of condolence to her husband, from one of the purest and most distinguished of the public men of Kentucky, who knew her from her girlhood to her death. After alluding to the intelligence of her death, he says:

"What a rush of recollections the sad event has driven through my mind. We were schoolmates at Lancaster, *when the most beautiful Ellen Bainbridge was just budding into womanhood—the admired and beloved of all her associates. How gracefully and perfectly she performed every duty of a wife*, I well knew from observations when a guest in your hospitable mansion. You and Ellen lived together *truly as one*, more than half a century. Your loss is irreparable on earth. Hope of a re-union in Heaven is the only ground of consolation. I mourn with you. I find that the world, to me, contains one friend less; and those of my years have none to spare.

"We have spent so many days with each other as boys and as men—associating as Legislators and as Judges, that I am sure you will not regard me as obtruding on your grief by expressing my heartfelt sympathy in your bereavement."

And all who knew her as well as this good and accomplished man, would concur in his testimony of her worth. With such memorials, her name, her virtues, and her model life, will long be embalmed in the hearts of her many descendants and friends.   A SON.

And, as our youngest son, who was her idol and whose death she constantly mourned to the last, lies entombed by her side, I choose, as befitting and just, to transmit them together by copying the following slight biographical sketch of him and paternal monody, addressed to his departed spirit eight years ago:

MEMORIAL OF GEORGE ROBERTSON, JR.

My youngest child—a son—was born in Lexington, Ky., on the 12th of May, 1838, when his mother was 45 years old and I was in the 48th year of my age. My family wished to name him George; but as I had lost two sons of that name, they were prevented by a superstitious apprehension from giving that unlucky name, and called him by the pseudonym, *Boson*. But when, in his seventh year, he was asked for his name by his first teacher, he answered, George; and thus he named himself, and that nomination was ratified by our family, and ever afterwards recognized, though at home he was generally called and known by the first imputed name, "*Boson*."

In form and expression he was remarkably handsome, even beautiful. And no son was ever more filial, docile, or affectionate.   He was the pride and hope of the family, and was favorably observed by all who saw, and beloved by all who knew him.   Though indulged in all his tastes and desires, he never became infected with an immoral principle, or acquired a bad habit.   He was always as amiable and gentle as a lamb, and as generous as the sun.   And if he ever uttered an impudent word, did an ungenerous act, or cherished an unkind feeling, I never heard of it.   He was devoted to his parents, and distinguished for his attachment to his brothers and sisters and their children; and we were all peculiarly devoted to him.   Among his various graces he had exquisite taste for music, and played very sweetly on the violin.

In robust health, he was sent, in September, 1855, to Mr. Sayre's select school at Frankfort, when, either from accident or severe exercise, he had, on one occasion, in December, a slight hemorrhage from the lungs; and exposure to cold at home during the succeeding Christmas holidays brought on a severe attack of pneumonia, from the effects of which, although for some time he appeared to be relieved, he never recovered.   For some months he manifested symptoms of bronchial inflammation, and we were apprehensive that, from sympathy or otherwise, his lungs were in danger; but I never believed that they were fatally or essentially diseased.   He was prudent and careful in the use of all restorative means, and in the autumn of 1856 he was increasing in flesh and strength, seemed restored to healthful appetite and digestion, could take his accustomed exercise in the air on foot and on horseback, and up hill and down hill, without apparent fatigue or inconvenience, and his blooming color was rapidly returning to his cheeks.   We thought he was almost out of danger, and he thought so too.   Expecting to go with his mother South in a few days, he went down into the city on the evening of Thursday, the 11th of December, 1856, and bought a new black coat and some other things, preparatory to his contemplated trip.   The evening was damp and chilly, and he did not return until fifteen minutes after five o'clock, or nearly dark.   We had several lady visitors that evening, for whom he played with admirable execution, at the request of one of them, "Old Folks at Home," and "Rural Felicity," in the order just stated; and these were his last on earth.   He then retired to his mother's chamber, in which he had been for some time sleeping; and, after cheerful conversation with Dr. Bell, undressed for bed about nine o'clock.   He slept quietly until disturbed by our entry for the purpose of going to bed.   He then conversed with his mother, and said he felt quite well.   But shortly afterwards he was disturbed by a cough, which continued at intervals, with increased violence, until about half-past four o'clock, when, after a severe paroxysm, he called his mother and told her he had coughed up some blood.   She instantly arose and made two abortive efforts to make light.   Seeing that she was agitated, he, sitting up in his bed, instructed her how to use the match, whereby she succeeded in lighting a candle, when, with extreme trepidation, she ejaculated, "Yes, my son, you *have* thrown up blood."   Whereupon he said, "Send for the doctor."   While she was calling for a servant I went to our son, and as I approached him, still sitting, he said, "*I can't get my breath;*" and these were his last words.   Sinking into my arms he expired just as his mother re-entered and approached his bed.

More surprise and grief were never felt or manifested than followed this terrible bereavement.   Even Dr. Bell fell on the floor apparently dead, and cordial sympathy seemed to be universal, extending to the colored people, many of whom manifested deep sorrow.   His devoted mother is even yet, eighteen months after the shock, crushed in body and mind, and feels hopeless of restoration of vigor to the one or cheerfulness to the other.   And my own condition is that of settled melancholy.   Mournful memories haunt me wherever I may be, day and night, without intermission.   It is idle to tell me this is wrong: I know it; but I cannot help it.   No effort of philosophy or will which I can command affords any

essential or permanent relief. I know that soon the
separation would be inevitable under the most favorable circumstances. And the fact that grief will not restore my
loving son, wipes away no tears, but only makes them flow
the faster. No father ever lost a son of more endearing
graces, more suited to his tastes, or more needful to his declining life. Attractive traits of character, growing habits,
cementing associations, and blasted hopes—all peculiar, in-
communicable, and countless—combined to inflict a wound
immedicable by human skill, or manly energy, or earthly
hopes.

I had lost father and mother, and brothers and sisters (all
except one), and four interesting and lovely children, among
whom was a daughter eighteen, and a son six years of age,
and for each and all of these visitations I felt deeply and
long, and yet *daily* feel transient sorrow; but my last bereavement has been and yet is, for nameless reasons, more
afflictive than all that preceded it. Even yet my house looks
desolate, and every thing in it suggests memories of my dear
George. Rallying all my manhood, I try to be resigned;
but nature rebels, and I can only command apparent seren-
ity, without hope of cheerfulness or capacity for earthly
enjoyment. I have exhausted philosophy. Faith in God
and his salvation is the only hope, and, with vivid and assuring faith, I have not yet been comforted. I have long been
striving for it, but have not yet been blessed with such as I
feel to be vital and consolatory.

George, though not nineteen years old, was nearly six feet
high, of perfect form, and, when in good health, would have
weighed one hundred and forty-five pounds. His hair was
black and silk like; his eyes dark brown, beaming a benig-
nity peculiarly attractive; his cheeks, when ruddy in health,
were smooth, blushing, and redolent as the spring rose; and
his countenance was a mirror of the chasest emotions of the
best and purest heart Had I the power, I would not have
altered him in head, heart, or form.

5

After he died he was kept in our parlor, in an open metallic casket, until the 9th of January (one month), and was then, with the body of his nephew and companion, William R. Letcher, conveyed, side by side, in hearses followed by a long procession, to the Lexington cemetery, where their bodies were deposited and sleep together in death, as they walked together in life. They rest with my grand-daughter, Ellen M. Troutman, in my family vault; and who will follow next and repose by their sides God only knows.

As soon as I felt calm enough to write I composed a monody, addressed to my son, which was completed on the nineteenth anniversary of his birth, May 12th, 1857, and is transcribed into this little book. On a sober revision of it this day, I indorse every sentiment and fact it contains, and believe that, as far as it goes, it is a faithful portrait, without the exaggeration of panegyric or apparent bias. And it is a true, though imperfect, expression of the feelings of his crushed mother and saddened father.

G. ROBERTSON.

April 16th, 1858.

LEXINGTON, KY., May 12th, 1857.

A FATHER'S ADDRESS TO HIS DEAD SON.*

---

* Only about half of this monody is here given. The other portions of it are an expansion or reiteration, in different form, of the same sentiments.

My son! my son! my youngest son!
   Of faultless mould and heart and form,
Whose graces countless blessings won,
   Whose model life was cloudless morn.

My son! my handsome, darling boy!
   Thy mother's pride, thy father's hope;
Their prop, their comfort, and their joy,
   The star of their declining slope.

Born late to bless their lonely age,

To grace their home and cheer their hearth,
To gild with light their closing page,
  And hallow their last days on earth.

Benignant, lovely, free from strife,
  In noble manhood's fragrant dawn;
In buoyant, blooming, hopeful life,
  Unwarned, from earth thy soul was drawn.

With lightning speed the message came,
  That called thee from thy mother's side,
And stereotyped thy LIVING NAME
  On hearts forgetless in Time's tide.

Couldst thou have lived 'till we had died,
  To close thy dying parents' eyes,
How blessed had been that eventide
  That cheerless now in sorrow dies.

Last rose of Summer! Autumn's hope,
  That Autumn comes, and thou art gone,
And left old age behind to grope
  A bloomless down-hill all alone.

If childish innocence and love,
  Chaste life untinged with impure leaven,
Might fit a soul for peace above,
  Thine rests, dear George, secure in heaven.

Thy fiddle, tuneless, now alone,
  Thy clothes, thy letters, and thy books,
Daily revive, with plaintive tone,
  Loved memories of thy ways and looks.

Where'er we go, whate'er we see,
  Chairs, tables, halls, and porch and gate;
All, all we meet, remind of thee,
  And seem to weep our mournful fate:

At morning, noon, and solemn night,
  Thy cheerless parents, side by side,
Fill with their sighs, for lost delight,

The room *where thou wert born—and died.*

Our house, now silent as thy tomb;
    Our hearth, bereft of all its glee;
So cheerful once! all draped in gloom,
    Have lost their life enshrined with thee.

Now home, dear spot with magnet sure,
    Charmed sanctuary, sacred shrine
Of love and peace and virtue pure,
    And tranquil joys almost divine:

That home thy presence made so sweet,
    Is cheerful home, "Sweet Home," no more;
Its desolations now we meet
    In every room, at every door.

To deeply mourn for such a loss,
    Which nothing earthly can supply,
Is nature's cry at nature's cross,
    Love planted here to melt and try.

Philosophy cannot console,
    And time alone can cicatrize,
But faith may heavenly love unroll,
    And trust in God may harmonize.

This grievous stroke of chastening love
    Melts all our hearts and weans from lust,
And calls us loud to look above
    For hopeful rising from the dust.

No longer here we love to stay,
    Our path so dark, our time so short,
We long to find the narrow way
    That leads bruis'd hearts to heaven's safe port.

Thy sudden death has proved how frail,
    How fleeting all things here below;
Then, while our loss we *must* bewail,
    We pray for blessings from the blow.

May thy example, ne'er forgot,
  Draw us from worldly cares and ties,
And may it be our pleasing lot
  To rest our bodies where thine lies.

Then—hard to say—Adieu, adieu!
  Till death shall come again to sever
Thy parents from this footstool, too,
  And bring us all, and more, together.

That hope is now the gleaming star
  To guide our tottering steps above,
And lead us safely to that bar
  Where reign eternal light and love.

For *time*, dear son! a last farewell!
  But to forget thee?—*never, never!*
Soon, how soon, we cannot tell,
  We'll meet again to live forever.

                    GEORGE ROBERTSON.

The following tribute to the memory of George Robertson, Junior, was written by the widow of Col. Wm. R. McKee, who fell at Buena Vista:

Better are the dead, which are already dead, than the living, which are yet alive, saith the voice of Divine Inspiration—yet seldom does the heart of the bereaved mourner respond to the sentiment. When the aged and weary pilgrim sinks to his quiet resting place, we bow in silence to the mercy of Providence, and repine not at the dispensation. The bounds allotted to human existence have been enjoyed, and an extension of life would be an extension of misery. But far different are the feelings called forth, when youth, and beauty and strength are prostrated by the cold hand of death. Then it is that the heart, in its bitterness, exclaims: "Dark and mysterious are thy works, O, God! and thy ways past finding out." Though the mind may be chastened to endure, and every rebellious thought be subjected, yet sorrow is ours, and we are permitted to indulge it—it is not the offspring of guilt, for He sorrowed who never knew sin.

Such were the reflections which crowded upon us whilst contemplating the shrouded form of GEORGE ROBERTSON, JR, and the tears which followed were allowed to fl w unchecked, for he was worthy of them. Friendship demands no lengthened tribute to the virtues of the deceased—his eulogy is already written on the hearts of all who knew him;

and it needs not that we sift his ashes to seek for golden memories of his
character, they were stamped on every page of his fleeting life. Possessing the vivacity of youth without its volatility; enjoying its pleasures
without its dissipation; and using the world so as not to abuse it, he was
at once an example to the young, and an object of admiration to the aged.
But the silver cord has been loosed, and the golden bowl has been broken
—the dust has returned to the earth as it was, whilst the glorious consola-
·tion is ours, that his spirit has returned to God who gave it.   M.

Having ten children—five of each sex—we lost six of them
in the following order:

1. Our second son, Bainbridge, a large, grey-eyed child,
born December 13th, 1822, and died February 9th, 1823.

2. Our fifth daughter, Martha Jane, a beautiful and
sprightly blue eyed girl, of fair skin, born July 24th, 1824,
and died May 17th, 1826.

3. George S. McKee, a black-eyed, handsome and promising boy, born November 2d, 1827, and died December
12th, 1832.

4. Mary Oden Eppes, born May 5th, 1815, and died of
cholera June 20th, 1833. She was the largest and most
majestic in form and port of all the daughters. Admirable
mould, fair skin, blue eyes, auburn hair, capacious head, and
beaming face, combined to make her a favorite, and talents
of a high grade assured a distinguished destiny, had she lived
long enough to allow full development of the rare elements
of her girlhood character and promise. Her premature
death was a sad bereavement to her parents and other kindred and friends. Her remains, together with those of her
sister Martha Jane, and her brothers Bainbridge and George
S. McKee, were, in September, 1866, disinterred, and, in-
closed in a common box, now rest with their mother in the
family vault.

All these births and deaths occurred in Lancaster, Ky.

5. Our youngest child, George, already described, and
who was born and died in the same room, in Lexington, Ky.

6. James Bainbridge, of whom the following obituary will
present a condensed outline:

AN HUMBLE OFFERING AT THE SHRINE OF GENIUS.

[From the Lexington Statesman.]

The memory of JAMES BAINBRIDGE ROBERTSON, deceased, deserves more than an ordinary tribute of surviving affection. His history may be useful to all young men of exuberant talents, and will exemplify the necessity of vigilant pilotage and stern self-control.

Born in Lancaster, Ky., on the 4th of October, 1831, he died suddenly, in the city of Lexington, on the night of the 27th of February, 1867, leaving an admirable widow and an interesting daughter and son of rare promise. From his early boyhood he exhibited extraordinary talents of peculiar docility, brilliancy and power. Without any other than solitary self-tuition, he had learned to read before his parents knew that he understood the English alphabet; and in a few weeks after he was sent to his first elementary school; his teacher advised his mother to place him under higher tutelage in some other institution. He was accordingly sent to the City School, and thence soon translated to Transylvania University, where, before he was eighteen years old, he graduated with signal honor; and, in his twentieth year, his scholastic course was crowned with the Bachalaureate Diploma of the Law Department of the same institution. In his whole scholastic pupilage he was first in every class of every grade, and developed *equal aptitude for every branch of science*. When he left college to start his career of responsible manhood, his prospects of eminent usefulness and distinction were as bright and auspicious as ever dawned on the opening pathway of any native-born Kentuckian. Good habits, a handsome and majestic person, graceful and affable manners, cultivated taste, thorough education, a true and benevolent heart, and a commanding intellect, fitted him for the palm of victory in the race of life; and thus armored, he might have contemplated his future, as his friends did, with high hopes of illustrating his lineage, of stereotyping his name on the roll of honorable fame, and of blessing his country and his kind.

But his genial nature inclined him too much to social sympathy and convivial associations, which, before he had entered the arena of professional competition, partially unhinged his habits of systematic industry, stifled his ambition, and unsettled all fixed purposes of progress in any useful pursuit of proper manhood; and thus, too irresolute for the necessary self-denial, he, like many of the most gifted men in every age' gradually trifled with his powers and drifted on the sea of life without a rudder, compass, or anchor, and his history and destiny were the results of magnificent talents, unpiloted by a vigilant and self-denying prudence. During his unfortunate probation he acquired a large fund of miscellaneous knowledge by observation and extensive reading of almost every thing worth observing and reading. Polite literature, in all its forms, was his favorite study. He wrote much for newspapers and periodicals. His style of writing was versatile, chaste, and graceful; and his colloquial style was copious, rich, and exceedingly interesting and attractive. Notwithstanding his prodigal waste of moral power, his veracity and integrity were never doubted, and he died, as he had lived, with a host of devoted friends, and without an enemy. Had his sunny heart and massive head been guided by prudence, he might, under a fostering Providence, have achieved whatever man could do, and embalmed his name in the heart of posterity.

But his fitful drama and its closing scene impressively illustrate Watt's photographic picture of all human life on earth:

> "How vain are all things here below?
> How false and yet how fair?
> Each pleasure has its poison too,
> And every sweet a snare."

And, although, in infinite wisdom and inscrutable benevolence, it may have been best for all that the subject of this brief memoir should have died when and as he did, yet many surviving friends mourn over the sad event and will hallow his grave with their tears.

To rescue his memory from unjust obloquy or hasty oblivion, a friend, who knew him well from his birth to his death, now offers this imperfect tribute at the tomb of his shipwrecked genius.

These dead children have been, and still are, the melancholy subjects of my occasional meditation *every day*. But the death of my wife is more crushing than all preceding blows. My only consolation for these Providential bereavements is the hope that they will be of short duration, and that soon I and all mine will be re-united in a happier state forever.

CHAPTER VIII.

At the August election, 1864, I was elected an Appellate Judge, by surprise and against my will. The extraordinary circumstances characterizing that event induced an explanatory address to the electors, which may be seen in the next enlarged edition of my "Scrap Book."

The office was unwelcome to me, and the duties are irksome and onerous. But the experiment so far has gratified me with the conviction that my faculties are as well adapted to the station as they were in their noontide. But the tranquillity and locomotive liberty more congenial with my age, incline me to abdicate as soon as I can do so gracefully.

As a slight memorial of my public life, I have and use an old judicial chair, presented to me in 1860; and why presented, and how received, the following correspondence will show:

[The touching letters that passed on this occasion have been mislaid.]

What I have said about my memory and self-denial, and the rapidity with which I wrote, may seem egotistic; it is, nevertheless, true, and fidelity to biographic truth not only requires, but justifies these statements, which can be proved by many of my cotemporaries who are yet living.

Accepting the Appellate Judgeship the last time with extreme reluctance, and satisfied that I could not continue to hold it without too great sacrifice, I resolved to abdicate as soon as I could befittingly. Some of my friends knowing this, and apprehending that a partial paralysis which crippled my limbs, but did not essentially impair my mind, might

precipitate my resignation, protested against it.   The following is one of many such remonstrances.*

Nevertheless, without communicating my immediate purpose to any person, whilst standing on the platform on which
I performed the ceremony of inaugurating the Governor, I
resolved to execute my long-deferred purpose then and there,
and, addressing the representative crowd there assembled, I
announced, in that presence, my retirement from the Appellate bench, and my resignation of the office of Chief Justice
of Kentucky.   This novel and unexpected scene took the
crowd by surprise, and the occasion was hallowed by a profusion of tears then shed.   Shortly afterwards the remaining
members of the Court, and members of various bars at the
Capital, met together and adopted the following testimonial
as a tribute of their respect:

STATE OF KENTUCKY,
COURT OF APPEALS,
6th September, 1871.

Gov. T. E. Bramlette presented the report of the committee appointed to draft suitable resolutions in relation to
Chief-Justice Robertson, which, on his motion, seconded by
W. R. Thompson, Esq., after appropriate remarks made by
each of them, were ordered to be spread on the Records of
this Court, and a certified copy sent by the Clerk of this
Court to Chief-Justice Robertson; said report reads as
follows:

On yesterday, after administering to His Excellency, Preston H. Leslie, the oath of office as Governor of Kentucky,
the venerable George Robertson, in the presence of a large
multitude of his fellow-citizens, announced his final leave of
the Bench of the Court of Appeals, and his resignation of
his office as its Chief Justice.

It is now meet and right that the members of the bench
and the bar should inscribe upon the Records of this Court

* This has been mislaid.

some memento of their veneration for his character, and their high appreciation of his great public service. Of him it may be said with truth, his life has been devoted to the public service.

As he put off his robes of office, pronounced his heartfelt benediction on his beloved countrymen, we beheld the representative of a race of intellectual giants. It was allotted to him, in the providence of God, to survive them all, with the solitary exception of his distinguished and venerable compeer, Joseph R. Underwood.

Though enfeebled by age, and wasted by disease, his mind seemed to be as active and vigorous as ever. Having finished his course, and won for himself the plaudit, "Well done, good and faithful servant," he stepped down into private life with the calm dignity of the veteran patriot. He is followed to his loved home with the approving smiles of a grateful people.

The life of this illustrious man has been one of remarkable activity, and full of incidents and results. In every sphere of life in which he was called to move, he made an indellible impression. In his early manhood, and at the very threshold of life, he occupied the front rank in the profession of law, and coped successfully with the greatest men of Kentucky. His great legal ability, and his singular devotion to the interests committed to his charge, won for him a reputation co-extensive with the State. In fact, such was his acknowledged worth, he was soon called into active political life. At a most eventful period in the history of the State, when it became necessary to vindicate the fundamental principles of the Constitution, and uphold the independence of the judiciary against the encroachments of legislative and executive power, no man wielded a more trenchant pen, or exerted a more commanding influence. His clear and masterly arguments, in the heated controversy of that day, contributed in no small degree to the verdict which was ultimately rendered by a virtuous and enlightened people.

They evince the same intimate acquaintance with the true
theory of our Government; the same profound reverence for
the principles of the Constitution; the same earnest devotion
to law and order, and the same enlightened and conservative
spirit which have characterized all the subsequent efforts of
his public life.

Whilst yet a young man, in the very heyday of his life, he
was elected to the Congress of the United States At that
time the Kentucky delegation, headed by the illustrious Clay,
was distinguished alike for their talents and force of character.
George Robertson, though young in years, was the fit compeer, and the acknowledged equal of them all. He was
assigned a high position in that body, and by his unwearied
attention to his duties as a Representative, his laborious researches into the archives of the nation, and his broad and
extended views of public policy, with his keen perceptions of
the dangers to which our free institutions were then exposed,
and his profound anxiety to avert them, by wise statesmanship and patriotic concession, he stood in the front rank of
American statesmen. He stands to-day the sole survivor of
that Congress, that emptied their heart's devotion upon the
altar of their country, that sectional strife might never come.
Venerable man! He has lived to see the day which has
proved him a patriot and a prophet.

But it is as a jurist he has acquired his highest distinction.
His mind was of that cast which eminently fitted him for
legal analysis. His grasp of principles, and his quick and
intuitive perception of the reason of the law, eminently qualified him for the high and responsible duties of the bench.
In the alembric of his massive brain legal principles were
coined and applied with confidence to the wants of an advancing civilization. A giant in intellect, he refused, whenever
necessary, to be bound by the *res adjudicata* of the past.
With a profound knowledge of the philosophy of the law, he
never hesitated to carry out its principles to their legitimate
results. He had the mental intrepidity of a great judge.

It has sometimes been said that he made new laws. The fact is, he looked upon law as the science of reason. Not only so, but as a progressive science, which must keep pace with all other sciences, and lend its aid to them all. He was not only versed in the common law, but his mind was well stored with the enlightened jurisprudence of Rome; but at the same time he levied tribute on all the achievements of modern science, and made them contribute to the elucidation and application of legal truth. Hence it was that the profession were sometimes startled by his decisions. Hence it is that we are indebted for those masterly arguments which are now recognized as valuable contributions to the jurisprudence of the nation.

Judge Robertson has long been recognized as one of the legal giants of the United States. His opinions are accepted as high authority in every State of the Union.

He has conferred imperishable honor upon this tribunal, and the Bench and the Bar of Kentucky will ever respect his virtues, and hold in grateful remembrance his distinguished public services.

> THOS. E. BRAMLETTE, *Chm'n.*
> JOHN RODMAN,
> W. F. BULLOCK,
> HARVEY MYERS,
> J. R. HALLAM,
> CHAS. G. WINTERSMITH,
> JAS. A. DAWSON.

A Copy—Attest:
A. DUVALL, C. C. A.

On the 9th of February, 1872, at last satisfied I was encouraged by the faith which works by love, purifies the heart, and overcomes the world, and that this, independently of all creeds and dogmas, is the *soul* of pure Christianity, I joined the First Presbyterian Church in Lexington, under the pastorate of the Rev. Mr. Dinwiddie; and all that I need add here on that subject is, that ever since I have enjoyed more peace and comfort than ever before.

As this sketch of myself *may* close here, I will now add the declaration, that having, **on** *all* occasions, striven to **do my** duty in all **the** relations **of** life, regardless of my own **interest** and comfort, and consequently at the expense of great and almost constant self-denial, I could this day leave the earth with a clear conscience, and without remorse for **any** voluntary act or omission in my whole life.

G. ROBERTSON.

CHAPTER IX.

LAST ILLNESS AND DEATH.

When twilight comes, clouds, that attend the sinking sun, catch his last beams, and in faint and fading colors show them to the world. Life has its twilight too,—some tongue or pen besides its own must tell its close. From their last hours, prophets alone, like the great Hebrew leader, who saw his own grave (forever hid from other eyes) between him and the promised land, may lift the vail.

Though, in the language of his own calling, but tenant at will, Judge Robertson was permitted, for a long term, to enjoy his earthly abode, and was served with a long notice to quit. Nothing now was left him to do but to settle his score with this world, and examine his title to another home. The foregoing pages give the result of that enquiry, in effect, as follows:

Reviewing my relations to mankind from the plane of ethics, or according to the standard of men, I am satisfied with my motives and conduct. Reviewing my life from the plane of Christianity, with regard to my relations to God, I entrust my case before the unerring Judge, to the unfailing Advocate.

Dr. Franklin, with characteristic and not unfounded self-complacency, expressed his willingness, near the close of his long and useful pilgrimage, to live again just as he had lived. Judge Robertson did not, perhaps could not, speak so decidedly. Perhaps his feeling was nearly expressed in these lines of Phœbe Carey:

"I would not make the path I have trod
  More pleasant or even more straight or wide,

> Nor change my course the breadth of a hair.
> This way or that way, to either side,
> So, let my past stand, just as it stands,
> And let me now, as I may, grow old.
> I am what I am, and my life for me
> Is the best, or it had not been, I hold."

In some respects the philosopher and the jurist were vis a vis. The one extremely practical, and occupied with material things, habitually turned his powerful, but near-sighted and microscopic mind, from the dim and ideal prospect of hereafter, to the substantial realities of the present, and the plain experience of his own prosperous past. The other, far more speculative, sought, with longer focal power, his reward in futurity. The one seemed to regard this life as a consummation and fruition; the other as a beginning and a probation. The one was willing for a brief continuance of his identity, and for the stale enjoyment of a twice-told tale to escape the risk of not being, or of a state of being whose horoscope he could not cast. The other recoiled from an existence that is only long enough, at best, to beget desires which can never be satisfied, and attachments doomed to be torn up by the roots and painfully educate and discipline faculties never to be used, and then end in nothingness. To him, life was a worthless boon—if this be all of life, if not all, and the trial has been successful, or if the result of another experiment must be the same, why wish to roll a rebounding stone, by renewing a youth of toil, a manhood chequered with bereavements—ending in an old age which survived nearly every object of affection?

In estimating the character of a man it would be a capital omission to overlook a quality which he most desired to possess, which he most desired to be considered to possess, and which above all others he claimed to possess. Beyond question, he of whom we inadequately write, wished above all things else to be, and to be deemed by his fellow-citizens, morally upright, in the most perfect sense in which those words can be applied to human frailty. The majority of mankind, must in most cases, judge of character as the law does, upon evidence of reputation, or what a majority of his acquaintances say of the person on trial. But the real and underlying fact in every case is his conduct. By their fruits ye shall know them, is a proposition which has received the assent of all time. The rule may be plain—its application is often difficult, because most of the individuals of the human flora are, like Christmas trees, laden with fruits they never produced.

Praise and censure are so freely bestowed upon man for acts that were never done, or were done by others; so, often has life-long hypocrisy been stripped of its cowl, or its harlequin garb of levity; selfishness won the palm of prudence; stinginess borne off the prize of pious self-denial; apathy worn the crown of moral strength; and wealth and patronage hid a multitude of sins. So many indeterminate figures —every-day Cromwells and Robespierres—double faced Januses—half saint, half devil Dick Turpins—robbers to-day, almoners to-morrow—throng the thoroughfares, that the marks of rectitude are also marks of accomplished villainy. In vain may law and what was once good reason declare that every man is innocent till proved guilty, and that scoundrels grow and are not Minerva-like, born complete. The outraged common sense and experience of the people doubt or reject presumptions, faithless, as mercenary troops, which serve with equal efficiency on both sides, and so confound evidence that the wheat of society is fated not only to stand beside, but also frequently to be mistaken for tares—until the harvest.

Still, to be not only negatively blameless, but to maintain persistently to the end every appearance of activity, performing all social obligations, and to corroborate these indications by an averment of motives, having almost the sanctions of a dying declaration, if not proof, must be deemed the best substitute for proof that can be found.

Of all the aspects of virtue, the appearance of mere ab-

6

stinence from evil is feeblest. Who can tell where omission
ends and commission begins? Or whether the temptation of
A is not the aversion of B? Or whether refraining from one
vice may not be addiction to the opposite vice, just as the
farthest from Charybdis may be nearest to Scylla. When
the torpid snake is rewarded for not striking in winter, then
also may the phlegmatic man, who, like Eve, is "fair by
defect," be canonized for his exemption from the excesses
of ardent and impulsive natures.

Judge Robertson believed — as man was not designed to
belong to "the painted populace, who lead ambrosial lives"—
the butterflies — as the bones and thews of his body and
mind declare, " In the sweat of thy brow shalt thou eat
bread"—that to do his duty, he must work. And that he who
hid his talent of money, of brains, or of muscle, "in a napkin,'
was himself that napkin, with all the pliancy, little worth and
fitness for low uses of a rag. His was not a dead faith.

Thoughtful, earnest, self-reliant, standing upon his own
feet; never borne upon the shoulders of another, not for a
moment; a barnacle dependent for headway on the speed of
the craft, to whose bottom he stuck; nor a misseltoe or a
fungus, sucking unquited sustenance from his country or
friends; in early youth ceasing to be a weight, he became,
and to the last continued to be, a power to lift and sustain
others. For all they did for him, he paid his fellow-man
heaped measure, running over, and believed that the primal
curse had been his greatest blessing.

In the domestic circle he was worthy of unbounded veneration and love. As a citizen, he had been public-spirited,
obedient to the laws, temperate, chaste, truthful in all
things, in all things decorous and just.

Without question or complaint, he accepted several not
very eminent, nor at all lucrative, and still responsible
and laborious offices, that had been assigned him, and resolutely and satisfactorily discharged their duties. He never
filled a place of which he was unworthy, or left one without

having added as much honor and advantage to it as he gained from it. Though one of the youngest and most inexperienced, he was one of the most active and faithful, and was fast becoming one of the most distinguished members of Congress.

In the Legislature of Kentucky, at its most brilliant period, by his unflinching boldness, pertinacity, learning, and eloquence, he did the State as much service as any other man has ever done in that body. Never idle, and amassing large stores of general information, he had been widely known and useful as a writer and speaker on political and literary and historical topics. He had patiently, and not unprofitably, instructed many classes and individuals in the elements of law.

When a sense of duty demanded, he had met men of all grades in council and in debate. And among the names that have shed the lustre of unquestionable integrity, varied and accurate attainments, and profound reasoning upon the bench of the Court of Appeals, his had been conspicuously enrolled.

If the State loved to honor other of its citizens more, who of them all had been more faithful and useful to the State? And if he did not render to his country and his race more conspicuous services, for which he proved his abundant capacity, it was because his country denied him the opportunity.

What a man, who has been equal to every demand, moral, physical, or intellectual, that has been made upon him, and has stood all the tests, and these neither few nor light, to which he has been subjected, might have accomplished, under other and more favorable conditions, beomes, after his goodness and strength are buried in the grave, a matter of idle conjecture, or of vain regret.

Some weeks before the term of the Court of Appeals which he last attended, one of his legs became partially insensible. Domestic cares and business complications conspired to disturb his mind and impair his health. His children importuned him to resign his seat, and devote his remaining days, which, in the course of nature, could be but few, to well-earned relaxation. He did not need the emoluments of his office, and had obtained all the honors it could confer. But employment, which had been the master of his youth and middle age, had become the friend of his old age. An active mind may possibly find rest in change of occupation, but not in indolence. Habit, energy, and a strong sense of duty, yield only to disability.

Men who desire to be contentedly idle, or to change their pursuits when they shall have grown old, must begin to be idle or to change while they are still young. The vulgar, but true adage, "an old horse cannot learn new tricks," is mainly true, because an old horse cannot forsake old tricks. The worn-out calvary horses of the peninsular war never forgot their training. Discharged from service, and pastured at the public expense, they formed into line of battle at the sound of thunder or the call of the bugle. The instance of the blind old Duke, at Crecy, who, stirred by the well-known roar of battle and the "stern joy that warriors feel," had himself borne, between two cavaliers, into the thickest of the fight, is remarkable, not because he was old, but because he was blind. History, recognizing the force of habit, especially when united with the love of power, has never ceased to wonder that Diocletian could betake himself to architecture and the culture of cabbages, and Charles the V to a monastery, and neither of these emperors was far advanced in age, and both were broken down by fatigue and disease   Avocations or diversions from the regular calling, late in life, have generally been unblessed. Therefore, sound reason, as well as inclination, generally persuade the lawyer to remain at the bar, the preacher in the pulpit, the merchant at his desk, so long as they can respectively discharge the duties of their vocations. But no man should hold or attempt to administer a public or private trust after he has become disqualified to do so.

Judge Robertson, though an octogenarian, was not a
"lean and slippered" one, "sans everything;" and if he
could not say with the Hebrew law-giver, "That his eye
was not dim, nor his natural force abated," still he was hale
and hearty, and seemed to retain the mental and bodily
stamina of his best days. No man ever read with keener relish
than he, the famous interview in which Gil Blas, in obedi-
ence to instructions, hints to the decrepid Archbishop of
Grenada, that there is a slight falling off in the vigor of his
homilies; and as no man had a nicer sense of personal
honor and official integrity, so no man would have been further from replying to a similar intimation from a competent
person, in a right spirit, as the ancient Primate did, with the
words, " I wish you all manner of prosperity, with a little
more taste."

He frequently expressed his intention to retire, on such occasions, and at other times he received many spoken and
written assurances, from members of the bar, in whose judgment and candor he trusted, of their unabated confidence in
his ability, and their earnest desire that he should not abdicate. If the question had been captiously asked, "Why
superfluous lags the veteran on the stage?" he might have
replied, first, that the people, unsolicited, and knowing his
age, had put him there; and then, after the manner of So-
phocles, who, when his children, in order to obtain his
estate, brought their father before the court on a charge of
being in his dotage and incapable of managing his affairs,
held forth, in overwhelming refutation of the charge, the
Oedipus Coloneus, which he had just written, the veteran
Judge might have pointed to his opinions on legal tender,
the effect of war upon contracts, the liability of employers for
injuries to their agents, resulting from the negligence of other
agents, and many others of his later opinions.

His house was almost desolate. As all must do who live
to fourscore years, he had survived the companions of his
youth, and most of the friends of his maturer years. Be-

sides himself, one sister alone was left of all his father's
numerous family. He had seen his wife and more than half
his children laid in their graves. His other children and
grand children had families of their own. Although the eyes
that used to "mark his coming, and look brighter when he
came," were all gone; although he missed the tidy and mat-
ronly form from the accustomed seat beside the hearth, and
tokens of the graceful and gracious boy who had been the
light of that abode, were scattered all around, he could not
be persuaded to abandon his home, and could not occupy it
without being saddened by recollections which every object
in it awakened.

Disregarding the gentle monitions of incipient disease, he
resumed the duties of his office. His parting words on leaving home intimated that the time and occasion of his return
were doubtful. He continued to discharge his official duties
until the morning of February 1st, 1871, when, while writing
an opinion, his sight was affected with a dimness which
glasses could not relieve, and the lines on the paper became
oblique and irregular, though still legible. His left leg and
arm soon ceased to obey his will, and he continued helpless,
with gradually increasing loss of vision, resulting for more
than a year before his death, in total blindness.

The paralytic attack was complicated with pneumonia, and
for several weeks neither he nor his friends thought he could
live more than a few days. The sympathy and attention
which his situation at this time awakened were wide-spread
and constant. Especially did he receive the strongest
evidences of attachment from his former pupils and other
members of the bar throughout the State.*

* The following note from a distinguished lawyer, who had been his pupil, is a specimen of many of a similar kind, which cheered him while
death pressed his slow but certain siege:

MY DEAR JUDGE :

* * * * I do not intend to believe that I am to lose my noble friend,
and the State its first citizen, until the fact shall have existed. You do not
desire from me words of eulogy, and you have too much philosophy to
need words of condolence. It was a white day for Kentucky when you

Some of his old acquaintances came long distances, with no other purpose than to have another and last interview with their venerable friend.   Of these some, and among them, Governor Bramlette, were soon to be re-united with him in another world.

The Legislature expressed their profound sense of his great services to the State, and caused his portrait to be placed in the Capitol.

Henceforth he needed unremitting attention, and was anxious lest he should give trouble to his attendants.   In addition to bodily suffering, which was often acute, his affairs had become involved, and he was compelled to know that his descendants would enjoy but little of the earnings of his long and self-denying labors.   Still, he was generally cheerful, sometimes facetious, and always uncomplaining.   He seemed to be at peace with God and man.

Any notice of his character which omits its religious element would be imperfect.   Looking at his religious experience from a rational standpoint, he had encountered all the difficulties which a man of resolute will, great deductive power, and strong emotions, who has been compelled, at the bar, to deny or affirm, according to his position, either side of every proposition, and who has been educated in the school of adversity, to be fearless and self-reliant, may be expected to combat before he rests on the simple gospel, which is to the Jew a stumbling block, to the Greek foolishness.

Christianity was a subject of too great apparent importance to be overlooked or underrated by one of his inquiring mind and aspirations after a purer, higher and more abiding destiny than this way station — mortality.   He saw, at a

again assumed the bench; it will be a black when you leave it.   If you still live to continue to serve the State, that you have honored more than it has honored you, so much the better; but if there be another fate, the past at least is secure.   I know, my dear venerable friend and preceptor, that you will not censure me, even if I intrude into the sick room.   My object in now writing is to ask you to direct one of your children or grand children to write to me how you are, and whether I can serve you in any way, either here or elsewhere.

glance, that its opponents must concede that it was the most remarkable fact in the roll of ages; the source of the mightiest conflicts in the past, and of the most unselfish and untiring activities of the present. A cause for which men and women of every grade, social and intellectual, had fosaken all else, and poured out their blood with triumphant joy; a centre around which the brightest intellects of eighteen centuries had revolved—he could not close his eyes to the fact that it claimed to be a standing miracle, fully attested by its own history and progress; and whether considered as a cause or an effect, to have produced the largest growth from the smallest beginning, and the vastest, most beneficent, and permanent results, by apparently inadequate, and even insignificant means, that have ever been known. Especially was he attracted by its claim to be the safe guardian of the present, with all its precious interests, and the only prophet of eternity, bringing life and immortality to light. He was drawn to it still more for the reason that it had been the guide and consolation through life, and the support in death, of many of those whom he had most loved and revered. And he felt that the possibility that God had manifested himself in the flesh, made it his duty, as well as his interest, to inquire if this were true. This feeling was kept alive and fostered, by the question which he was compelled to ask again and again, when the objects of his tenderest affections were taken from him, Shall we meet again? Or, with the greatest of all thinkers unblest by revelation, the Stagyrite ("who asked the dreadful question of the hills,—

> That look eternal, of the flowing streams
> That lucid flow forever, of the stars
> And whose fields of azure his raised
> Spirit had stood in glory—

and found that all were mute), must I adopt the sad conclusion—If any part of the soul be immortal, it is the impersonal part?"

Rejecting the conclusiveness of authority in religion, as in most things else, and considering evidence an indispensable means of certitude, and despising skepticism, which is the result of ignorance where knowledge is attainable, he devoted close and patient attention to the evidence of natural and revealed religion. Knowing that no mind, and especially one enthralled by the most exacting of task-masters—the municipal laws—could collect and weigh all the evidence relating to any fundamental question of religion or philosophy, he would concentrate all his forces upon single decisive facts. Of the crucifixion and resurrection, and the particulars in regard to the character and conversion of Saul of Tarsus, were examined by him with minute and searching thoroughness, because he knew that the correct decision of an issue on either of these stupendous facts, like a judgment at law, on a traverse to a special plea to the merits, would be conclusive, not only as to the particular question, but as to the whole case. Many questions he asked to which he received no answer, other than that insoluble difficulties were not peculiar to religion, but were common to every subject of human inquiry.

He also devoted much time and thought to the investigation of facts and statements in relation to the deluge. In doing this he had to consider whether the earth's surface exhibited any vestiges of the flood; whether there were any traditions in relation to it; whether the ark in size and construction was adapted for the purpose for which it was intended; what was the depth of the inundation, and whether caused by a subsidence of land as well as by rain; and whether the overflow was partial or universal. His conversations on these subjects showed large research, long rumination, and were replete with instruction.

From his daily conversations on religious topics it was clear that, besides many side investigations and peculiar conclusions, the main current of his thoughts pursued the worn channel which is open to all explorers.

He found, historically, that man, left to the discipline of reason, unaided by revelation or physical science, had collected into a moral code the rays of that light which lighteth every man who cometh into the world, and that in the exploration of visible things other systems of relations had been eliminated, and not being able to perceive why necessary relations, resulting from the nature of things, did not imply a personal, intelligent, and superior power as clearly as such a power was implied by the provisions of a book of statutes, he thought it probable that such a law-giver would make a clearer manifestation of his will than can be seen in unwritten laws. And turning to the Scriptures, which have been accepted by the Christian Church as the word of God, he found two dispensations, the one, undoubtedly of great antiquity, wonderfully preparatory for, and confirmatory of, the other, and he believed that the discipline of the unwritten moral law, and of the written moral and ceremonial laws disclosed the necessity of a mediator and prepared the way for his reception.

He learned all that he could from books and from persons of exemplary piety on the subject of experimental religion. And it is probable that his conduct and his experience were those of a regenerate man for more than forty years preceding his death; but it was not until after he had been ill a year or more that he joined the church. This was not the result of any sudden impulse, apprehension, or moral change. He considered the transforming effects of faith the strongest evidence both of the truth of revelation and of conversion, and he had been awaiting for years a clear manifestation of the operation of this miracle upon his own nature, the unclouded peace, the full tide of purifying love, which he desired to feel, never came He learned that he must look out of himself, and that religious experience is itself probationary. One of his favorite books was the writings of Bishop Butler. Two books which he read most frequently in his latter years, were Buchanan on modern infidelity and Coleridge's aids to reflection.

During his long decline of more than three years, he occupied, most of the time, a chair in which he could either recline or be supported in an erect position. Occasionally, for the first year, he rode out in his carriage. Afterwards, his only exercise consisted in daily airings about his house, or about the grounds surrounding it, in a wheeled chair. Some months before his death this was abandoned. His speech was sometimes inarticulate—he swallowed his food with difficulty. His physicians said that paralysis was invading his throat and stomach; and he was subject to frequent violent and dangerous attacks, resulting from the disorder of his digestive functions. His reasoning faculty seemed to be as vigorous as ever, when aroused, but there was a momentary confusion in its first efforts. His recollection of facts and principles, of the names of persons and titles of cases, with which he had been familiar years before, seemed unimpaired. His recollection of recent events was imperfect. His emotions were easily excited. He slumbered during part of every day, how long or frequently, could not be told, because often, when supposed to be asleep, he was engaged in meditation or listening to conversation.

A once popular writer remarks: That nature, attentive to the preservation of mankind, increases our wishes to live, while she lessens our enjoyments, and as she robs the senses of every pleasure, equips imagination in the spoil. This was not wholly true of Judge Robertson. Still, without manifesting any fear of death, or any increased wish to live, he did not wish to die. A few weeks before his death, he had remained silent for a long time, with open and upturned eyes, an attendant (his neice) asked him what was the subject of his thoughts, he replied, "My exit from this world." In response to her question, whether he desired to depart, he said, "I do not." Still, when he spoke of dying, which was seldom, it was with perfect composure, and he selected two of his favorite hymns to be sung at his funeral. In the latter months of his life, he was frequently reminded of mortality by the decease of friends, among others, a servant, who had been in his family for more than fifty years, met with an accident, which caused her death, and soon after, his daughter, Mrs. Letcher, a lady of beautiful person and winning manners, and endowed with a vigorous and cultivated understanding, was summoned from the earth. A few days before his departure, he said that in a dream or vision he saw all the departed members of his family, his mother, wife, and children, more radiant and vigorous than when in the flesh, but in other respects exactly as he had known them. During his last day (May 16th, 1874), he could only speak a few words. His vital organs, invigorated by his prudent habits, had often before rallied and now refused to surrender without a struggle. But his last hour was the calm close of a serene life. With that regard for places, hallowed by associations, which he never ceased to feel, he had wished to die at the spot where his wife and youngest son had breathed their last. And, reclining in his chair, near that sacred spot, with his children and grandchildren around him, his pulse and breathing slowly sunk. For one instant he opened his sightless, but now beaming, eyes, and turned from side to side his face, lighted with an expression of surpassing brightness. Were the beloved forms that he had seen in the vision now welcoming him into their midst? As the clock struck ten, his usual bed time, he solved or ceased to heed the engrossing question of his life. The glorious mind, the tried and faithful heart were nothing or immortal.

The following from the Lexington Daily Press accurately tells the closing scene:

DEATH OF THE DISTINGUISHED JURIST LAST NIGHT.

Hon. GEORGE ROBERTSON died at his residence, on High street, corner of Mill, last night, at 10 o'clock. Members of his family and kind friends, who have faithfully attended him during his long and painful illness, were with him at the closing hour of life, and ministered to his suffering in every way that warm affection could suggest.

In the winter of 1871 the venerable jurist was stricken with paralysis. The lingering disease, with varying phases, weighed down the strong frame, and keeping him an invalid, did its work slowly but so surely, that those who knew and loved him so well were prepared for the sad event which has lost the nation a master mind.

His last relapse occurred on Monday, when he was attacked with something like cramp colic. Every day succeeding he suffered from chills, and on yesterday morning about 4 o'clock, began to yield to the dread summons. During the forenoon he was visited by Rev. Mr. Dinwiddie, who held religious services with him. In conversation with Mr. Dinwiddie, he expressed himself as perfectly at peace, and fully prepared to die. During the entire day the work of dissolution continued. The sufferer endured at times intense and almost unbearable agony of body, such was the struggle between giant strength and the King of Terrors. By the advice of his physicians opiates were administered, but they served to little purpose.

At nine o'clock he asked for water. It was given him in a spoon, and he asked for the glass. Soon after drinking of it he began to sink, and did not speak again. About fifteen minutes after he had taken water, Mrs. Judge Alexander Robertson went to his side and asked him if he recognized her. His answer was a pressure of the hand. Three times was the question repeated, but the power of speech was gone, and only that gentle clasp told the sorrowing ones that he was yet conscious. Slowly the hand of death rested upon him, and just as the clock sounded the hour of ten, the heart ceased its throbbing, and the great brain was at rest.

Two years ago Judge Robertson, with several members of his family, united themselves with the Church. From that to the end of his life he was an earnest, devoted follower of the Meek and Lowly One. For nearly two years he was almost totally blind, but so desirous was he to know "the ways of pleasantness and the paths of peace," he would have his friends to sing and pray and read from God's Holy Word to him, and from its teachings he seemed to derive consolation. The great mind which had so long been accustomed to view all questions from a purely philosophical standpoint, accepted the simple laws of Holy Writ, even as a little child accepts the parent teachings. The man who, for nearly a quarter of a century, was the expounder of human law, was himself an humble listener to the lessons of the Judge of the Universe.

In death, as in life, the face of Judge Robertson bore the impress of that intellect which placed him in the ranks with those great minds, the movers of the nation in the years gone by. The countenance, when viewed by the writer last night, wore a calm and peaceful expression. The massive forehead, broad and smooth, betrayed no sign of the suffering through which the body had passed. From the face alone could be detected aught of the pain endured. The body was resting upon the extension chair, which he had occupied during his illness, and in which he was resting when he died.

In the room, at the time we visited it, was a little granddaughter quietly sleeping. She was not aware that the Death Angel had swept over her family and called a loved and revered one, and those who were there did not awaken her.

No definite arrangements have yet been made for the funeral, nor will any be made until the arrival of all the family and friends. The Judge had but three children living. Of these, two, Judge Alexander Robertson and Mrs. Bell, were with him at the time of his death. Mrs. Buford is expected to arrive this morning.

CHAPTER X.

FUNERAL SERVICES.

The death of JUDGE ROBERTSON, though not unexpected, created a feeling of sorrow throughout the country. The press of his own and of other States paid heartfelt, full and lofty tributes to his memory, and many Bars passed resolutions expressive of their profound respect for the character of the departed jurist. In the 9th volume of Bush's Reports may be found a transcript of the record of the proceedings upon the occasion of his death, of the Court of which he was so long a member, containing a just and beautiful resume of his life and character, by Judge Hardin, and immediately following is the record of the same sad offices to the memory of that lamented Judge. "They were pleasant in their lives and in their death they were not divided."

A few of these notices of the press, found at the end of this volume, may be taken as a fair specimen of them all.

THE FUNERAL SERVICES.

[From the Lexington Press.]

The scene was impressive in the extreme. Around the door groups of men, mostly men of that profession which the deceased had so highly adorned, but still embracing representatives of other walks in life, were scattered, discussing in under tones the noble qualities of the illustrious dead.

When members of the bar reached the residence, the pall-bearers stepped from the ranks, while the remainder were conducted into the house, and assigned seats immediately to the right of the bier, which was placed in the folding doors between the parlors. The space to the left of the casket was occupied by ladies; that to the right by the officiating minister, visiting clergymen, choir, and gentlemen not of the profession. The coffin, covered with the rarest flowers, offerings of love, separated the assemblage as described. One of the most affecting sights was the bowed and feeble frame of the venerable Judge Underwood, the school-fellow and companion of Judge Robertson, seated near the body. The old man, himself on the shadowy side of four score years, had obeyed the summons to attend the obsequies of his friend, and was then the occupant of a seat near to all that was mortal of the one he had loved so well.

Shortly after the entrance of the Bar, the religious services began with the solemn, tender refrain, "It is well." Dr. Christie then read the 90th Psalm, after which prayer was offered by Rev. Gelon H. Rout, of Versailles. The man of God then read the hymn, "There is an hour of hallowed peace," which was exquisitely rendered by the choir. It is said that this hymn, as well as that which was sung at the close of the services, was selected by Judge Robertson to be sung at his funeral. When the last note of the low, sad music had floated away, Rev. Mr. Christie began the delivery of the funeral oration, a full report of which appears in another part of this paper. More than once during the time the speaker was upon the floor, strong men's lips were seen to quiver, and bright eyes to moisten with tears. The sermon speaks its own merit; the universal commendation given it by those who heard it shows the appreciation with which it was received.

Upon the conclusion of Mr. Christie's remarks, the following named gentlemen, who officiated as pall-bearers, took charge of the remains and conveyed them to the hearse in waiting: Hon. Joseph D. Hunt, Hon. James O. Harrison, Hon. Madison C. Johnson, Hon. George B. Kinkead, Hon. F. K. Hunt, Col. W. C. P. Breckinridge, Judge Joseph R.

Underwood, Judge Alvin Duvall, Attorney General Rodman, Major B. F. Buckner, J. R. Morton, Esq., Gen. John B. Huston, Hon. R. A. Buckner, and Judge W. B. Kinkead.

The line of procession was at once taken to the cemetery, in the following order:

Pall-Bearers.
Ministers.
Hearse.
Family of the deceased.
Ex-Judges and Officers of the Court of Appeals.
Judges and Officers of Courts, and Members of Bars of other Cities.
Judges of County and Magistrates' Courts.
City Council.
Lexington Bar.
Citizens.

The cortege, one of the largest ever seen in this city, moved down High street to Mulberry; down Mulberry to Main, and thence to the cemetery. There the remains were deposited in the family vault; a few remarks were made by Dr. Seeley, a prayer was offered, and the iron door closed upon the great jurist, to await the last summons which is to call him before the Judge of the Universe.

EXTRACT FROM THE FUNERAL DISCOURSE OF THE

REV. ROBERT CHRISTIE.

Even if this were the occasion on which to indulge in eulogistic speech concerning the illustrious dead, your speaker is not one to attempt that sacred duty. A just and discriminating tribute to one possessing such forensic ability, technical knowledge, ripe scholarship, varied accomplishments, and a life of grand achievements, can alone come from the lips or pen of one who has trodden the same lofty path with himself, and who is competent to weigh the results of a

7

life that has helped to shape and determine the great events of half a century. The materials for such a tribute are abundant, and only need the shaping of some plastic hand. For his career was not like that of the meteor which dazzles the eye for a moment, but is gone before you can analyze to light or determine its path; but rather like one of the grand luminaries that rises steadily and gradually, increasing in brilliancy as it reaches the meridian, then slowly sloping down the West till it sinks in a flood of glory. His place in the intellectual heavens can be determined at any point along the path of three score years of our Commonwealth's history.

The arena which he selected for the exercise of his powers was one where distinction could only be won by pre-eminent talent. For there were giants at the bar of Lexington in those days. One who could successfully cope with the witchery of Clay's eloquence, and break the spell which the sage of Ashland could cast over the minds of a jury, has no fictitious claim to greatness. Those fully competent to judge, tell us that no man ever brought to the Supreme Bench of Kentucky greater fitness for the responsible duties of the place than did Chief Justice George Robertson. A cursory glance at some of his published papers shows that he always took a large grasp of any subject, whilst no detail was too insignificant to escape his penetrating glance. And it is impossible to overlook that delicacy and sensitiveness of moral touch which is visible all through these papers, especially when he is dealing with the feelings and reputation of others.

One of the great dailies has indicated in a few words his professional status. It says: "His professional course was marked by high integrity of purpose, and while presiding as Judge of the Appellate Court, he enjoyed to an eminent degree the confidence of the bar and public."

I am told by those who knew him well that he never shrunk from any work of usefulness; that he was one whose superior judgment and zeal were pressed into almost every

benevolent enterprise and public institution. He also sustained and filled with affectionate assiduity the tenderest
relations of domestic life, whether of husband, father, or
grandsire. But to use his own language touching another:
"His name needs not our panegyric. The carver of his own
fortune; the founder of his own name; with his own hand
he has built his own monument, and with his own tongue
and his own pen he has stereotyped his own autobiography.
With hopeful trust, his maternal Commonwealth consigns
his fame to the justice of history and to the judgment of
ages to come."

But there is one event in his life that we cannot pass by
in silence. It is well known to most of you that the deceased did not confess Christ before men till he had passed
the limit of four score years. But let us not conclude that
he then for the first time considered seriously the subject of
religion. There was perhaps no layman in the State of Kentucky who possessed a more thorough and comprehensive-
knowledge of the science of theology. He was familiar with
all the more recent attacks on revealed religion. He understood thoroughly the principles and scope of positivism,
development, and evolution. I mention these things to show
how great was the triumph of faith at the last. When he did
unite with the Church, although his mind had lost some of
the elasticity of youth, it had lost little or none of its grasp
and clearness. O, how beautiful to see this eminent patriarch sitting for the first time at the feet of Jesus, trusting to
Him alone for salvation.

And yet the beauty of the scene is marred by a tinge of
sadness when we think of how much he might have done for
Christ had he taken this step in youth, or early manhood.
But let us praise the long suffering and love of God that let
him wander so long, but brought him home at last. I need
not dwell on the good confession that he witnessed during the
past two years. But perhaps the most beautiful trait of these
latter days was his love for music. Not for the heroic ballad

or grand oratorio, but for the simple and tender hymns of childhood. It was said that the great Dr. Nott was soothed to sleep during the latter months of his life by the cradle hymn,

> "Hush, my child! be still and slumber;
> Holy angels guard thy bed."

When the great Dr. Guthrie was fighting the billows of death, he asked those around him to sing something. They asked him what it should be, when he replied: "O, sing me a bairn's sang!" So our departed friend loved to hear these bairns' sangs—the songs of childhood. Does not this interpret the words, "Except ye be converted, and become as little children, ye shall in nowise enter into the kingdom of heaven." He knew for months that death might come at any moment, and he calmly awaited his approach.

APPENDIX

—

A.

SCENES OF EARLY LIFE.

The following addenda were originally in the form of short foot notes, which, having been revised from time to time, whenever it was supposed that this volume was about to be printed, have grown by successive accretions, without reference to any leading idea or regular plan, too large for the places for which they were intended. Although disconnected, deficient in pertinent matter, and now seen to be written in an inflated and otherwise faulty style, they may shed some light upon their subject, and are, therefore, not without hesitation, retained.

If habit is second nature, birth-place is second parentage. *Mantua, bore me (me genuit)*, are words of Virgil's epitaph. People of the German race speak of their father-land; but every one of English blood loves to call his native spot a mother. And aptly so, for birth-place and mother are the first teachers of the dawning mind.

In his usual aphoristic style, M. Hugo says: "The config uration of the soil decides many a man's actions. The earth is more his accomplice than people believe. The education of hights and shadows is very different. The mountain is a citadel; the forest an ambuscade. The one inspires audacity, the other teaches craft." But it is needless to refer to him, or to Montesque, or to Spencer, to prove that the natural scenes, amid which a character is formed, are both directly, and, by modifying the social environment, the mould of many of its leading and ineffaceable traits. Examples of the fact are ever and every where present.

The author of this volume had simple tastes, cared little for display, for fashion, or fashionable people; loved music and beauty in all its forms, and was endowed with a vivifying imagination, which the study of statutes and records may have in a large measure repressed, but could not destroy. No Vendean or Swiss ever loved his country more, or had a larger share of that regard for place, which Phrenologists call by the rugged name, inhabitativeness. He had not first studied nature in science, "which reveals a rigid immutable order, that looks like self-subsistence, and does not manifest intelligence, which is full of life, variety, and progressive operation," but by early observations of the forces and changes displayed in the objects around him, he was impressed with an abiding sense of an all-pervading and intelligent power, and escaped the meshes of that cheerless positivism, which holds that God is unknowable; religion is superstition. Unlike city-bred persons, he was much given to solitary meditation, and could readily withdraw his thoughts from the distracting influence of society.

He had learned to act and think before he had learned the authority of names, and was always an independent thinker —yielding only to the strength of reason. He had not been taught that the chief end of life is to acquire riches, and after obtaining enough to make him independent, he subordinated the gaining of property to nobler objects. These tastes and mental habits were no doubt, to a considerable extent, the result of the physical surroundings of his early life.

His boyhood was passed in the romantic region near the confluence of Dix and Kentucky rivers. The approaches to these streams have been denuded of their first vesture of evergreens, and the waters have shrunk to half their former volume. But the deep ravines, with their summer brooks and winter torrents, and the vertical limestone cliffs, are still there, and the southeastern horizon is still a waving line of purple-crested knobs, looking, in the distance, like the delectable mountains, upon whose pastoral hights Christian rested on his way.

When the author was a boy, most of the fine country in this neighborhood was covered with the primitive forest, unbroken save by scattered "settlements," which were either clearings, surrounded with a worm-fence, and dotted with fresh stumps, from whose midst rose the little cabin, or the more stately hewed-low house of the settler, and from whose edges were heard the ring of the woodchopper's stroke and the crashing thunder of falling trees; or they were deadenings, whose belted and sapless timber was left to sink beneath the destroying hand of decay and of the storm.

Those who have only seen the dwarfed, scraggy, scattered, and degenerate trees, which are all that the Vandal axe has left in the central portions of Kentucky, can form no due conception of the girth and reach of the Titans that have fallen, or of the majesty of their vast assembly.* Large upland tracts of these wilds were free from undergrowth, and their mossy paths, more beautiful and more springy to the tread than carpets of heaviest ply, were columned by stately trunks and arched and groined by interlacing boughs into "long-drawn aisles and fretted vaults," whose dim and solemn grandeur is feebly imitated in the noblest cathedrals. Depressed spots, the censers of these first temples, were filled with spicey shrubs and flowering vines, which at certain seasons exhaled varied and delicate perfumes. In the morn-

*The writer published the immediately following portions of this article in an early number of the Dispatch.

ing of a still summer day, these woods were musical with birds;
at noon, their silence was unbroken; in the evening, their
depths resounded with the droning orchestra of the insect
world, "their ever changing magnificence never grew stale."
In a calm, they were solitudes, into which the Egeria of meditation loved to retreat at the call of her votary. When
"the trees against a stormy sky their giant branches tost,"
the display of force was of that resistless kind from which the
mind derives its conception of almighty power. In winter,
the naked spray traced lovely embroideries on the overarch-
ing sky, or gave forth a play of many colored lights from its
crystal incrustations of sleet. These woods were gay and
brilliant in the spring. Their saddest and most splendid season was the fall—the foliage, ere it fell, put on all the glories
of the evening clouds, and at the rising and the going down
of the sun, tree tops and clouds blended into one, presented
through the hazy air a sublime panorama of the apocalypic
vision of the Holy City coming down from heaven. How
vivid and pure the effect of scenes like these, compared with
second-hand impressions made by books, or the corrupting
influences of towns! Who can doubt that the mind will become more fraught with images of beauty, more earnest and
elevated by listening to the voices, and watching the working of nature, and by associations with plain, artless, and
thoughtful people, than by conning in hexameters, how Ty-
tyrus dallied with Amaryllis in the shade, or by mingling in
the frivolities of fashionable society?

Forests have been the source of fertilizing streams and of
renovating men. They cherished all of manly virtue that
social corruption left in the effete old world, and gave it a
nobler civilization than it lost. And in the new they trained
wise founders and loyal subjects of free States, who combined
the swain's simplicity with the forecaste and daring of the
hero, and were worthy of both the bucolic and the epic lay!
Vivite Sylvae! Farewell, ye woods! Great countries bereft

of trees have become material and moral wastes. May ours escape their fate!*

In these woodland homes the sturdy, thoughtful, and honest pioneers, of winter evenings, by the great log fires, told of the privations they had endured, of the never-to-be-forgotten "hard winter," of their imperfect shelter, their scanty and rough fare, their hair-breadth escapes from savage men and beasts, and inspired their attentive young ones with a firmness of purpose which enabled them to face dangers, moral and physical, and in the midst of difficulty and trial feel with the son of Anchises in like case. We, too, in after times may think of this with pride. The first settlers produced and raised a vigorous breed, not only by commonly transmitting to their descendants strong nerves, strong bones, and shapely forms, but also, partly from necessity, partly from choice, by permitting the law of natural selection to have free course, they inadvertently adopted the regulation of Lycurgus, which required all the feeble and deformed children to be put to death. Having undergone exposure in youth, and being stout and hearty themselves, they inferred that the exposure had made them so, overlooking the need of strong constitutions to enable them to survive the exposure. The sleazy home-made clothing of that day was far

---

* In "The Settler," by A. B. Street, are these lines:

The paths which wound mid gorgeous trees,
The stream whose bright lips kissed the flowers,
The winds that swelled their harmonies,
Through those sun-hiding bowers;
The temple vast, the green arcade,
The nestling vale, the grassy glade,
Dark cave and swampy lair,
These scenes and sounds majestic, made
His world, his pleasures there.
Humble the lot, yet his the race
When liberty sent forth her cry,
Who thronged in conflict's deadliest place,
To fight, to bleed, to die;
Who cumbered Bunker's hight of red
By hope through weary years were led,
And witnessed Yorktown's sun
Blaze on a nation's banner spread
A nation's freedom won.

less warm than the thick woolens now in common use. Most
boys, even of the wealthiest families, had no shoes in summer. Many of them not even in winter.

One of the author's staunchest friends, who had been his
neighbor in boyhood, used to tell that he himself went
the round of the traps he had set for quails and hares, by
dextrously stepping on one and then on the other of two
shingles, to protect his bare feet from the snow and the
briars. The stone bruise, which compelled its victim to limp
on his toe; the stumped toe, which made him hobble on his
heel; chapped feet, which made him wince, when they un-
derwent the indispensable scrubbing at bed time, were the
rule, sound feet, the exception. And then all children too
large to sleep in the trundle-bed in the family room, took a
Russian bath every winter night by going into a room without fire, stripping to their short shirts, and jumping into the
frozen brown linen sheets. In the morning they went to the
spring, as the author has herein related, to wash themselves.
It is strange that such air-loving, out-door people as the first
settlers should have taken great pains to exclude fresh air
from those who were ill.

B.

GARRARD COUNTY.

If the place of youth is important, for preparation, hardly less so is the place of manhood, for achievement. The woods are a better school than stage, more favorable to study than to action, forces that have much range or speed, like cavalry and artillery, require space. Whether Judge Robertson's interests were best promoted by his long stay in the agricultural and then sparsely peopled district in which he was born, depends on the question whether fortune and fame are to be taken as part of those interests. Unquestionably he could, at any great commercial center, have speedily attained a front rank in his profession.

Lancaster, his home for thirty years or more, is situated on a high table land, near the center of the State, and fifty years ago contained a population of five or six hundred. Its people were as intelligent, hospitable, and honest as those of any other town in Kentucky, then or since. Their houses were mostly of brick, well built and comfortable. Less than half the surrounding country had been cleared of the forest which bounded the view in every direction. The arable lands of the county produced crops far in excess of the home demand, and there were no accessible foreign markets, except for tobacco, which was floated down the Kentucky river in flat-boats, and for hogs, horses and mules, which were driven South, by way of Cumberland gap. Provisions of all kinds were exceedingly cheap and of excellent quality;

quails and squirrels abounded; deer frequented the outskirts
of the county, and in the fall wild pigeons in countless numbers settled upon the oak trees; the woods were well stored
with honey, and produced abundance of delicious sugar and
molasses.

The fleeces of their own flocks, flax and cotton from their
own fields, supplied this Arcadian people with most of their
clothing, their carpets and bed clothes. These were spun
and woven in the country. Their hats and shoes were made
in the town. The only importations they needed were iron
and certain articles of hardware, mordants, used in coloring
yarns, porcelain and the materials for holiday attire. The
furniture made in the village was handsome and durable.
Materials for building, except nails (the cut nail had been
newly introduced), were excellent, and could be had for little
money or labor. The difference between the rich and poor,
at this time, was in the quantity, not in the quality, of their
possessions, and as there were no fashions of the rich for
families of moderate means to ape,

> "Their sober wishes never learned to stray
> Beyond the cool sequestered vale of life."

Lancaster was therefore a paradise for the poor. If it had
not been, Judge Robertson could not have lived, comfortably
as he did, on his slender salary. And still, Lancaster was
not all the poet has painted Sweet Auburn, nor was the age,
to all, golden. It was the iron age of children, they were in
charge of or compelled much of their time to be with negroes,
who either had been born or were but one or two removes
from those who had been born in Guinea. Ignorant races
are superstitious. The supernatural creations of the negroes
were all of a sinister kind. Their dreams, sombre, like their
skins, producing none of the Naiads, Dryads, Pucks, Ober-
ons or Santa Clauses, of happier mythologies, peopled the
night with ghosts, goblins, and witches. The old mammies
used to take forks to bed with them to keep off the witches.
They believed in obeah charms, and interpreted almost all

the ordinary and all unusual events of the day into omens of evil. The "uncles and aunts" of these benighted children of the sun, so infested the minds of most children in years with their delusions, that they were afraid to pass a church yard, to sleep alone, to go unattended through the dark, and un willing to turn back, after starting to a place, without making a cross-mark and spitting on the intersection, to prevent bad luck. If a belief in the supernatural be, as some suppose, a delusion, and not innate, early associations may have led Judge Robertson to look, if not with much credence, with not little interest into the evidence of the responses and appa. ritions that are alledged to have come from another world, and to have surmised to his dying day that there may be realities corresponding with the shadows which flit in the gloaming between two states of existence.

He had been fortunate in having Joshua Fry and Samuel Finley for his teachers. Most of the schools were mere prisons to which children were sent with the mistaken view of keeping them out of mischief. School books were gener- ally destitute of explanations, and the teachers, with some honorable exceptions, too ignorant to supply the deficiencies. Punishments were inflicted for trivial delinquencies, and were often cruel, sometimes dangerous. A boy could not be for a long time an inverted V, by putting his finger on the floor, without danger of cerebral congestion, and this was no un- usual punishment. The great want of the town was a suffi- cient supply of wholesome water It contained no cisterns, no perennial springs, and but a single well. This would have been a source of insufferable inconvenience, if slaves had not been numerous. In seasons of drought this well would become dry, and then water had to be hauled from distant springs. The insufficiency and quality of the water were no doubt a principal cause of the frequent epidemics with which the village was scourged. And it was a terrible thing to be even a little sick at Lancaster, because any indis- position, if a doctor were called in, almost inevitably resulted

in great exhaustion.   Hahneman had not been heard of, but
Sangrado had.   Medicine of the most nauseous kind was administered in its most nauseous form, and in the heroic doses,
which the gentlemen of the veterinary art (vulgarly called
horse-doctors, notwithstanding they also doctor oxen) give to
their patients.   Every physician carried in his pockets, as
regularly as he did his spectacles, a spring and a thumb
lancet, and in almost every stage of almost every disease, the
only option of the sufferer was whether he would hold out
his arm to the one or to the other.   So great was the rage
for phlebotomy, that it was considered a good prophylactic
precaution to bleed well people every spring, and it was held
indispensable that one blade of every jack-knife should be a
fleam.   Warm water was freely given, not in pursuance of
Sangrado's theory, to supply the place of the abstracted
blood, but to assist vomiting, and thereby prevent a renewal
of the blood.   For all other purposes the use of water was
strictly interdicted, and fresh air was declared by these Galens
to be peculiarly noxious to people who were ill.   A man or boy
who was so unfortunate as to be sick at Lancaster, in those
days, may possibly forgive, but can never forget, his treat-
ment.   Some of the most noted cures were of persons who
were given up by their physicians, and were allowed by their
nurses free use of air and water, and plenty of good food.*

Members of Judge Robertson's family were often ill, himself never—but once, and his remedy was peculiar   Having
been affected for several days with nausea or sick stomach,
he received through the post-office a fresh number of the
North American Review, in which there was an article re-
commending cold boiled cabbage for his complaint; he tried
it at once and was relieved.

Lancaster rarely had a stationed preacher.   The inhabit-
ants were divided among so many religious sects that no one ,
denomination was able to build a church or pay a regular

---

*It is needless to say that the doctors of Lancaster were, in theory and
practice, abreast of the most advanced skill of their times.

pastor, but they united to erect one church, in which the different denominations worshiped in rotation. Religion here was not so imposing as in the "dim religious light" of a Trinity or St. Paul's, but was probably fully as sincere, and not less effectual. The prayer-meetings were commonly lighted by a single tallow dip, not much larger or whiter than a catalpa bean. When this feeble luminary needed snuffing, some brother valiantly used his thumb and forefinger to remove the charred wick, and sometimes put out the light; on such occasions, as dwelling houses were remote from the church, and matches had not been invented, the congregation would disperse.

This usually quiet little town was the scene of many a bloody set-to. Numerous individuals and families in the county, each thought the other too many, whenever these opposing parties met, which some of them were almost sure to do, in town, on every public day, then and there, in the dialect of the time—

> "They gouged and they bit,
> Scratched, pommeled and fit,"

with fists, feet, missiles, knives (pistols were not in common use), to the unmitigated annoyance of every body, except possibly the doctors, lawyers, and undertakers, to whom they afforded some employment.

Social intercourse at Lancaster was unrestrained and cheerful. Mr. Robertson's house was the abode of neatness, abundance, and cheerful welcomes, and so were the houses of most of his neighbors. The home society was well informed and persons of culture, chiefly preachers and lawyers, were frequent visitors from abroad. One man, a bachelor of middle age, visited Judge Robertson's house every evening during many years. Regardless of weather, or if detained, of the lateness of the hour, he was sure to make his appearance between sundown and midnight, and his camlet cloak, often dripping wet, and his tin lantern were welcome sights to the whole family, especially of a bleak winter night.

He brought all the news, foreign and domestic, and was a
pleasant companion, of strong understanding, much good
humor, considerable reading, retentive memory, and warm
attachments.   He was fond of a smoke, a chat, a good laugh,
a game of back-gammon or whist, and fondest of all of a
savory luncheon, which, if not tendered, he did not hesitate
to call for.   His presence was especially welcome to the
younger members of the family, because he had a wonderful
store of tales and anecdotes, and could recite Tom Jones,
Ivanhoe, The Children of the Abbey, Tales of a Grandfather,
or any of the many books he had read, with vividness and
close minuteness.   This nightly visitant and his host had
been boys together, and they never tired of talking about the
persons, events, and scenes of by-gone years.   He died
about a year before the Judge removed from Lancaster, and
there was one less tie to bind him to that place.

It has been said that people are every where the same.   If
this is true, the world is full of brave and generous hearts,
for certain it is that nobler men and women do not live in any
clime, or in song or story, than some of those who once trod
and now repose beneath the soil of Garrard.   Their memory
will ever, to those who knew them, make that county a
Holy land.*

* Those who wish to know more of this county may be gratified by reading a metrical history, called " The Song of Lancaster," by Mrs. Eugenia
Potts, the accomplished daughter of Col George W. Dunlap. The writer
has not seen, but has heard favorable mention of the work by competent
judges.

C.

HIS LOVE OF COUNTRY.

His patriotism was both instinctive, or an involuntary extension of his attachment for other objects, and rational. He experienced in its full force that unreckoning passion which made the exiled Foscari "Feel that his soul moldered in his bosom," and forced him back to Venice, though to return was to die, and which hurried the dying Scott from Italy, that he might hear once more the ripple of the Tweed. Judge Robertson gave utterance to this unconquerable sentiment, when he said, "And then, whenever or wherever it may be our doom to look for the last time on earth, we may die justly proud of the title, Kentuckian, and with our expiring breath cordially exclaim, Kentucky as she was—Kentucky as she is—Kentucky as she will be—KENTUCKY FOREVER."

His native State was the only country he ever knew. He was born two years before she became a State. He had passed the whole of his life within her borders, except the four sessions which he spent in Congress. She was the theater of all his domestic and social enjoyments, of all his efforts and his griefs, the home of all his living friends and the grave of all his dead ones. From her he had derived all he was; from her he looked for all he hoped in this life. This, on all proper occasions, he gratefully acknowledged. He also had a strong rational regard for Kentucky. He had learned her physical geography and resources, and was familiar with the character of her people. Traditionally, or as an actor, he knew every event in her history, and he believed and unhesitatingly asserted that, all things considered, there was not a more desirable dwelling place for man upon the earth than this "Hesperian land," and he strenuously opposed that notion, which is the bane of American households, that families should scatter in quest of wealth. He thought that the union and co-operation of kindred hearts and hands would more than compensate for the loss of any prospects of material advancement that could be afforded by a voluntary exile from country and home.   He also had a peculiar regard for the counties in which his youth and early manhood had been spent, and was not alone warmly attached to the people who had appreciated his solid, rather than showy, worth, and had elevated him as high as they could, in preference to other men of ability and of fortune and fortunate connections; but he had a strong affection for the natural objects with which he was familiar.   When he crossed to the south side of the Kentucky river, his countenance seemed to say, ''the very winds feel native to my veins.''   Some now living have not forgotten his chagrin and distress when, during one of his occasional visits to Garrard, he saw that a magnificent elm, which had stood in a bend of the road, on his homestead place, and under which his children used to play, and which had been the first and most beautiful object that, in other days, had greeted his vision as he drew near home, had been felled by his tenant, under the pretext that it shaded the land.   Judge R. never forgot this act of wantonness.   He had designated a spot in Garrard county as the burial place of himself and family, and it required an absence of many years to change this intention; and it was only after the beautiful cemetery at Lexington had been established that he gathered the bones of his deceased children into the vault which now guards his own ashes.   He also became so attached, from clustering memories, to his home in Lexington that, in his helpless and desolate old age, no persuasion could induce him to abandon it.   He expressed a desire to die in the house and in the very spot where his youngest son and wife had expired

This man of simple and loving affections, not only loved, he also lived for his country.   What it is to do this he has told us both by his words and by his acts: ''What is it to live for one's country?   It is not to get rich, nor to hold office, nor to be gazed at with vulgar admiration, nor to win a battle, nor to make a noise in the world. Many who have accomplished all these have been a curse rather than a blessing to mankind. But he, and he alone, who honestly dedicates his talents and his example to the happiness and improvement of his race, lives for his country, whatever may be his sphere. He who seeks his own aggrandizement at the expense of truth, or principle, or candor, does not live for his country—nor can he live for his country, in the full sense, whose example is demoralizing, or in any way pernicious. But he truly lives for his country, who, in all the walks of life and relations of society, does as much good and as little harm as possible, and always acts according to the disinterested suggestions of a pure conscience and a sound head. Whatever may be his condition—high or low, conspicuous or obscure—he, whose life exemplifies and commends the negative and positive virtues, personal, social, and civil—who lives in the habit of pure morality, enlarged patriotism, and disinterested philanthropy—and whose conduct and example are, as far as known and felt, useful to mankind—he, and he alone, lives for his country. And hence it is perfectly true, that a virtuous peasant in a thatched hut, may live more for his country than many idolized orators, triumphant politicians, or laureled chieftains."

These are his words. His life afforded a perfect illustration of them. Entertaining and acting up to these sentiments, although many who were not in any respect his superiors, left him far behind on the road to power and affluence. He never thought that his life, either as an experience or an example, was a failure. Disappointment never gave him any taint of misanthrop, or made him affect the part of a Cincinnatus.

D.

LOVE OF MUSIC.

The violin, accompanied or not by the piano, sometimes, after the labors of the day were over, afforded him an innocent resource for the entertainment of himself and friends, and was also frequently the inspirer and the interpreter of his most serious musings. His mother taught him the scales. With this exception, his fine natural ear was only self-taught. Yet, without even frequent opportunities of hearing first rate performers, he attained a skill in all keys and in several different positions, which evinced a capacity for the highest excellence. He played lively tunes with a dash and fire which few amateurs could equal, and could render plaintive melodies in tones that bewailed the loved and lost, and revealed delicate shades of feeling and conception too subtle to be expressed by words. Like Sivori, he fully appreciated the richness and power of the base or G string, and drew from it strains of surpassing volume and softness. His most intimate friends can never hear Lea Rigg, or Turbaned Turk, or The Arkansas Traveler, without remembering how exquisitely and how peculiarly they were played by him. His favorite time for these musical interludes was the evening, as he walked to and fro in a large room or hall. He dearly loved the old church tunes which his mother and sisters used to sing, and the beautiful melody, Old Folks at Home, for a reason which he has stated in this volume, never failed to move him deeply. He requested that it should be sung on two occasions, when his attendants supposed he was dying. On the first of these occasions, the fair cantatrice, the obliging and deservedly renowned Miss Carey, overcome by the sadness of the circumstances, was unable to proceed. Many of the hours that he passed in darkness, reclining in his invalid's chair, were solaced by songs of kind men and women, who had learned that he was fond of music. Itinerant minstrels were often called in, and not unfrequently some amateur band would play near his window at night.

At his own house his services as a musician were often requested by his children, grand-children, and their young friends. For hours, during two or three evenings of every week, he would play for them to dance, and would participate heartily in their innocent mirth. Most of those who were, from time to time, present at those gatherings, preceded their kind entertainer to the grave. The rest are scattered, and the large and cheerful room in which these re-unions were held, has ceased to exist. The old violin remains, and is the most eloquent souvenir of its departed master.

In his valedictory to the law class he expressed his estimate of music in these words: "Music, Luther's intellectual catholican, next to the Bible, in his judgment, as an adversary of the devil, should not be derided or undervalued. It exhilerates and tranquilizes the mind, elevates and purifies the heart, and thus contributes much of what scarcely any other amusement can as innocently contribute to improvement and happiness."

E.

DOMESTIC RELATIONS.

To know Judge Robertson was to know him at home; to know him there was to love him. The strongest wish of his youth was to have a settled home, and when he had obtained one, to make that home happy was the central object of all his efforts. Nobly did he redeem the hostages which, he says, he gave to fortune when he married, and the pledge which he made to cherish his wife and children. His wife deserved his care, for she valued his love and the endearments of her home above all other pleasures, and accomplished her-

self in all housewifely skill and in every domestic virtue.
His letters to his wife, children, and friends, if they had been
preserved, would have afforded the best evidence that could
now be exhibited of the ties that bound him to his family.
These, written in a plain style, related to all the occasions of
joy and of sorrow, congratulation and of consolation incident
to life, and evince a more varied experience, a wisdom more
chastened and profound, and a wider sympathy than he
manifested to the world   But most of these have been
inconsiderately destroyed, and among them many communications that deserved a better fate, addressed to him by
distinguished and by obscure friends, and which would show
the regard felt for him by those who knew him well.

The following letter, written while he was on his way to
Congress for the last time, has been casually found, and contains a promise which he faithfully kept, by resigning his seat
for two years in Congress, to avoid separation from his wife
and young children, and to devote himself to the more arduous and less congenial labors of his profession for their
benefit:

LANCASTER, OHIO, 28th Nov'r, 1319.

My Dear Wife:

Being entirely alone, I can't employ my time better than
by writing to you.   I came last night to a little town called
Tarleton, 15 miles from here, and there expected to stay all
day, as the stage does not travel on Sunday; but being very
lonesome, I could not bear the idea of staying a whole day
in such a place by myself—I therefore employed the driver to
bring me on here.   We started about 12 o'clock and got here
about 4   I have travelled this far without company, and
without seeing a human face that I ever saw before, since I
left Stephen at Lexington.   The trip is of course very disa-
greeable.   I am here now alone, about dark, and the weather
is getting very bad.   It snowed all day to-day, and will rain
very hard I fear to-night.   It is the most dismal night to me
that I ever saw.   I need not disguise from you that I am

completely miserable. I never was as unhappy in my life. I can think of nothing but you and the children. I have eat very little since I left home, and have not had one hour's good sleep—some nights I have not slept at all. But, in other respects, I am in good health.

I expect to get company at Zanesville, where I will stay to-morrow night, and hope to be able to get to my journey's .end on next Saturday or Sunday.

It is just ten years to-night since we were married, and it was about this time in the evening. This reflection, as well as every thing else I can think about or see, tends to increase my anxiety.

I never will leave you again as long as we live. I will be at home as soon as I promised, or sooner, and intend then to stay with my family. I cannot be happy or contented one moment any where else.

I am very anxious to see the children already, and particularly Charlotte. I do not think I can stay from her. Take good care of them all, and of yourself, and be as happy as possible, and live as well as you can desire, without regarding the expence.

If Darwin's horse can not be sold he ought to be sent home. He is not worth wintering. Give my compliments to Sally and tell her to stay with you day and night, and she shall never regret it. If I could think you were contented, I could go along pretty well, doleful as is my situation; but the idea that you are unhappy almost distracts me.

Elijah Hyatt promised me to keep you in flour, and he is to let you have some pork. What you get of him, with what you may kill, if Archy attends to our hogs, will be sufficient. A man by the name of Cook is to let you have one hog—and if you want beef, Ben. Bryant will furnish you.

If you should want money, call on Mr. George, and if he has none, get what you want of Joe Letcher.

After I get in, I shall write to you every day. Oh, how happy would I be, and how different my situation, if, instead of Lancaster, Ohio, I was in Lancaster, Kentucky, with little Charlotte on my knee! But the time shall, I hope, not be long before I shall make this exchange.

Give my love to the children. Farewell.

To his eldest daughter, when eight years of age, in answer to the first letter she ever wrote:

WASHINGTON CITY, 15th December, 1819.

My Dear Daughter:

It was with great pleasure that I received a letter from you this morning. I hope it will not be the last which I shall receive from you during the winter. I am very much obliged to you for this your first letter. I would advise you to stay at home this winter with your mother, and learn to knit, and improve your education by attending occasionally to your books and writing. Stay in the house and be a good girl; don't run about with the little girls of the town they will teach you bad habits and make you a bad girl. If you do as I advise you, I will make you some very handsome presents when I return, and you may go to see your grandma in the spring.

Tell Ellen I wish her to stay at home, and be a good girl and learn her book, and you must teach Mary her A B C's.

I had very good weather during my journey, and am in good health. Give my love to the children, and be very good, and kind, and attentive to little Charlotte.

Your affectionate father,

GEORGE ROBERTSON.

His love of his home did not render him selfish or exclusive, or less willing to assist others. His opinion of people generally was too favorable, and his regard for their welfare too unselfish for his own good. His very failings, as has been before said, leaned to virtue's side.

Although he had mingled long in many relations, and under various circumstances with people of every grade; although he was guarded and never known to be entrapped when managing the affairs of others, still he did not seem to suspect any body of improper motives, when his own interests were concerned, and was not particularly careful of his own property Confiding in his knowledge of men and his discreet management of his own concerns, like the good Vicar, in his favorite novel, Goldsmith's immortal story, he was sometimes caught by the "cosmogony" of a rascally Mr. Jenkinson. He would entrust his own business to persons deficient in discretion—when in straitened circumstances himself, he would indulge or release his creditors, and could not always, perhaps not often, resist opportunities to assist or endorse for those who either would not or could not, save him harmless. He would descant on the virtues of carefulness and leave his purse on a market-stall, and deposit his quarter's salary among loose papers, or drop it in the highway. He would dwell on the impracticability of pocket picking, and the same day his own pocket would be picked. He thought it was easy to make profitable speculations—his own investments were rarely remunerative, and often a source of loss.

Money he could and did make rapidly at his profession, and when made, expended but little of it for himself. Self-denial, long a necessity, had become a habit, and he only thought of himself after he had provided for the wants of others. He was particular as to small sums, because it was by their accumulation that he accomplished his determination to acquire a reasonable competency. "Too low for envy, for contempt too high," without which he thought with Junius, it was hard for a man to be either independent or honest, he was less regardful of large ones, possibly because when his character was forming, these had been too scarce to enable him to form any habit as to them. If he who discovered the mechanism of the heavens forgot that the kitten could pass through the same hole in the floor that admitted the cat and caused a smaller opening to be made, it is not strange if another occupied mind should not always remember that a large sum is made up of many small ones. He lived well and bountifully for one of his means, and kept open house, **and** referred to the example of Cicero and the advice of Polonius to prove that a man should maintain an appearance corresponding with his estate and his station. He also gave liberally to his children, needy friends, to charity, and to public enterprises. If his domestic affections were the source of his highest, purest, and most constant enjoyments, they were also the fountain of his deepest afflictions, and his un- utterable and long continued grief, as more than half his children and his wife faded from his sight, affords proof con- clusive of the strength of his affections. He has recounted at length his feelings when his latest born, the little Benjamin of his declining years, was taken from him, and in his pub- lished writings may be found **at** length his views of **the** manliness of a man's sorrow for the dead.

The loss of his favorite child cast a shade over all his after **life.** If his grief was a weakness, it has been a weakness of **all** the better portions of mankind: of the Christian, who looks forward to a reunion amid happier scenes, and of the doubter, who sees in the dust of mortality the end of ex- istence; **of** the feeble and the strong, of the helpless widow, and of David, of Cicero, and of Burke. The latter, alluding to his deceased son, says: "The storm has gone over me, and I lie like one of those old oaks, which the late hurricane has scattered about me. I am stripped of all my honors; I am torn **up by** the roots, and lie prostrate on the earth! There, and prostrate there, I most unfeignedly recognize the Divine justice, and in **some** degree submit to it. * * * **I live** in an inverted order. They who ought to have succeeded me, are gone before me. **They** who should have been to me as posterity, are in the place of ancestors."

And how tender is Evelyn's lament for his departed Mary: "**Oh, dear,** sweet, and desirable child! how shall I part with all this goodness and virtue without the bitterness of sorrow and reluctancy of a tender parent? Thy affection, duty, and

love to me was that of a friend as well as a child; and thy
mother! oh, how she mourns thy loss! how desolate hast
thou left us! To the grave shall we both carry thy memory."

No words can express grief more profound than David's
exclamation: "O, my son! would God I had died for thee!"

Again, when his wife, who had nestled by his side, in sunshine and shade, for fifty-five years, turned to him her last look
and her last thought, and left him to finish his journey alone,
he, though less given than most men to betray his feelings,
sunk beside the bed of death, pouring forth a prayer such as
can only be wrung from a prostrate soul, when deep calleth
unto deep, and all the waves and billows of sorrow have
passed over it. Nearly a year after his wife's death he wrote
this letter:

LEXINGTON, 1st January, 1867.

My Dear Daughter and first child:

I received, with grateful emotions, stronger than I can
express, your very affectionate salutations on the advent of
another Christmas, and your prayers for my health and happiness. I am glad to be able to assure you that my health
is perfect, and that I feel younger at 76 years of age than I
did at 66. But as to happiness, I neither enjoy nor expect
any of that blessing on earth. I am desolate and hopeless;
all my philosophy and manhood fail to make me contented,
or even cheerful. All that I see around me reminds me of the
ruins of Time, and overwhelms my sad heart with memories
of departed joys and buried friends. Ardent and incessant
employment is my only relief, and now another year has
dawned in gloom to your old and isolated father, whose
only comfort is in the love and *harmony* of his posterity.

This is peculiarly a suggestive day dawning over the grave
of the old year and all that is gone. It inaugurates a new
year, on the events of which our destiny may hang; and for
myself, whatever it may unfold, of weal or of woe, to me or
mine, I consecrate it, by sober contemplations, on the past,
the present, and the *frequent* future, and by a sacramental

vow at your mother's shrine, to do all that in me lies to improve the coming year, by doing better and living better
than ever before. Will you and your household join me in
this hallowing resolve?

I deeply sympathize with you in all that affects your happiness, and for Mr. Buford I especially feel great concern.
I would visit him often, but my official and domestic duties
leave me scarcely an hour of liberty or pleasure.

I would have been delighted to repeat my affectionate testimony to all my children and grandchildren, by appreciable
offerings to each of them, but could not thus remember one
and forget others of them. Circumstances were as such
could not make useful presents to all. But I, nevertheless,
am unwilling to answer your kind letter by words only, and
therefore, not knowing anything better, enclose you a sum
of money as a poor testimony of my paternal regard. May
God bless you and all your household.

Your devoted father,

G. ROBERTSON.

Under afflictions like these, he drew very little consolation
from philosophy. He found its whole sum in the beautiful
but cheerless letter of Serv, Sulpicius to Cicero, on the death
of Tullia, which commends submission to fate, because it is
inevitable. He derived more from religion, which demands
resignation to the will of God, because he is wise and good.
But he felt that religion, even after its own verity is accepted,
leaves us in doubt whether we shall ever again see our departed friends, or know them if we do. Perhaps the healing
influence of time and occupation afforded him most relief.
After all, long watching by the beds of the suffering and the
dying saved him from many disappointments, by moderating
his desires and teaching him the vanity of most of the objects
of human ambition.

F.

HIS GENERAL INFORMATION.

He devoted far more of his time to reflection and observation than to reading. Still, considering his opportunities, and the urgent demands of his exacting profession, his knowledge of books was remarkable. In early life he probably had access to as many books as he could use to advantage —they were more select that numerous. He was thus protected against the seductions of a miscellaneous collection, and mastered those that he read. By the time he was twenty-five years old, he had accumulated all the volumes that his occasions or curiosity required. His library contained the best works on philosophy and criticism; a good collection of English poetry and early periodical literature; the best of the English novels, prior to the time of Scott, and works of the best English dramatists; fine editions of choice translations of the Greek and Roman epic and dramatic poets and historians; popular treatises on all the sciences; standard works on divinity; theoretical disquisitions on government; histories, general and particular, of nations and of philosophy, and biographies and memoirs of the intrigues of courts and of parties; the writings of Smith, Ricardo, and others on political economy, up to the time when he resigned his seat in Congress. He had but few books of reference, and relied on his own stores of knowledge and information at first hand, for his facts. He had read these books with attention. His acquaintance with universal history, including the course of both human action and of thought was respectable. His knowledge of the history of particular periods, and especially of the time of Pericles and of Cicero, of the Middle Ages, of the Protestant reformation, and of the English revolution of eighty-eight, was excellent. He read with avidity every accessible authority relating to the social and political condition of America. He was personally familiar with the whole annals of Kentucky, and had studied the biographies of the great judges. His inquiries into the origin and destiny of man led him to explore the facts of geology, and the metaphysical and conflicting speculations of theologians and philosophers, and the evidence for and against Christianity. These studies became so engrossing as to exclude all others, except law, during the last decade of his life.

G.

THE POLITICIAN.

The bent of his active mind made him take a lively pleasure in the study of the science of government. That these studies were crowned with a large measure of success, abundant proof yet remains, and his public and private declarations and his conduct evince that he subordinated his desire for place, immeasurably, below his love of principle. Those who knew him intimately will believe that he expressed his unalterable sentiments, in the conclusion of a speech of great power against the bill to reorganize the Court of Appeals, in these words: "Mr. Speaker—I have taken my passage in this vessel (meaning the Constitution); my wife and children are on board. I will cling to her as long as she floats; and should she sink, I will seize her last plank as my best hope!

"In the humble part which it has fallen to my lot to bear in this great question, I expect not victory, I solicit not applause. My only wish is that I may promote the welfare of the country that gave me birth, and entitle myself to the reputation of an honest man. I fear not responsibility — Heaven made me free, and I will not make myself a slave. I have not consulted men in power. Although not one drop

of patrician blood runs in my veins, I am entitled to the
humble privilege of obeying the dictates of my own conscience, and of fearlessly uttering my opinions.   And I shall
deem it one of the most fortunate incidents of my life that
I have had the opportunity of protesting against this ruinous
and violent act, and of transmitting to my posterity, on the
record, a memorial of my opposition to it. * * * * *
As for me, I prefer the approbation of a sound conscience,
even in obscurity, to the proudest station purchased at so
dear a price; with this, the humblest station cannot make
me miserable; without it, the most exalted could not make
me happy."

To Milton's question—

"Canst thou not remember
Quinctius, Fabricius, Curius, Regulus?"

he could have replied: From boyhood have I known them
all.   ·

As the people who handed down these matchless stories
must have practiced the virtues which they admired, so now,
it is impossible to be thoroughly pervaded with the spirit of
these traditions without exhibiting their influence in conduct.

Although he held but few political offices, and those for
but a short time, and while upon the bench carefully lifted
the judicial ermine above the mire of parties, he was a more
active and efficient politician than many who have devoted
their undivided time to public affairs, and who have obtained
far greater distinction than ever fell to him.   A vigilant and
attentive observer of men and measures, he discussed from
the platform and through the press most of the great public
questions which were agitated during his times.   This is attested by his various published addresses, and by his letters
and pamphlets on theory of popular government, on the relief laws, on the tariff, on the Missouri compromise and
squatter sovereignty, on common schools, on the American
policy against the new Constitution, against an elective judiciary, on nullification and secession, on the doctrine of

popular instructions, on slavery and emancipation, and on many other topics.

These publications have a grasp and power, and show an amount of information far greater than can be found in the fleeting productions of the ordinary politician. They have much of the philosophic breadth, of the writings of Hamilton, and the disquisitions of Burke, and contain, or foreshadow, nearly all those valuable truths for which the subsequent works of Mill on government, and De Toqueville on democracy, are prized. This could be shown by a comparison of their respective writings, and the coincidence is noticed, as an example, that able minds think alike. He says of himself: "My public life has been short and humble; it furnishes no incidents to flatter pride or gratify ambition."

Several probable reasons might be suggested why he was not a more conspicuous politician :

1. The urgent demands of a growing family compelled him to retire from the pursuit when in the high road to success,

2. He never hesitated to advocate what, upon mature deliberation, he considered right and expedient, or to oppose any proposition which he considered wrong or false. His writings, his teachings, his conduct showed that he preferred to suffer for doing right rather than to be rewarded for doing wrong. They declare his conviction, that the price of every good is a conflict in which every combatant must take the risk of defeat, of neglect, of obloquy; and his belief that the history of those who have fought and lost, if it could be written, would be a nobler epic than the story of those who have won. Nor did he believe in the right of any competent citizen to shirk the battle in which he was interested. In his view, the difference between the man who slunk from, and him who faced, responsibility, who did the act, and who permitted it to be done, was, if the act were right, that the one was brave and truthful, the other a coward, who adhered not to the right but the winning side; if the act were wrong, that

the one played the part of a robber, the other of a thief, or an assassin.

In becoming a politician, he squarely accepted these issues. He constantly and openly avowed his opposition to the doctrine of popular instructions, and his unwillingness to hold an office that fettered his judgment and constrained his conscience.

Recognizing the natural and established right of the majority to govern, with bold and incisive words he defended and expounded the constitutional barriers to its dominion. As allowing an appeal from the impulse of a mob to the second thoughts of the individuals composing it, he demonstrated that, without sleepless restraint, its sway might be more fearful than that of the worst central tyranny; not only because of its divided responsibility, but because its eyes and its hands, being in every place, no disguise can escape its vigilance, no fleetness its pursuit. That its power and its penalties might combine the despotism of kings, of priests, and of classes, destroying liberty and life like the first, chaining the thoughts and conscience, and destroying the soul like the second, and interdicting the expression of opinions, excommunicating from society and making its victim a pariah or an exile like the third. Fearful of indiscriminate suffrage, and believing that the pioneers who had borne the heat and burden of the day, in subduing and improving the country, had earned the title to secure the blessings they had won, he insisted that Americans should govern America. Relief laws rushing in, the tide of bankruptcy swept the State like a torrent. Young, obscure, poor, and alone, he threw himself into the flood and breasted it. If not in favor of the immediate emancipation of slaves, he was opposed to their increase, and when the majority were phrenzied on the question, he urged the re-enactment of a law interdicting their importation into Kentucky, and in this way lost all future prospect of promotion. Though a southern man by birth, alliance, and sympathy, he published elaborate argu-

9

ments against the doctrine of Nullification, the Virginia and Kentucky resolutions of '98 and '99, and the right and expediency of secession.

He might have said (in fact, often has said), with Burke, "I was not swaddled, and dandled, and rocked into a legislator—*nitor in adversum* is the motto for a man like me. I possessed not one of the qualities, nor cultivated one of the arts that recommend to the favor and protection of the great. I was not made for a minion or tool. As little did I follow the trade of winning the hearts by imposing on the understandings of the people. At every step of my progress in life (for in every step was I traversed and opposed), and at every turnpike I met I was obliged to show my passport, and again and again to prove my sole title to the honor of being useful to my country, by a proof that I was not wholly unacquainted with its laws. I had no arts but manly arts. On them I have stood, and please God to the last gasp, will I stand."

Not a few nor unobservant men believe that the holding of a public office has long ceased to be any evidence of merit, either because according to the famous line which cost Naevius his liberty, "*Fato Metelli fiunt Romæ consules*," which may be paraphrased, destiny alone confers honors in America; or, because public virtue has reached that stage of decline in which Dryden says nothing goes unrewarded but desert; or, in the defiant words of that invulnerable political paladin, who hissed so many bitter charges and challenges through the bars of his visor, in which trifles float and are preserved, while every thing valuable sinks to the bottom and is lost forever.

When C. T. Varro, after the overwhelming defeat at Cannæ, caused by his own misconduct, doubtful of his reception, had drawn near Rome, the Senate and people came out to meet him and publicly thanked him—"For that he had not despaired of the Republic." Who says Republics are ungrateful? Not the successful aspirant, his success, whoever fails, does not prove it—to him. Not the C. T. Varros, who every day are rewarded for no visible merit, if not "For that they have not despaired of the Republic," and never will so long as there are places to fill and money to pay for holding them.

Our republics are not ungrateful, if they sometimes bestow their gratitude upon the wrong men. It is probably because the notion has been gradually and generally adopted, that allegiance to a party is the highest patriotism and the most useful talent, and a few managers, looking alone to their own interests, who assume to represent a party, are permitted to dictate for whom the masses shall cast their suffrages. These men are the designing Rebeccas, the people are blind Abrahams, who mistake the Jacobs for the Esaus.

If Judge Robertson's hope of preferment was ever disappointed, his chagrin soon passed away, and he spoke well of, and felt not unkindly towards, those who had opposed him. He may have been ambitious, but was too tall for envy; too masculine and too busy to be a gossip; too self-respecting and generous to be a detractor. Besides, while he was still in a green and hale old age, he had lived long enough to know the vanity of human aspirations, and the degrading littleness of jealousy, at the advancement of others. If he did not, like England's gifted son, stand amid the crowded monuments and fading hatchments of another Westminster Abbey, and feel every emotion of rivalry die within him, he did stand in the midst of a far more affecting and pitiable scene. Around him were the scattered, obscure, and neglected graves of all the most successful cotemporaries of his prime. He had survived them all A new generation had sprung up that worshiped strange gods, who, in their turn, were soon to be torn from their shrines and be forgotten.

Reviewing his political life at an advanced age, he says: "My public life has been short and humble; it furnishes no incidents to flatter pride or gratify ambition. If in the stormy and difficult times in which it was spent, it has been disinterested, firm and straight forward, I shall have fulfilled in its results all my expectations, and have deserved as much commendation as I have ever desired. If, in reviewing it, I see nothing to be vain of, or to extort the applause or admiration of others, I see, what is more grateful to my feelings, that it exhibits nothing of which I am ashamed, or of which, on mature reflection, I repent. But while I recollect no act of my public life which I would alter, I confess that I have, more than once, done that which I regretted, and still regret, being compelled to do by convictions of public duty. In other words, my votes have not always been in accord with my feelings. Political life, however humble or unambitious, is beset with many difficulties, trials, and perplexities; it is the crucible of merit, the ordeal of virtue and energy. He who expects to pass through unhurt and self satisfied, and wishes to be able, when at his journeys' end, to look back, without shame or remorse, on the various meanderings and multiform incidents of the mazy path which he has followed, must be prepared to do many things incompatible with his individual interests, and repugnant to his personal and local predilections. He must expect to be instructed by the suggestions of an unbiased judgment, frequently to do that which, while his head approves, his heart abjures. He must be prepared, too, to smile with unmixed contempt at causeless abuse, and to see his popularity in ruins without emotions of sorrow, surprise, or resentment, looking in triumph to its day of resurrection. All who engage in political warfare should be thus shielded, if they wish to avoid ultimate discomfiture and disgrace. A firm and honest man should always be contented under the consciousness, if he fail, of having done his duty. He has also for his encouragement an assurance from the testimony of all experience, that if, in the storms of faction or momentary popular commotion, he shall be, for awhile, overwhelmed, and lighter bodies should be permitted, for a moment, to mount the bursting wave, the sunshine of reason and the calm of sober judgment will soon return and find him on a proud eminence high above those ephemeral favorites who could vegetate and flourish only in the beams of popular favor, and cameleon-like, live by snuffing air—the breath of popular applause. No wise man will be insensible to the approbation of his fellow-men, or indifferent about obtaining it; but no honest man will ever attempt to obtain it in any other way than by endeavoring to deserve it. The popularity which is gratifying to an honorable and elevated mind, is not that evanescent capricious thing that must be conciliated by caresses, and purchased by dishonest compliances, but that high and constant sentiment of esteem which follows virtuous actions, and is their best reward, next to the approbation of a sound conscience, which it will, sooner or later, gratify and prosper.

I have been anxious to obtain your approbation, but more so to secure that of my own conscience. The last I know I enjoy—the first I have endeavored to deserve."

H.

THE LAWYER.

In this age of railroads and turnpikes, of comfortable inns and commodious court-houses, it is difficult to realize the inconveniences, toil, and exposure to which the lawyers of an earlier day were subjected. Then it was necessary to go from court to court; the circuits were large; the courts far apart; accommodations at hotels wretched in quality and small in quantity. The roads never good, frequently almost, and sometimes altogether, impassable; the streams unbridged; ferries few and fords difficult; court-houses small, ill ventilated and crowded; the people rough, familiar, always calling a man, whatever his age or station, by his christian name, noisy, and belligerent. Mr. Robertson kept two or three saddle horses, the best he could procure. Mounted on one of them, and enveloped in a drab great coat, with three capes, shingling him to the waist, and with skirts reaching to his heels, his legs encased in the indispensable green baize leggings, enormous buckskin gauntlets on his hands, and with well-filled saddle-bags, he would, in mid-winter, with defiant will, intensified by necessity, go forth in storm of sleet or rain, through mire or slush, upon the circuit, not knowing how long he would be deprived of the comforts of home. These journeys were often protracted far into the night. Regardful of his horse, as he was of every living thing over which he had control, he was still compelled to be a hard rider. When he was Judge, he would accomplish the distance from Frankfort to Lancaster, about 57 miles, when the broken road was at its worst, without leaving the saddle. On his return from courts, he almost invariably brought presents to his wife and children. These were often in packages or bundles so large or numerous as to subject him to much inconvenience, but the delight he afforded the "expectant wee things" amply repaid him for his trouble.

He undertook the practice of the law amid circumstances which threw him entirely upon his own efforts. He was a boy, incompetent in law to make a binding agreement for his professional services. His poverty was next door to indigence, and he had married a wife whose only dowry was her beauty, her virtues, her cheerful willingness to share his uncertain fortunes, and that womanly intuition more ready and infallible than reason, and which makes a discreet wife the wisest and safest counsellor of her husband.

His scholastic training, notwithstanding his rapid insight and faithful memory, had been too hurried and too brief. His legal knowledge had been acquired without the aid of an instructor, and the law was then far more difficult and perplexed than now, and law books less perspicuous than those of the present day. The bar of the circuit in which he lived was crowded with men, who, in a broader and more elaborate sphere, would have become widely eminent, and would have been considered able jurists and persuasive advocates at any bar of any time. Dockets were small, fees in ordinary cases were slender, great cases were few, and all cases were prose-cuted and defended with the utmost pertinacity. Mr. Robertson was small and slight in person, his health not robust, his disposition retiring, and his mind reflective rather than objective. He lacked those charms of manner and voice which fascinate crowds and serve to adorn superior qualities or conceal the want of them.

His friends had greater need of assistance than ability to render it. Yet, by the time he was twenty-five years old, he was not only a good lawyer, but had convinced the people of that fact, and had obtained a business second in amount and grade to that of none of his professional brethren. That he was then a good lawyer is shown by the fact that, although during the interval between that time and the date of his appointment to the Appellate bench, he was engrossed with politics, he was fully qualified to discharge his judicial duties, and rendered decisions not inferior to his subsequent ones. His success is attributable to great mental power, guided by rectitude and impelled by indomitable energy—energy stimulated, but not created by necessity. Weak men are crushed, not strengthened, by burdens. Circumstances are the occasion, not the causes, of power. A great chancellor's advice to a father, who consulted him as to the best means to make his son an efficient lawyer, namely: To permit him to spend his patrimony; marry a rich wife and exhaust her estate, and then, under stress of circumstances, live like a hermit and work like a horse, would not produce the desired result in the case of every son.

The following description, which Judge Robertson has given of the discipline and qualities of another, is an accurate statement of his own moral and mental training:

"Without the adventitious influence of wealth, or family, or accident, and without any of the artifices of vulgar ambi-

tion or selfish pretension, he was, as soon as known, honored
with the universal homage of that kind of cordial respect
which nothing but intrinsic and unobtrusive merit can ever
command, and which alone can be either gratifying or honorable to a man of good taste and elevated mind. It was his
general intelligence, his undoubted probity, his child-like candor, his scrupulous honor, and undeviating rectitude, which
alone extorted—what neither money, nor office, nor flattery,
nor duplicity, can ever secure—the sincere esteem of all who
knew him. And so conspicuous and attractive was his unos-
tentatious worth, that, though he rather shunned than courted
official distinction, it sought him and called him from his
native obscurity and the cherished privacy of domestic enjoyment. His education was unsophisticated and practical. He
learned things instead of names, principles of moral truth
and inductive philosophy instead of theoretic systems and
scholastic dogmatisms. His country education preserved
and fortified all his useful faculties, physical and moral—his
taste was never perverted by false fashion—his purity was
never contaminated by the examples or seduced by the temptations of demoralizing associations. Blessed with a robust
constitution, his habitual industry, and 'temperance in all
things,' preserved his organic soundness and promoted the
health and vigor of his body and his mind. What he knew
to be right he always practised—and that which he felt to be
wrong he invariably avoided. In his pursuit after knowledge
his sole objects were truth and utility. In his social intercourse he was chaste, modest, and kind—and all his conduct,
public and private, was characterized by scrupulous fidelity,
impartial justice, and an enlightened and liberal spirit of
philanthropy and beneficence. Self-poised, he resolutely
determined that his destiny should depend on his own conduct. Observant, studious, and discriminating, whatever he
acquired from books, or from men, he made his own by appropriate cogitation or manipulation. And thus, as far as he
went in the career of knowledge, he reached, as if *per saltem*,
the end of all learning—practical truth and utility.

"Panopiied in such principles and habitudes, his merit could not be concealed. In a just and discerning community, such a man is as sure of honorable fame as substance is of shadow in the sun-light of day. And have we not here a striking illustration of the importance of right education and self-dependence? Proper education is that kind of instruction and discipline, moral, mental, and physical, which will teach the boy what he should do and what he should shun, when he becomes a man, and prepare him to do well whatever an intelligent and upright man should do in all the relations of social and civil life; and any system of education which accomplishes either more or less than this, is so far imperfect, or preposterous and pernicious. But, after all, the best schoolmasters are a mediocrity of fortune, and a country society virtuous, but not puritanical; religious, but not fanatical; independent, but not rich; frugal, but not penurious; free, but not licentious—a society which exemplifies the harmony and value of industry and morality, republican simplicity and practical equality.

"Reared in such a school, and practically instructed in the elements of useful knowledge, a man of good capacity, who enters on the business of life with no other fortune than his own faculties, and no other hope than his own honest efforts, can scarcely fail to become both useful and great. But he who embarks destitute of such tutelage, or freighted with hereditary honor or wealth, is in imminent danger of being wrecked in his voyage. Fortune and illustrious lineage are, but too often, curses rather than blessings. The industry and self-denial, which are indispensable to true moral and intellectual greatness, have been but rarely praticed without the lash of poverty, or the incentive of total self-independence."

Believing that the true end of litigation, as of war, is peace, (*pax quaeritur bello*), when consulted about a controversy, he advised a settlement, if a fair compromise could be effected, before the passions of the parties had enlisted them, irretrievably, in the conflict. If this could not be done, he engaged, with untiring zeal, in the service of his client. Indefatigable at every stage of the contest, his ablest exhibitions were his addresses to the court.

He never blazed with the splendid conflagration of Tully or of Curran, nor could he attack with the insidious and panther-like approaches of Plunkett; he had not the commanding presence and clarion voice of Clay. Several of his contemporaries excelled him in wit, invective, in brilliant episodes, and in stirring declamation.

Although he was never a meteor, corruscating with a brilliancy that dazzles and blinds; nor "A Hesperus that (with borrowed splendor) led the starry train"—his light was more sustained and steady than the flash of the one, and unlike the sheen of the other; it was native as well as reflected. His purpose was not to shine, but to win. The judgment he sought was, not that he was a great man, but that his case was a good one—too plain in fact to require any skill in its management. Keeping himself as much as possible out of sight, and having perfect knowledge of the ground upon which every decisive contest must be made, and a dialectic skill that was never at a loss for middle terms, he assaulted with great force and apparent confidence one or more weak (or, if there were none such, strong) points in the position of his adversary. Whatever side he was on, if the result was doubtful, he boldly assumed the aggressive, in order to keep his opponent employed in his own defense.

Taking no notes of evidence, and relying on but few authorities, he adduced reasons in profuse abundance, and none of them so frivolous as not to be plausible, for every proposition that he affirmed, and he responded immediately and forcibly to the objections and authorities of the opposite party. He freely indulged in fallacies, when he believed they would lead, though illogically, to a just judgment. Some of his discussions of dry propositions of law were, from their clearness, method, and ingenuity, more pleasing to

cultivated minds than the most finished efforts of the rheto-
rician.

His discussions of facts were rapid, bold, often vehement,
ingenious, and always plausible in bad cases, and conclusive
in good ones. In fact, his ardor, grip, and resources seemed
to increase with the difficulties which opposed him. Most
of the witnesses of the exhaustless readiness and persistence
with which he affirmed premises and drew inferences, are
dead. Some now living may not have forgotten how

> " He could veer and tack and steer a cause
> Against the weather-guage of laws,"

as shown in the remarkable contest between Mr. Clay and
himself over the instructions in an action against the client
of the latter for selling plated bagging, or bagging that was
of better quality on the outside of the bale than on the inside.
The argument was protracted three days, and exhausted all
that could be said for and against the proposition—custom
makes law.

He was not of a polemical disposition, and was not fond of
the practice of law. This is proved by the fact that he remained so long upon the bench, when, with less labor, he
could have reaped incalculably greater rewards at the bar.
He disliked the personalities of the bar, and preferred to appear in courts of equity and in revisory courts, rather than
before juries. His speeches in court were in form and in
matter very similar to his written opinions as a Judge. Both
were conceived with marvellous rapidity and lucidly, always
accurately, and often beautifully expressed. The only one of
his addresses to the jury now remaining, is his speech in
defence of Dr. Abner Baker. This is a fair specimen of his resources. Some of his regular clients were those against
whom he had been employed, and who had felt his strength.
Among these was an old man of property, who having no family but a wife, for whom he had a great aversion, and who being
determined to devise his estate to some other person, importunately besought Mr. Robertson to be that person; but he

firmly refused to accede to this request, on the ground that his honor as a man and a lawyer would not permit him to do so, and the estate was finally given to an entire stranger to the testator. Mr. Robertson, though gratified at his self-denial in this instance, deplored the circumstances that made it imperative.

His facility was very great as a special pleader and convey-ancer. Believing the science of pleading to be the logic of the common law, as showing what was necessary to be affirmed and proved, he directed the attention of his pupils to it at an early period of their progress All instruments of writing drawn by him are distinguished for their brevity, clearness, and accuracy. He knew what was essential in the accepted forms, and therefore never used a form or any superfluous word, although its employment might be conse-crated by immemorial usage. And as he wrote in the small and compact, but legible hand, which some have called the Virginia hand, a specimen of which may be seen in the man-uscripts of Mr. Jefferson, and which possibly they and others derived from a common source, namely, Joshua Fry. His deeds and pleadings were contained in a very small compass.

As a conveyancer, he did not consider it necessary for his own safety or that of his client, to assume an attitude directly hostile to every title which he was called to examine. He knew, as Dr. Johnson has said, that there were objections to a plenum and also to a vacuum, but that one or the other was true, and that extraordinary ingenuity or ordinary igno-rance might raise objections to the best title. Therefore, holding that it was as culpable and as hazardous to cast sus-picions on a good claim as it was to misrepresent a bad one, he sought not, through excess of caution, to defeat, but de-sired rather to uphold the transfers of property that had been in good faith acquiesced in. His investigations were careful, his interpretations liberal, and while in his professional capa-city, he caused little or no interruption to the business transactions of the country, no complaint was ever made against him for wrong advice or for mal-practice.

He was in no sense a timid· lawyer. If he had not had strong confidence in his ability to advise and to act, his sense of duty would have compelled him to retire from the bar. When he came to the bar, and for long afterwards, the distinction between professional opposition and personal hostility was exceedingly obscure. Still, though one of the most peaceable and courteous of men, he never hesitated, from regard for the consequences to himself, because the opposite party was powerful or dangerous, or his attorney was a ruffian, to undertake a case, or denounce a wrong; and when dispatch was urgent, and the efficiency of the sheriff was doubtful, he has been known to go with him and recapture property illegally taken.

He was fashioned on too large a scale to be a mere lawyer, and often spoke of the intimate relations of various knowledges, and illustrated the quaint saying, that the sparks of all the sciences are raked up in the ashes of the law. Nor was he content to explore one system of law. Among the first books he ever owned are a Latin copy of Justinian's Institutes, Pothier on Obligations, and Vattell's Law of Nations. Many of his terms, illustrations, and reasons are drawn from the civil law. He placed a high estimate upon Comyn's Digest, the writings of Pothier, and the English ecclesiastical reports. The latter, according to his judgment, contained some of the finest models of judicial style. Not inconsistent with his regard for general knowledge, he thought that a large collection of law books was apt to embarrass and enfeeble, and his own library was more select than numerous. He trusted more to rumination than to reading, and the *"cave canem,"* to which he sometimes pointed his pupils, in the atrium of the law, was the maxim, "Beware the man of one book."

THE TEACHER OF LAW.

No one can be a first rate lawyer who does not maintain a clear knowledge of elementary principles, which consist chiefly of definitions and propositions, which denote the divisions, classes, or combinations into which rules of law have been or may be arranged.   It was by teaching that Judge Robertson refreshed and constantly extended his analytical apprehension of the law.   He taught because he loved to teach, and because teaching was one of the best modes of learning.   While he was a young man his reputation attracted students from this and other States to solicit his instructions. He cheerfully gave them the use of his library and the aid of his learning free of charge.   For a long time after he had retired from the law school of Transylvania, he continued to instruct classes of from fifteen to thirty.   That school, when he and Judge Mayes, and afterwards, when he and Judge Woolley and Marshall were its professors, attained a high and deserved reputation.   Its roll of matriculates was greater than that of any other law school in the United States.

His mode of instruction was by oral examinations and comments upon a text   His questions were frequently in the form of a sorites, each one being a deduction from a preceding one.   In this way the pupil was led to prove propositions which, perhaps, at first he denied or doubted.   His comments were full and so lucid that, to the superficial or ignorant, they seemed to be superficial, because he made intricate doctrines plain.   He inaugurated each course of lectures by a public introductory.   These were published by the successive classes.   The first of these coming to the hands of Mr. Webster, drew from him this kind note:

WASHINGTON, Dec'r 16, 1835.

My Dear Sir:

I hope it is to your own remembrance and kindness that I am indebted for a copy of your truly excellent Introductory Lecture.   I have read it with much pleasure.   I have forwarded it to my son, a student in the Profession

I hear so much of you, my dear sir, and know so much, that I heartily wish we might meet, face to face.   Though I remember to have seen you in Washington, I hardly know whether we were in each other's company more than once.

Will you not come and look at us in the North? You would find many who would be truly glad to see you.

I pray you remember me to Mr. Letcher, and believe that I am, with cordial regard,

Yours,

DAN'L WEBSTER.

CH. JUS. ROBERTSON.

He felt a lively regard for the welfare and advancement of his pupils, and entertained them (as did the other Professors) often and handsomely at his house. Mutual and enduring regard was the result of their intercourse. He labored not only to teach them municipal law, but also conservative principles and legal etchics, and so far as known, all of them have led honorable, and some of them, distinguished lives. Probably the greatest benefit he conferred upon his country was as a teacher. The effect of the moral and intellectual forces that he assisted to train and direct can never be estimated The following words of his show the regard which he had for his pupils:

"Whatever may be your destiny, may you ever cherish fraternal sympathies for each other, and a filial remembrance of your Alma Mater. She will never cease to feel a deep interest in all that concerns you, and in whatsoever you may do, or may be; and it will rejoice her to hear of your prosperity and honest fame. May she, like Berecinthia, be now and always—

Felix prole virum   *   *   *   *   *

*   *   *   *   *   *   *

Proud of her sons, she lifts her head on high,
Proud as the mighty mother of the sky—

*   *   *   *   *   *   *

"And may we too be allowed to hope that you will not forget us, nor neglect our precepts. If we have contributed to your improvement, we shall be happy to hail you as sons, and to be long and kindly remembered; and when our earthly course is finished, may you, our cherished pupils and friends, still live to adorn, to save, and to bless our beloved country.

"Though—after our approaching separation—we may not meet again on earth, yet, as we are taught to believe, it will not be long until we shall be re-assembled at the bar of Almighty God, to be severally judged for the deeds of our probationary pilgrimage. May the light of that day, like a bright fixed star, guide us from the snares through which we pass to the tomb, and cheer our hearts with a hope beyond the grave!"

I.

THE JUDGE.

The Great Teacher's precept, "Judge not, that ye be not judged," though, probably, not intended in its prohibitory part to apply to the official judge, in its consequential part holds good especially as to him. He never judges without being judged. Every one has a right to know, and the opportunity of knowing, all his judicial acts. Like the patriarchal arbiter of oriental nations, he sits in the gate—his courts are open, his rulings are public—star chambers and secret inquisitions are not of this age and land. Parties and attornies judge him because he judges them ; by-standers and others judge him because they may come under his jurisdiction. These particular judgments are abstracted, generalized, and perpetuated. Who may be better supplied with digests, with types and examples, with parallels and antitheses of his subject, than the judge of a judge? Have not his publicity, his necessary interference in the affairs of others, and his peculiarities, made the justiciary of low and of high degree a favorite character of fiction, which honors his virtues and loves to deride his short comings? Who has not laughed at the justice Shallows of the drama, and the justice Starleighs of the novel, and commiserated imaginary-victims of the tardiness, the costliness, and the uncertainty of courts? And has not history, with no truer or broader conception than fiction (which is the shadow of the real), but with more Nathan-like, thou art the man point, execrated, truckling subserviency, venality, imbecility, and brutality and extolled splendid independence, incorruptible fidelity, varied attainments and clear discernment in summing up the evidence whether the names of particular judges shall be inscribed in her pantheon, on the scrolls of glory or of infamy?

If the judge is the most judged, he is also often the worst judged of men. The qualities which he ought to have, many of his judges lack. They are frequently interested, and not seldom (and sometimes none the worse for him) incompetent. The ignorant, not less readily than the instructed, judge him. Individual judgments take their complexion from the tempers of the individuals, and of the times. Confident youth, ignorant of nothing, tells his measure quickly, peremptorily, and extravagantly. Age, coupled with experience which knows but little, is apt to view him with circumspection and with charity.

In piping times of peace, individual judgments of a bad judge may be deep but not loud, and be satisfied by mingling into a murmuring current of public opinion; in stormy times, individual judgments of a good judge may burst forth into "reorganizing acts," and into mobs.

Who then is authorized to estimate the absolute qualities of a judge, and assign his relative place? It is not enough to know, as everybody knows, that he ought to be honest, have competent knowledge of law, "not be afraid of the face of men," be free from vices and wrongs which the law condemns, be diligent, patient, and as delay is a species of injustice, be able to reach conclusions and assign sufficient reasons for them, with dispatch. To know what a thing ought to be, and to know what it is, are, by no means, identical propositions. If they were, impostor and kindred

10

words might be dropped from our speech. Law, not less
than theology, philosophy, and art, has its esoteric language
and doctrines. A critical knowledge of his judicial rulings,
which is the crucial test of a great judge, must be confined
to the initiated and laborious few, whose business it is to
explore, to apply, and to evade them. After long and close
attention to the judgments and history of the bench, and to
the lives of the strongest and the feeblest, the best and the
basest, who have adorned or disgraced it, had fitted him to
approve or to condemn forensic proceedings, with at least a
formidable show of facts and of reasons, Judge Robertson,
upon proper occasions, guardedly expressed his opinions of
the comparative merits of other judges. A like careful consideration is due to his own course. One of the chief and
less obvious qualifications of a good judge is his ability to
think. In considering the thinking faculty regard must be
had not only to the quality of the thoughts that is to the
degree of generality of the ideas, the degree of definiteness
of the ideas, the degree of coherence of the ideas, but also to
the amount or volume of the ideas. Mechanical forces are
compared and measured by the quantity of motion, which
they respectively produce in a given time, so in estimating
the relative vigor of minds the quantity of work done must
be taken into the account. A man of ordinary ability may
accomplish a particular result, in a long time or with needful
helps, in a better manner than one greatly his superior could
do it, in a short time and under less favorable circumstances.
Single speech Hamilton's sole effort may have been equal to
any one of thousand speech Brougham, but as Hamilton
took his own time to elaborate his speech, and never made
but the one, it would be unfair to rank him with Brougham,
who could make a good speech upon any subject at any
time.

The trickling waters of a brook, if pent up with weirs and
locks, slowly swell into ponds as deep as the ordinary channel of a river.

To call a judge, as Lord Eldon was called, a doubter, is at best, but equivocal praise; habitual doubt implies delay, if not inconsistency. To call him a Lingerer is not expressive of merit. To say of a general, as was said of Fabius, "*Unus homo, nobis, cunctando rem restituit*," may be a high eulogy; to apply the same words to a slow judge, would be a severe rebuke. In comparing decisions of different courts, with reference to the ability of the judges, the number of judges composing each, the attainments and industry of their several attornies, the amount and character of their business, the time occupied in disposing of it, and the amount of compensation of the judges, as upon this may depend their exemption from many distracting cares, must all be considered. In all these, and perhaps in other respects, the Supreme Court of the United States has the advantage of most, perhaps, of all other courts in the Union. The Federal Courts are better paid, their cases are better prepared and argued by attornies, and although they may not display "a masterly inactivity," which defeats the purposes of litigation, they take more time for deliberation than would be patiently tolerated in a State judge. The Kentucky Court of Appeals, during most of the time Judge Robertson was connected with it, consisted of but three judges, who were so ill paid as to have to resort to other means of making a living, and so hard pressed as to have but little time to devote to single cases; its bar was never without able lawyers, but very many of the cases were hastily and imperfectly prepared. His first labors were peculiarly arduous. Judge Underwood, a pure and wise citizen, who yet lives to enjoy the consciousness of a well spent life and the respect of his countrymen, and he, were the only judges. And to them had been left a large and unwelcome legacy of old cases, amounting to not less than one thousand. He was inexperienced, and his fitness for this, as for every other place which he ever held, was to be tried by watchful partisans and jealous aspirants. The feelings provoked by a long and bitter contest of parties for the possession of this court had not subsided. Though the salary, less than that of an ordinary clerk or the judge of a petty police court of the present day, and much of this was consumed in paying the expenses of the judges in term time, would now be considered grossly inadequate to the toils and responsibilities of the office, still the position had been made honorable by illustrious names, and the men of that day resembled in many respects the old Romans, who never received any pecuniary reward for serving their country. (Judge R.'s reasons for accepting the office may be found elsewhere in this volume.)

He had won distinction as a political writer and speaker, and had rapidly become conspicuous at the bar, but there is not much affinity between politics and law, and although it may be difficult to determine in what the diversity consists, there is a well recognized difference between the mental gifts and acquirements of an able judge, and those of an effective practitioner. Great advocates have made poor judges, eminent judges have failed at the bar, both before and after their elevation to the bench. If it be said that the chief mental process of the judge is inference, of the advocate proof, that the one inquires, the other affirms, the one asks what is A., the other says that A. is B., that the one begins with the premises, the other starts from the conclusion. That the reasoning of the one is from particular propositions to general ones, and that of the other deductive, still they seem to travel the same road, but in different directions. Whatever may be the difference, Judge Robertson, by applying himself during almost all the hours of the day and night, with an assiduity that injured his eyes, and would have broken down any but an iron constitution, rapidly dispatched, with the assistance of his distinguished associate, the accumulated business of the court, and soon vindicated his right to his position, and his claim to be considered an able judge. His earliest decisions show that his legal learning was both comprehensive and accurate. In the cases of Breckinridge's heirs *v.* Ormsby, and Lampton's Ex. *v.* Preston's Ex., are exhibited the same perspicacity and completeness that are found in his later opinions.

Opinions running through twenty-five volumes of the reports, well argued, often exhaustive, though betraying marks of haste, resulting from pressure of business, show that he performed his full share of the known duties of the court, but do not disclose his labors in deciding the far greater number of cases which have never been published. He never neglected any official duty, and is not known to have ever been absent from his post, unless he was personally interested in the matter under consideration, until after he had been attacked with the malady which ended his life.

He understood and administered the law, not as a collection of arbitrary and detached points, but as a rational and harmonious system. That empiricism, whose school is experience, whose only lesson is examples, does not belong to any one profession. There are attornies and judges whose stock of learning consists of practical rules and forms, whose writings are copies, whose reasons are *ipse dixits*, and who often have the enviable readiness and accuracy of light weights on a beaten road, but who, unguided by general propositions, are, when left without "an ancient *saw* or a modern instance," apt to mistake the sign or circumstance for the source, the accident for the substance, and to draw conclusions as trustless as the *post hoc ergo propter hoc* inference of Master More's aged man, viz: That Tenterden steeple was the cause of Goodwin quicksands, for the reason that the one was built before the other appeared. In describing a man of this type, G. S. Mill remarks. "Almost every one knows Lord Mansfield's advice to a man of practical good sense, who, being appointed Governor of a colony, had to preside in its court of justice, without previous judicial practice or legal education, the advice was, to give his decision boldly, for it would probably be right, but never to venture on assigning reasons, for they would almost infallibly be wrong. In cases like this, which are of no uncommon occurrence, it would be absurd to suppose that the bad reason was the source of the good decision. Lord Mansfield knew that if any reason were assigned, it would probably be an after thought. The judge being in fact guided by impressions from past experience, without the circuitous process of framing general principles from them, and that if he attempted to frame such he would assuredly fail. However Lord Mansfield would not have doubted that a man of equal experience, who had also a mind stored with general principles, would have been greatly preferable as a judge, to one who could not be trusted with the explanation and justification of his own judgments."

These artisans, who are the bulk of every profession, owe their practical skill to the loftier labors of a far higher order of minds. The thinker must precede the craftsman. The mass of accountants apply a calculus, all practical men employ rules, which they neither could have invented nor understand. They accept results without reasons. They are, at best, but plane glasses, which pass the light as they recieved it, or with some loss of brightness, greater minds, by refracting the dispersed rays into a focus, give a near and distinct view of their source. Judge Robertson deserves to be classed with those lawyers who have inductively reduced many points to a comparatively few propositions, and have administered the law as a deductive science, which, with some exceptions, growing out of eccentric decisions and meddlesome statutes, that are repugnant to its genius, may be exhibited in the telescopic form of successive propositions, each of which is contained in the next preceding one, and all in the first. Hence, though the laws which he has expounded may be repealed, and the precise facts which he has interpreted may never recur, his opinions, from the elementary truths which they explain, must, like fossil remains of the extinct mastodon, exhibiting marks of design and proving final causes, continue to engage and instruct the philosophic student.

To show that he did rapidly detect the true and essential resemblances of detached and, to the ordinary observer, discordant particulars of fact and of law, and refer them to, and derive them from, a common source, would require large numbers of his decisions to be arranged in groups or in trains according to the ideal thread or *vinculum* that connects them. This can not be done here, but as some have thought that he, at least in his earlier opinions, generalized too much, and sometimes subordinated particular rules to the harmony of the law as a whole, and as a man's wrong conclusions may be supposed to afford the severest test of his reasoning powers, an attempt will be made to show the logical relation to his other opinions that have been sustained, of the only two of his judgments of any general importance that are known to have been overruled, and show that in furtherance of individual rights and particular justice, by a strict and sound discrimination, he pointed out exceptions to broad and well established principles.

One of the first generalizations which a judge must make is an abstract expression or formula of the grounds of legal responsibility, because this must be at least a tacit premiss of most of his judgments, and he whose business it is to interpret the laws and enforce them, should not take the place of the legislator. The difference between their functions is clearly defined. They move in the same direction, but the law-maker leads the other, except where the organic law is violated, follows. The one enquires what is necessary, or expedient, or morally right or wrong? The other abjures all allegiance to "higher law," or what ought to be law, and to casuistry and political necessity. To the law, as it is, his fealty is complete, he has sworn "to be its man of life and limb, and terrene honor." Judge Robertson has very often recognized this view of the duties of the judiciary, especially in his elaborate review of the Dred Scott case, and in the conclusion of his masterly argument on the legal tender question, he says:—"Persuaded that we are right, no apprehension of inconvenient consequences, merely fiscal nor of human responsibility could excuse the announcement of any opinion which is not conscientiously our own. To guard the constitution is the highest trust of the judiciary; and thinking as we do, were we to bow to any other power than the law as we understand it, we should feel guilty of a criminal breach of trust, a shameful dereliction of our post. * * * Public necessity is an arbitrary and unsafe dictator, and to save while salvable, from its lawless dominion, an upright judiciary should now, if ever, self-sacrificingly, if need be, illustrate the righteous maxim of Christian patriotism, ' *Fiat justitia ruat cœlum.*' "

Legal responsibility is, therefore, the result of the logical agreement of the law and the facts, and as law precedes obligation, the next step of the inquiry is to ascertain what is proof of the law. There is a familiar distinction between what is called conclusive and persuasive evidence, and the question has often been raised whether any single judicial decision is conclusive evidence of the law in any case, except the one in which it was rendered. In all countries where the common law prevails, many judgments of the highest courts have been overruled or modified. This amounts to a recognition of the fact that judges are neither Pontiffs, who cannot err, nor Kings, who can do no wrong. The judiciary, as has been before said, cannot make laws, they can only expand them by application to new cases. They do, however, if unconfirmed judgments are conclusive, often, by a hasty, ill considered, illogical conclusion, by overlooking authorities or disregarding facts, both make laws and repeal them. Whatever may be the dividing line between the authority of precedents and the authority of reason, it cannot be denied that the latter holds a prominent place in a science which professes to be the perfection of reason and the collected wisdom of ages. As Judge Robertson's views on this subject have sometimes been misapprehended, his own clear statement of them will be quoted. In speaking of the malleability of the common law, he said:—"An adjudged point, unreasonable or inconsistent with analogy or principle, should not be regarded as conclusive evidence of the law, unless it shall have been long acquiesced in, or more than once affirmed—and unless, on a survey of all material considerations, you feel that it is better to adhere to it, than, by overturning it, to produce uncertainty and surprise. STARE DECISIS should be thus and only thus understood and applied. Stability and uniformity require that authority, even when conflicting with principle, should sometimes decide what the law is. But, in all questionable cases, follow the safer guides—reason and the harmony of the law in all its parts.

"In consequence of which, it has been greatly improved from age to age by judicial modifications corresponding with its reason and the spirit of the times, yet the judge who leaves it as he finds it is at least a safe depository. He is neither a Mansfield nor a Hardwicke—he is more like Hale and Kenyon. If he does not improve, he does not mar or unhinge the law. It is safer and more prudent to err sometimes in the recognition of an established doctrine of the law, than to make innovation by deciding upon principle against the authority of judicial precedents."

In a response to a petition in one of his earlier cases he says:—"The practice we have discontinued was unreasonable; it was peculiar to this State; it could not promote the ends of justice; it would frequently promote injustice and irreparable injury without any reason for it. The rule was old, but its antiquity alone does not commend it. It is not sacred and inviolable merely because it is ancient; error is not less error because it is gray with age. Time, which makes it venerable, renders it more alarming and mischievous." Still he would not disregard the nicest distinctions when founded on authority and principle. For example, he decided that a writing acknowledging the receipt of a note for collection was not a covenant to pay the money over when collected, and afterwards decided that in such case an assumpsit will be implied to pay within a reasonable time after collection.

It still remains to find a common expression for the facts that are essential to every legal obligation. The correspondence between the law and the facts, however it may differ in degree or in circumstances, is in every case essentially the same in kind. The nature of this agreement can be found by ascertaining what a municipal law is. It is, at the least, an authoritative command, addressed to intelligent beings, requiring them to do or not do a particular **act**. Its subject **is** mind, its object an act. The doing or not doing is obviously composed of two elements, namely, will, intention, consent (for each of these terms is used according to circumstances to denote the mental operation which is regarded), and a physical deed or external act. In this country, **intentions** alone have never imposed obligations, or been a cause of punishment.

And the doctrines of fraud, mistake duress, and mental alienation, show that involuntary acts have no greater effect. These two therefore seem to be co-ordinates, by which the facts are to be measured. But the intent or volition is the unseen complement of the act of which the external conduct and circumstances are the signs or effects. Hence great part of practical law consists in weighing and applying presumptions. From what can be directly proved the mental operation must be inferred according to probabilities founded on experience. To expedite the application of these presumptions, and to secure the attainment of at least general truth, law gives to certain facts a conclusive and fixed **effect, to others** only the importance which they **should have when** taken in connection with all the circumstances, and requires that others shall **be** the only evidence of certain conclusions. These artificial rules of evidence have a tendency to sacrifice individual interests for the common welfare, and have, in the opinion of many, **been** carried to an unwarrantable extent, and to destroy some of them and modify others, legislation **has been** invoked.

Judge Robertson passed much of his judicial life in sifting, defining, sometimes restricting, but never or rarely enlarging these judicial and statutory devices, that give to some signs, causes, and effects of intention, a conclusive, and to others no weight or a fixed or partial one. Knowing that the innocent had fallen victims to constructive treasons, constructive libels, constructive capacity, constructive fraud, and presumptive murder, and that a trifling interest would not make every witness a liar, and that every common carrier was not by nature or occupation a thief, and that the assumption that every man knows the law was not, in any instance, true to its whole extent and not in some instances true to any extent, and that all married women and minors are not in fact incapable of contracting, and that politic enactments, such as the statute of frauds and of fraudulent conveyances, sometimes operated oppressively, and having considered the husband's liability for torts by his wife, and the master's for misfeasances and malfeasances of his servant, and the servant's accountability to his fellow servant in the same or in a different employment. He looked upon these and other numerous and vast artifices that had been brought within the walls of jurisprudence, if not with the suspicion of a Laocoon, with a circumspection that tried all their ribs and sounded their hollows. And regarding science as a unit, he endeavored to give these presumptions their proper place as members of the science of law.

Satisfying himself that the intervention of mind is essential to legal responsibility, and that legal presumptions, which are generalizations of particular or natural presumptions, like ready-made clothing, cut upon a calculation of mean proportions or averages, and which fit the various members of the classes or sizes for which they were designed, with unequal degrees of accuracy, are only expressions of approximate truth, and in some of their applications of untruth, he seems to have held that they were to be rigidly applied only so far as they had been rigidly established, but not extended even to analogous cases.   He also saw as the law was deductive, commencing with a single definition and spreading into numerous branches, that the extremes of related subjects run into each other, and also that different ramifications, to a greater or less extent, interlap and seem to conflict, in so much that in well arranged digests it is impossible to tell, in the first instance, under which of several heads to look for propositions common to all.   Whenever the matter under consideration occupied this debatable ground, he assigned it to that title, and disposed of it according to the law of that which he thought was most rational and just, and in this way appeared to modify existing laws when he only reconciled them.

* * *   We find that this critique must be a nut without its kernel.   Hamlet, with Hamlet left out—a conclusion from suppressed premises.   A somewhat elaborate attempt has been made by an analysis and harmony of cases to elucidate and verify the foregoing statements, but many a tale, "like Cambuscan's bold," must be left half told.   This book approaches its prescribed limits, and we sacrifice the abstracts in preference to other matter.   Space may be afforded to show the general tenor of that which has been omitted.   The purpose was to show what effect Judge R. gave to actual and artificial or constructive intent in the most diverse cases, and how, without violence to the law, when two or more well established principles conflicted in a particular case, he selected the one which he thought was most just and rational. Among others, the following facts were brought forward. In pursuance of the settled proposition, fraud shall not be presumed, he repudiated the distinction, taken in early Kentucky cases between a *suppressio veri* and a *suggestio falsi,* which required evidence of knowledge of the truth in the one case and not in the other, and affirmed that (actual) fraud is a wilful misrepresentation of facts, or a fraudulent concealment of them, with a view to deceive, and that a party, by making representations of facts which he honestly believes

to be true, is guilty of no moral turpitude and incurs no legal responsibility. The maxim that no man shall stultify himself, or that every man shall be treated as sane, had been shaken, but not overturned. So soon as he came upon the bench, he discarded it in civil cases, on the ground that the proposition affirming a contract to be an agreement, *aggre* (gatio) *ment* (tium), or contunence of *minds*, is at least equally well established, equally ancient, and far more rational. When he came to examine that other outpost of expediency, namely, ignorance of law excuses no man, he, for the first time (so far as we know), qualified it, or rather harmonized it with the indisputable principle, that every contract must have a consideration, by deciding that where it is perfectly evident that the only consideration of an alleged agreement was a mistake of the legal rights and obligations of the parties, and when there has been no fair compromise of *bona fide* and doubtful claims, the agreement may be avoided on the ground of total want of consideration or mutuality. This is as far as he would sustain a mistake of law, and it has ever since been recognized as the true principle. Under statutes creating constructive frauds, while he made particular facts evidence of intent, so far as the statutes and repeated decisions had fixed their import, he denied that a like inferential effect should be given to new or slightly different facts. Pressed by cogent argument, he refused to apply the statute of fraudulent conveyances to a case, in which the conveyance was made, not by the debtor or of his estate, but by another person, at the instance and with the money of the debtor, and maintained that as the common law will not presume fraud, a conveyance procured by a father, in consideration of his money, to be made to his children, will not at common law, or under the statute, be deemed fraudulent, from the fact alone that he was indebted at the time. That he sustained well settled artificial rules of evidence, to their full extent, may be seen in his dissent, which has the urgency of a remonstrance, from the decision of a majority of the court

that on oral proof of a mistake in drawing a deed, the conveyance can not only be set aside, but that the deed may be
reformed and then specifically enforced.   Likewise, though
doubting the policy of the statute making retention of possession by the seller of a chattel, fraud *per se*, he never
swerved from it, however he differed from subsequent judges
as to what constitutes change of possession.   Can a man at
law contract with himself?   If the presumptions upholding
the execution and consideration of writings seem to affirm
that he may, the idea of an agreement, expressed in the saying. It takes two to make a bargain, affirm as decisively that
he cannot.   A and B make their promissory note, which,
by the law of Kentucky is a specialty, to one of themselves,
A.   A majority of the court, Judge Robertson being one,
decided that a contract is the reciprocal consent of two or more
minds to do or not do a particular thing, that therefore A
could not make an enforcible obligation to pay himself, and
that, at law, contracts were not apportionable, and each joint
obligor was primarily liable for the whole amount, without
denying that B might have relief in equity, he was required
to pay the whole.   This decision has been repeatedly followed.   Where there has been no mistake or fraud, and
where there is no assignment and no relation between an
original party and the claimant, can the claimant be presump-
tively substituted in the place of a party expressly named in
the obligation?   A, and B, his surety, make their promissory
note to C, a bank, to enable A to raise money on it.   C
refuses to accept the note or furnish the funds.   A delivers
the note to D, who advances the money.   Is B liable to D on
the note?   If leaving the name of the obligor blank implies
authority to fill the blank with any name, inserting a particular name must be, at least, an implied denial of the right to
insert any other name.   An accommodation party has a
right to select his creditor, and if he do name him, why should
not the maxim, *expressio unius exclusio alterius* apply?   He
may have abundant reasons for his choice, which are not an-

swered by the assertion that the instrument in the hands of the obligee would be assignable. For example: he may have reasons to expect accommodation or indulgence from the party named; may have a set off against his claim, or may be unwilling that his own name should be hawked in the market. Every purchaser of the note knows from its face who the payee is, and must be presumed to know the law of derivative parties. According to that law no one but the payee can assign the legal title to the note, and to enable an action to be maintained by relation, the relator C must have the legal title. If a note be indorsed to the maker, the indorsement extinguishes it; the maker's indorsement will not revive it, but will create a new obligation. The refusal of the note by the payee is a much stronger fact for the maker. In the one case it is returned to the maker because it has ceased to be obligatory; in the other case because it never was obligatory. Until a recent statute the law was, that the indorsement by the maker of a note, payable to his own order, was mere evidence of a previous indebtedness. The ingenuity and force of the argument in this case (Conway v. The Bank of the U. S.), cannot be exhibited in an abridged form. This decision, after standing many years, has been repeatedly overruled, for reasons which do not very satisfactorily appear. Proof of homicide creates, in the first instance, the presumption of murder. May this presumption be to any extent repelled by proof that the accused, by his own act, was drunk? According to an early Kentucky decision, drunkenness, unless produced by the adverse party, with a fraudulent intent, by which he gained an undue advantage, could not be shown in avoidance of a contract. Subsequent decisions of the same court establish that drunkenness, which renders the party incompetent to contract, however it may have been produced, will defeat the contract. Why apply one rule in civil, another in criminal cases? The basis of the obligations to keep one's word, and to abstain from unlawful violence, are the same. Intelligent will is at the bottom of both. Drunkenness produces every degree of mental aberation and alienation. If it be said that drunkenness is intentional or wilful, and the drunkard a *voluntarius demo*, it may be replied, that in many instances it is the accidental surprise of temperate and upright men, who drink for social enjoyment, or its victim, impelled by a resistless appetite that is sometimes congenital or acquired from the cordials administered in infancy or sickness, or stimulants taken as a relief against misfortunes, is pursued by a nemesis as unrelenting and fatal as the destiny of wretched and innocent house of Labdacus. As to his being a voluntary demon, the answer is, that although a frequent antecedent and cause of crime, still the relation between drunkenness and crime is neither so intimate nor so frequent as to create any presumption that drunkenness is produced with a view to commit crime. The objection that the decisions of courts uniformly held drunkenness not to be allowable in mitigation, is met by the statement, that the question had never been decided by a court of errors in Kentucky, and the British decisions were coeval with, and founded upon, the same extreme notions of expediency with the overruled doctrine that no man can stultify himself.

With regard to the expediency of admitting drunkenness in mitigation, it was urged that this was a more proper question for the Legislature than for courts, and that as manners control laws, a people who refuse to prohibit or punish drunkenness will not, under any instructions of courts, be likely to ignore it in the framing of verdicts.

That drunkenness, in at least some cases and for some purpose, was admissible in criminal cases, was the logical sequence of very many of Judge Robertson's opinions. Not being a man who could halt midway in an argument, or refuse to apply a conclusion which he had labored so often to establish, he rendered the opinion of the court, that under proper qualifications, drunkenness, resulting from a desire for social enjoyment, or sensual gratification, may be given in evidence, under the plea of not guilty, to a charge of murder, and may, if from all circumstances the jury shall so consider, reduce the offense to manslaughter. This is as far as he was asked to go, and regarding expediency as not a subject of judicial consideration, or whatever is right to be expedient, the conclusion is inevitable.

His opinions penetrate into almost every department of jurisprudence. Those upon the meaning of statutes, and upon rules of practice and pleading, exhibit his ingenuity and capacity for details, but those upon the leading principles of equity, constitutional, and international law, give most room for his discursive powers, and show to the best advantage the range and rigor of his intellect and the extent of his erudition.

The kind and arrangement of a man's words are a good index to some of the qualities of his mind. The style of an obscure thinker is never clear, nor of a slow one rapid, nor of a dull one brilliant. Judge Robertson could clothe his thoughts in different garbs, according to the subject and the occasion. They have appeared in the curt and gladiatorial dress of Junius, in the homespun of Bunyan and Cobbet, in the flowing robe of the historian of his own name, and in the ample and stately toga of Gibbon. The style of his opinions was his ordinary style; he adopted and adhered to it, because it was the language and idiom in which he thought, and because it required no elaboration. It bears no resemblance to that of his associates or predecessors, and can be detected at once. He wrote as fast as he could perform the manual part, without erasures or interlineation, and never revised. Many of his longest opinions were struck out at a single heat, and he either thought that alterations would emasculate the first strong expressions, or his time was too much occupied to permit him to attend to the refinements of composition. His opinions were thought out, often, when he was in a recumbent position, with closed eyes, before he took up his pen. Whatever may be the defects of his mode

11

of expression it is grammatically correct, and so clear as to present his meaning with ease and precision. His opinions are among the easiest to digest that can be found. His style also is remarkable for its force; he writes like a man who is in earnest. It has been said that his opinions betray feeling; this is true; they exhibit the feeling which is the result and not the cause of strong convictions; his cogent and diversified arguments show the source of his conclusions. Feeling of some kind must be behind every energetic style. It has been well said, "With a callous heart there can be no genius in the imagination, or wisdom in the mind; and therefore the prayer, with equal truth and sublimity, says, 'incline our hearts unto wisdom.' Resolute thoughts find words for themselves, and make their own vehicle; impression and expression are relative ideas; he who feels deeply will express strongly; the language of light sensation is naturally feeble and superficial."

Some have thought that a judge should be a bust truncated above the heart; the mutilating paradox is false; a judge of human conduct and motives must be a whole man, able to know, to feel, to will.

Judge Robertson had a vivid imagination, which quickened and adorned his varied knowledge, and shed the light of copious illustration upon the intricate path of argument. All his arguments may not be correct, nor all his illustrations in good taste, but the luxuriant vegetation, which a fertile soil throws up, makes amends for the weeds, which, under the best culture, are mingled with its fruits and flowers. It has been suggested that he preferred to use words that are not of Saxon origin. If this be a fault, it is the fault of many graceful and vigorous writers. But upon examination it will be found that his terms are well selected and expressive. The law has a dialect of its own. The two languages in which it was first written, and in which its proceedings were conducted, and which have left imperishable traces upon its nomenclature, were neither of them Saxon. And although

Judge Robertson adopted many names and phrases from the early common law writers and from the civilians, he has taken none, which those for whom his judicial writings are intended, ought not readily to understand. Besides, the learned are not agreed that too much of importance has not been attributed to Anglo-Saxon blood, of which but little now remains, and to Anglo-Saxon words, which constitute but a small part of our vocabulary.

The English language is made up of three principal, and many smaller, tributaries, whose combined volume is required to bear the intellectual commerce of this age. The Anglo-Saxon language ceased to grow before modern thought began, and, like the language of every uncultivated people, it has names for little more than the commonest objects of sense. What is called English undefiled, is only peculiarly fitted to narrative and descriptive compositions, like those found in the Bible, in the works of Bunyan, and of De Foe. And the Bible, when it expounds abstract truths, resorts to such terms as predestination, sanctification, and justification, for which the primitive tongue affords no equivalents. Saxon words are no more fitted for the entire purposes of modern thought, than the painted vest, which Prince Vortigern won from a naked Pict, would be a suitable dress for all the occasions of modern society. His crowning merit as a judge was his high and unblemished probity. Every suitor received from him a patient and respectful hearing, an honest and well considered judgment. On the bench and elsewhere, however he may have fallen short of other men, or excelled them, he devoted his time and his energy to the discharge of his duties, and did the best that he was able to do. To him, without qualification, may be applied the noble lines of Dryden:—

> "In Isreal's courts ne'er sat an Abethdin
> With more discerning eyes, or hands more clean,
> Unbribed, unsought the wretched to redress,
> Swift of dispatch, and easy of access."

It is believed it could be said of George Robertson, as Alexander Severus said of Ulpian, that the laws could not go far astray while he was at the helm.   And that the laws of Kentucky are not less wise and consistent, and her judicial reports less respected at home and abroad, from the fact that he sat so long and faithfully upon the bench of her highest court, and was the associate of so many true and gifted men, of whom Buckner, and Ewing, and Marshall, and Nicholas, and Hardin, are now his associates in death.   His companion in youth, his first and probably his best beloved colleague, Judge Underwood, still lives.

> "May death not be jealous of the mild decay,
> Which gently wins him his."

J.

J. B. ROBERTSON

James B. Robertson was, if not the best, one of the best talkers of his day; he was also a correct and ready writer. The only productions of his pen in my possession, are two faded letters, written in pencil, on long strips of printing paper.   Even in these careless effusions may be found flashes of his playful humor, and evidence of his fluency, as the following extracts will show.   The larger portions of these communications are descriptive of men and things, in disturbed times, and are too pungent, personal, and truthful, to be published now:

LEXINGTON, Feb. 14th, 1866.

Dear Aleck:

Yours of the 15th reached me with reasonable dispatch. I am exceedingly glad that my enclosures escaped the perils of the wayside, and afforded you so much satisfaction.   I have sent you several of our papers, which, dull as they

habitually are, will give you a fuller abstract of affairs here
and hereabouts than I could hope to do with an unpractised
pen.

*   *   *   *   *   *   *

The old gentleman is again at Frankfort. In his absence
the place is almost exclusively surrendered to the negroes,
of whom he is now subsisting a populous colony—no fewer
than four able bodied women, two grown men, and one or
two voracious picaninnies. I know nothing of their sump
tuary arrangements, but imagine that it would require an
army commissariat to keep such an establishment long upon
its legs. The waste, pillaging, and vexation, must be enormous. *   *   * I have been unable to find the
whereabouts of Wash, and presume that he has been for
sometime dead. Jourdan, the patriarchal and pediculous,
however still lives and—eats. Prayer is professedly his great
consolation, and he did, for a time, essay to exist as Elijah
and some of those old fellows did, a good while ago, but the
experiment was unblessed, and he returned to his oats. A
has a * * and barring interminable imbroglios with her
"help," which she avers is no help at all, she seems to be
getting along about as well as her idiosyncracies of temper
will permit. B has his commons at home, and contributes
much the greater share to the maintainance of the concern.
The C's seem to thrive as well as ever. * * They have
an abundance of company, which they doubtless entertain
with their accustomed facility and frugality. The wind
which blew D away, was the gale of necessity. He had
literally "played out" around here, and accepted, so he
proclaimed, the good offices of a kinsman, who proffered
him certain inducements to go to Michigan. Reaching
Chicago, where he was to meet his benefactor, he found
himself minus the wherewithal to proceed farther, and also
failed to find the benefactor. But he continued to push on,
and at last found his Samaritan, in as hopeless a state of im-
pecuniosity as himself. He is still in Michigan, and is said

to be making but poor headway against the tide.   I have
not seen E. or F for months.   Since the Rebs stopped their
forays into their part of the country, their own descents into
this have been fewer and farther between.   *   *   I have
thus given you a condensed census of ———, and would
enlarge it into an epitome of the personal history of the
friends and acquaintances you left behind, but for fear of
losing you as a correspondent.   The fact is, however, you
would require a re-naturalization here, so radically have the
manners and population changed.   As an experiment upon
your patience, I will endeavor to catalogue a few of the more
familiar characters, then and now.   *   *   *   I
have heard nothing of the P's for a long time.   John was
badly crippled in the rebel army, and afterwards married a
Mississippi widow, wealthy before the war.   Jim has shot
from the surface, and is probably burrowing somewhere, as
a provincial pedagogue.   B N. holds his own, in his own
eccentric way, and with a hunt or a piscatory debauch, now
and then, is commendably abstemious.   C. D. is still an
attache of the court-house—in fact, he is every where, where
money is to be made, and is doubtless getting rich.   L has
changed his base, and is now holding forth at the ——— office.
From indications and known facts, I would infer that his *per
diem* consumption of what Dickens calls "conspiracy against
life," could only be calculated in quarts.   Old M has been
ousted from his habitat, and looks like a desolation.   X. Y.
has tapered off somewhat, but is as intolerable a nuisance as
ever.   L. M. is residing in New York, and Ben is leading a
life of inelegant leisure here.   [At this point the letter runs
into politics.]   W himself was threatened with arrest, and
fled in dismay.   There is no doubt whatever that he would
have been held for contumacy, I suppose, in daring to
make a second application to the Grand Panjandaram for the
coveted permits.   By some extraordinary *auto da fe* he has
been permitted to return, and reached his home in the country a few days ago, where he remains in penitential retire-

ment. H also, was, Cataline-like, "set free," and he too
returns a wiser, if not more loyal, man. I could cite numerous examples of this arbitrary exercise of power, &c.

AUGUST 11TH, 1866.

With the single exception of politics, affairs here, both
social and commercial, aesthetic and ordinary, are in a state
of unpromising stagnation.   *   *   One thing, however, is certain, the Big Sandy, and every other projected
enterprise of any magnitude, in Kentucky, will have to be
finished, if finished at all, with foreign capital, and operated
with foreign brains. All is apathy and stupidity here.   *
*   *   *   *   I have but little intimacy with the
disciples of Themis.   *   *   *   *   W is *pro-
fessing* medicine, at N; his wife is here. Whether he has
suspended connubial relations, I am unprepared to say.   H.
G. I have not seen for some time; he has been here until
very recently, teaching music, operating the organ at ——
church, and imbibing copious lager.   *   *   *
Papa's establishment has become quite a popular house of
call. Mrs. R, a claimant for cousinship, and a Miss G, a
marriageable *protege*, passed sometime there lately. Mrs. R,
nee I—n, is a rather comely widow of questionable age, and a
native of Va She struck up an acquaintance with the old
gentleman, I believe through correspondence, while visiting
some —— family in Chicago. Another party of ladies
from, &c. I hope yet to give you a Christmas greeting. My
revenue is small, it is true, but I need not assure you, that
"what so poor a man as Hamlet is, may do, God willing,
shall not lack." Unless then you have renounced Kentucky
altogether, pay us the promised visit, before another intes-
tine war, which *quidnuncs* would have us believe is fearfully
imminent. I protest I would incontinently inflict a domicil-
iary visit upon you and yours, were it not, &c.

NOTICE TAKEN BY THE PRESS OF JUDGE ROBERTSON'S DECEASE.

Of the many bar resolutions and obituary notices, the following are sufficient to show the place that Judge Robertson occupied in the minds and hearts of his countrymen:

GEORGE ROBERTSON

1790—1874.

George Robertson, for more than half a century a leading and controlling spirit in the politics and jurisprudence of Kentucky, is no more. In the long and crowded line of illustrious children, of whom our State is justly proud, the public life of not one other, we believe, has extended over so long a period as his; and certainly the life of none has been more varied in service, more constant in honor. Born in Garrard county in 1790, he lived through more than four-score years, and has but now fallen in his tracks. The date of his birth is far back in the early times, when Kentucky was still in the dark and bloody ground; an almost unbroken wilderness; that of his death finds her, largely through his own loyal and loving efforts, an empire in resources and in promise. The strength and abundant vitality, which bore him through so long a course, and enabled him to labor so honorably to himself, so profitably to us all, he derived with his being itself from the sound and sturdy pioneer stock, whence he sprang. Nor did he have to purchase the advantages of health and vigor by the lack of early culture, which so many of our strong and good men, contemporary with him, had to deplore. For primitive times, his opportunities of cultivation were unusual, and he became a scholar. In 1816 he was elected to Congress, being then only twenty-six years old. He was twice re-elected, but resigned at the beginning of his third term, without taking his seat, in order to devote himself more entirely to his profession. Young as he was, he acted quite a prominent part in national politics during the terms of his service. He was chairman of the Committee on Territories, and author of the present system of selling public lands. He particularly distinguished himself in the angry controversy over the erection of a Territorial government for Arkansas, a proviso in the bill prohibiting slavery being stricken out, after a long and doubtful contest, only by the casting vote of the Speaker, Mr. Clay. After leaving Congress, Mr. Robertson was often, but vainly, solicited to accept various positions of honor and public trust. President Monroe offered him the Governorship of the territory of Arkansas, and the mission to Columbia; President Adams appointed him minister to Peru; but all these positions he declined. During the animated struggle between the New Court and the Old Court parties, the activity of his mind, and his keen interest in public affairs, in a measure forced him to lay aside for a time his resolution to abstain entirely from politics; and he was elected by a spontaneous movement of the people to the Kentucky House of Representatives, and was chosen Speaker of that body. The public labors of his later years were in the department of jurisprudence. In 1829 he was appointed Chief Justice of the Court of Appeals, and held that eminently responsible position for fourteen years, when he resigned and again retired to private life. During the war he was recalled by the vote of the people to the Supreme bench, and, during the inauguration ceremonies of Gov. Leslie, the venerable jurist tendered his verbal resignation, which was afterwards reduced to writing and accepted. This was in Semptember, 1872, since which time he has resided quietly at his home in Lexington. He never recovered from his paralytic stroke, and had been almost a constant sufferer up to the moment of his death.

In noticing the characteristics of Judge Robertson's intellect, no one can fail to be struck by its precocity, especially when taken in connection with the great age which he attained, and his continued activity to the last. He ripened early, and he hung long upon the bough, thus furnishing a remarkable exception to the general rule in such cases. At his first appearance upon the arena of politics, he was already a strong and fully developed man. His writings and speeches at that early time seem to be as ripe and as free from boyish crudities as the productions of his latter years. Perhaps much of this effect is due to the thoroughness of his legal studies, and to the ardor of his devotion to a sober and methodical profession. But it is noticeable that among the dusty folios of the law, he never lost his taste for the graces of composition. This is evinced by every thing he has left behind him. It is no unusual thing to meet in his legal arguments and judicial opinions, flowers of rhetoric, which, in such places, almost excite exclamations of surprise.

The bent of his mind was always toward large views of the questions that were brought before him. He seemed to take pleasure, not in avoiding difficulties and intricacies, but in boldly meeting and solving them It came natural to him to rest every ca-e upon the deepest principles involved in it, to hold it firmly on them, and to decide it by them, instead of sending it off on some shallow quibble or mere technicality. If there was anything in a case that went down into the depths and the obscure places of the law, it was always possible, nay, it was always easy, to get him to see and acknowledge the fact, and to guide his researches and reflections accordingly. Many of his briefs as counsel, and of his decisions as judge, have attracted attention beyond the confines of the State. One of his most celebrated briefs was in the case of Russell vs. Southard, which he gained before the Supreme Court of the United States. Perhaps the most famous of his earlier decisions, was that in the case of Dickey vs. the Maysville and Lexington Turnpike Road Company. Among his later decisions, that in the case of Griswold vs. Hepham, in regard to the constitutionality of the legal-tender act passed by Congress, is the most conspicuous. The doctrines laid down by him were afterwards affirmed by the Supreme Court of the United States.

Judge Robertson was a man of warm and generous impulses, as he showed on every occasion of his life. Out of love for his family, and in order that he might do the more for them, he gave up his seat in Congress and devoted himself to the law. Had he continued in the field of national politics, he would, no doubt, have attained the most exalted positions; for it may well be questioned, justly eminent as he was on the bench, whether his peculiar gifts of mind and traits of character did not fit him for a statesman rather than a judge, despite his large conscientiousness, and his elevated sense of the dignity and sanctity of his office as judge. His strong feelings, to some extent, controlled him, and when he had become thoroughly convinced that one party was the victim of fraud or injustice, he argued for him almost with the zeal of an advocate. He was an ardent Whig, and the enthusiastic and unfailing friend of Henry Clay, by whom he stood staunchly throughout all of that statesman's long career, and over whose remains he pronounced an oration of mournful regret and tenderness.

His signal devotion to duty can have no clearer or more more touching illustration than in the circumstances of his first attack. On the night before the morning on which he suffered paralysis, a young relative occupied the same room with him, as was customary, in order to watch over the hard-working old man. In the morning the Judge arose very early, and began his accustomed work. He sat down to the table to write out an opinion in some decided case. His stroke, if such it may be called, was not sudden, but astonishingly gradual. His eyesight began to grow dim, and he called out to his relative that such was the fact; but he refused, at the remonstrance of the latter, to give up his work. He continued to work on till his failing eyes could no longer guide his hand, and the written lines growing shorter and shorter, narrowed to a point; the strokes of his pen grew lighter, dimmer, illegible, and he could do no more. He insisted even then, however, that only his eyes were at fault, that his mental faculties were still perfectly sound, as was no doubt the truth, and begged that he might be carried to the court-room to take part in the decision of cases; so he fell at his post, and literally with his harness on—a pure patriot, an able, upright jurist, a noble man. He is no longer with us, for whose good his strength, his life were spent, but his name will live long in the State he loved and served. His labor was enduring—it will not perish. He has done more for Kentucky jurisprudence, more to give it form within the State and fame abroad, than any other one judge—perhaps than all other judges together, that have ever sat in the Court of Appeals. Possibly his mere words may die, and his opinions, as such, may cease to be cited; possibly the day may come when his name will be spoken no more, but the principles he so largely helped to establish, must continue to exert their influence on the jurisprudence of our State, for many years yet to come. Happy, indeed, was he in his destiny; few men have been more blessed in the fruitfulness of their work, or the richness of their remuneration.

Six years ago, just before he was stricken down by paralysis, he remarked, in conversation with a friend, that the longer he lived the more diffident he became of his own ability, and the correctness of his opinions He explained his meaning by the illustration of a man doomed, at first, to live in the bottom of a well—his horizon is circumscribed, and yet he imagines he sees all there is of it; but as he gradually climbs up, the boundary of his horizon is expanded, and he then understands how much is to be learned. He then feels as Sir Isaac Newton declares—like he was standing on the shore, picking up an occasional pebble now and then, while the great ocean of truth lay all unexplored before him. He had, he remarked on the same occasion, been accused of making law; but he held that the common law was, to a certain extent, a progressive science; not that its principles changed, but expanded so as to embrace the change of circumstances.

Judge Robertson was long the only survivor of the Congress that passed the Missouri compromise measures in 1820. He had indeed come down to us from a former generation; and the men who practiced before him, during the last years of his official life, were the sons of contemporaries, nearly every one of whom have passed away. The venerable Thomas A. Marshall, of this city, was one of the last representatives of the stirring times, which first brought the men of the last generation into prominence —he being four years younger than Judge Robertson.

The announcement of the death of this able jurist, comes like wailing over the State. His professional course was marked by high integrity of purpose; and while presiding as Judge of the Appellate Court, he enjoyed to an eminent degree, the confidence of the bar and of the public. Of him it can be truly said that he died full of years and of honors. Be his own motto his epitaph:

Non sibi sed patriae.

The following are the particulars of his last hours and death, as given in a special dispatch to the *Courier-Journal*, dated at Lexington the 16th:— "Judge George H. Robertson died at precisely 10 o'clock to-night, after suffering intensely from 4 o'clock this morning. He was taken with cramp last Monday, and brought very low, but was not thought to be dying until to-day. Since this morning his agony was so intense that morphine was administered, but failed to take effect, as he threw it up, and he continued to sink rapidly. Rev. Mr. Dinwiddie, his former pastor, whose church (the First Presbyterian) he joined about two years ago, happened to be passing through town, and called to see him, this morning. He was with him until 11 o'clock. Judge R. expressed himself willing and ready to die, and said he hoped to meet his pastor in a better world. He retained consciousness up to about 9 o'clock to-night, when he became speechless. However, upon his daughter-in-law asking him if he knew her, although he could not articulate, he pressed her hand. He has taken great interest in religious concerns for some years past, and last night asked that "Rock of Ages" should be sung for him. He died in his chair, where he had lived since his stroke of paralysis two are three years ago, and looked very little emaciated after death. His body will be kept, according to his request, for some days, probably a week, before burial."

JUDGE GEORGE ROBERTSON.

On the night of the 16th of May, in the city of Lexington, surrounded by family and friends, peacefully passed away the soul of George Robertson, a name so indissolubly linked with the history of his country that, without the record of his life, it would be incomplete.

The hand of death was not laid upon him unexpectedly. His great age, and a stroke of paralysis visited upon him two years before his death, prepared him for approaching dissolution. And yet the going out of that light that had been so long shining as a beacon in the world of intellect, startled us, though we saw the trembling, fitful flash of the expiring flame, and watched its feeble efforts to survive.

George Robertson, more familiar to us as Judge Robertson, of the Kentucky Court of Appeals, was born in 1790, in what is now known as Garrard county, then a part of Mercer. He inherited a robust constitution, which was never impaired by the indulgences too common to the youth of these days. At the age of eighteen he commenced the study of the law at Lancaster, in the office of Martin D. Hardin. That he was singularly fitted for the profession which he selected, his after life gave the most convincing proof.

In 1809 he married Miss Eleanor, then only sixteen years of age, daughter of Dr. Bainbridge, of Lancaster. The young couple had many things to contend with, but with brave hearts they fought the battle with the world, and triumphed. The promising talents of the young lawyer soon obtained a recognition of the most flattering character. In 1816, though only in his twenty-sixth year, he was elected to Congress, and again in 1818 and 1820. He did not serve out his last term, however, but resigned before taking his seat. During his Congressional career he distinguished himself in debate upon some of the most important questions that at that time occupied the public mind, and left the National Legislature with a reputation second only to that of Henry Clay. But a more important duty than settling the status of territories required his presence at home. At that time the great struggle for constitutional government was going on in his own State, and into that struggle he threw himself with all the ardor of his impetuous manhood, and brought to bear in defense of the constitution all the powers of his great intellect and persuasive oratory.

He was elected in 1822 to represent his county (Garrard) in the State Legislature, and continued to represent her from that time until 1826— during the most exciting period in the early history of the State.

He constantly refused positions of public trust at the hands of the Government, preferring to remain at home in the practice of his profession, and advancing the interests of his people. In 1828 he was appointed Secretary of State by Governor Metcalfe, and a few months later of the same year, was appointed to the Appellate Bench. Subsequently he received the commission of Chief Justice, which position he held until 1843, when he resigned. Having removed to the county of Fayette, he was elected a Representative to the State Legislature in 1851, and was at that session chosen Speaker of the House by acclamation.

The war coming on found him a consistent advocate of Union, and an unflinching opponent of Secession. Yet he was moderate in the expression of his opinion, and was rarely to be found on the side of the extremist. In 1864 he was again elected to the Appellate Bench by an almost unanimous uprising of the people. Hon. Alvin Duvall had received the nomination of the party, but it becoming known some days before the election that Gen. Burbridge and his bayonets would prevent the casting of any votes for Duvall, the people, to avoid trouble, nominated Judge George Robertson, and triumphantly elected him, such was the reverence the people had for his virtue, and their belief in his incorruptible integrity.

Judge Robertson retained the position of Chief Justice of the Appellate Court until 1871. At the inauguration of Governor Leslie he, in a short and painfully impressive speech, and with halting tones, tendered his resignation, after having administered the oath of office to the Governor.

Immediately after this solemn act, by which the venerable Judge severed as it were, his active connection with the world, a committee appointed by the Court of Appeals drew up a memorial as a tribute to the life and public services of the great Chief Justice. Says the report: "As he put off his robes of office and pronounced his heartfelt benediction on his beloved countrymen, we beheld the representative of a race of intellectual giants. It was allotted him, in the providence of God, to survive them all, with the solitary exception of his distinguished and venerable compeer, Joseph R. Underwood. Though enfeebled by age, and wasted by disease, his mind seemed to be active and vigorous as ever. Having finished his course and won for himself the plaudit, 'Well done thou good and faithful servant,' he stepped down into private life with the calm dignity of the veteran patriot "

The immediate cause no doubt of his determination to resign his position as Chief Justice was, the physical incapacity to discharge its duties, having, in the summer of 1871, been struck with paralysis.

For sometime before his death he became completely helpless, but the surest evidence of the fast approaching end, was a loss of that intellectual vigor that had distinguished him above all men with whom he had to cope, either in the Senate or the forum. Recognizing the approach of that day when he should appear before his Maker, Judge Robertson took great interest in spiritual matters for some time before his death, and frequently during his illness solicited the visits of favorite clergymen, whom he desired should pray with him. He was conscious to the last, and died with faith in his Redeemer, and a trusting belief in his salvation.

Judge Robertson was a man of remarkable native talent, an untiring student, and possessed with a singular power of convincing men. In every department of effort in which he was called to serve, he distinguished himself. As a member of Congress he was remarkable for his ability and mastery of the details of legislation. But as a lawyer he far outshone all his contemporaries. It was in this profession that he made for himself an enduring fame. While Chief Justice of Kentucky he rendered decisions that have no superior in the history of jurisprudence, and are quoted as authority wherever the English language is spoken.

To a peculiar aptitude for research and an unwearying industry, he united a mental intrepidity that led him, whenever in his judgment he saw proper, to disregard dusty precedents, and with the unfailing and unalterable principles of truth and justice to guide him, to delve into the mysteries of the legal science, grapple with complex problems, and evolve theories of jurisprudence remarkable for their force and brilliancy. His great analytical powers, fine perceptive faculties, and breadth of view, enabled him to conquer difficulties that would have been insurmountable to less able men. But amid all the technicalities of his profession, and in spite of his years of groping among the dusty tomes of law, he preserved his love for the flowers of rhetoric, and in some of his decisions are to be found passages that startle the reader by their beauty of expression.

The State of Kentucky was justly proud of her distinguished son. In his death she has suffered a severe, we will not say, an irreparable loss. He contributed to her fame, and to her judiciary he added a lustre that attracted the attention of the world. She will honor his name; the nation will honor it, and when the student of her history turns its leaves in after years, he will find no name more deserving of enduring memory than that of Judge George Robertson.

REPORT OF THE COMMITTEE OF THE LEXINGTON BAR

Judge Hunt having taken his seat, the report of the Committee was read by Mr. Kinkead, as follows:

REPORT:

The members of the Lexington Bar have appointed us to express their sentiments of respect on the occasion of the death of George Robertson who died at his residence, in this city, on Saturday, the 16th of May, 1874, at 10 o'clock P. M.

He who for so long a time has been our head and chief has fallen at last and it is becoming in us to manifest our reverence for his worth. His long list of services, beginning with the early years of our Commonwealth, and reaching wdon almost to the present, passes before our minds; and on a fitting occasion and by eloquent lips, these shall be recounted in our hearing to his countrymen. Standing now in the presence of the dead, with the opening heavens above us, it seems almost out of place to look back to earth and to earthly objects and earthly honors; in the presence of immortality to turn to the mortal and perishing scenes around us. And yet this earth of ours is so allied to heaven; this mortal is so linked with immortality; those of us who remain are so united with those who have gone; the deeds of this world cast their shadows so distinctly on the world beyond, we unconsciously acknowledge that those only are worthy of a crown who by their lives have exalted virtue and made her lovely, and who, amid the passions and temptations by which they are surrounded, have kept their garments undefiled.

It was said of an eminent man of old that he had done things worthy to be written; that he had written things worthy to be read; and by his life had contributed to the welfare of the Republic and the happiness of mankind. He on whom this transcendent eulogy can be pronounced with even partial truth, is entitled to the gratitude of his race. During the present generation, within the broad limits of the Commonwealth, has there died a man over whom it might more truthfully be said, than George Robertson?

The temptation is great, the materials are abundant, but this is not the time or place to discourse of even the outlines of the life of this distinguished man His early days of poverty and hard labor—his lack of that early education and discipline, which, while it did not hinder him from rising rapidly to a seat among the highest, by the force of his natural intellect, yet shows itself in all his after life—the conservative character of his mind, which led him to throw himself on several trying occasions at different and distant periods—in youth, in full manhood, and in old age—on the side of law and order and stable government, his great legal and constitutional learning in which, for more than half a century, he had occupied a front seat with his associates, and which only needed a broader and more conspicuous theater, with its controlling and stimulating conflicts, to have

made his reputation coextensive with our language; his ample head; his
firm mouth indicating a strong will and unbounded confidence in his powers; sometimes leading him too far; his exquisite and subtle intellect
sometimes deceiving itself; all this must be dwelt on to make their proper
impression and do justice to so remarkable a man. Other men may
have had excellencies which he did not have; other men may have
been free of faults which he had; but take him as he was, with all his
faults and all his virtues; with his intellectual strength and his intellectual
weakness, Kentucky has produced from her soil, distinguished as many of
of them have been in every department of life, no son whose name she
will inscribe higher in her list of worthies.

All, then, that remains to us is to resolve that in the death of the Hon.
George Robertson, this bar feels the loss of one of its most distinguished
members, and one of its most pleasant associates; the State one of its
most valuable citizens and friends; that from a sense of duty to the profession, of which he was an ornament, of gratitude for his services to the
Commonwealth, as well as to satisfy our own private feelings, we bear our
testimony to his great ability, to his extensive learning in the common law
as in equity and constitutional law, and to his domestic, no less than to his
public virtues.

MISCELLANEOUS EXTRACTS

FROM THE WRITINGS OF JUDGE ROBERTSON, SHOWING HIS OPIN-
IONS ON VARIOUS SUBJECTS.

GRIEF, INDULGENCE OF.

That is a false and pernicious dignity which chills the warm emotions
of the heart, or hushes the soft accents of nature's voice. Achilles was
never so attractively interesting as when agonizing in the dust for the
death of Patroclus; nor did the aged Priam ever appear so amiable, as
when, with trembling frame and streaming eyes, he begged the lifeless
body of his son Hector. These were nature's doings, and among her
proudest achievements; exhibiting, in the one case, the most impetuous of
heroes, tamed and subdued by the tenderness of a holy friendship, and, in
the other, the majesty of a King mildly mingled with the tenderness of a
kind father. You remember the stern and towering Pyrrhus—being rebuked for the unstoical weakness of shedding tears for the death of his
wife, and urged to assume the aspect of a Philosopher unmoved, he ex-
claimed—"Oh, Philosophy! yesterday thou commandest me to love my
wife—to-day thou forbiddest me to lament for her!" And being told that

tears could not restore her, he replied—"Alas! that reflection only makes them flow faster."

The reasonable indulgence of the affections and emotions of the heart is not only happying but meliorating, and is one of nature's expedients for civilizing mankind, and saving them from selfishness and vice. The most wise and honored should always act as rational men, and never rebel against Heaven, or commit treason against nature, by attempting to destroy or to conceal those emotions which belong to the wisest and best of men, for the wisest and best of ends. Let them then be enjoyed and acted out in a becoming manner by the most exalted of our race, as long as they wish to be considered as men. Such a course secures the intellectual Sun from eclipse, disrobes knowledge of the cold and mystic cloud of pride and hypocrisy, and presents it in all the simplicity and radiance of its native grace and intrinsic loveliness. He who never seems to feel, either never feels at all, or as man ought to feel; and others will never feel much affection or respect for him. But in the tender sympathies of pure hearts, there is "a joy unspeakable and full of glory"—and remember,

> "The path of sorrow, and that path alone,
> Leads to the land where sorrow is unknown."

LITERARY FAME.

The classical reader remembers that, when almost all the Greeks, captured with Nicias at Syracuse, had died in dungeons, a remnant of the survivors saved themselves by the recitation of beautiful extracts from Euripides. How potent was the shadowed genius of the immortal Athenian, when it alone melted the icy hearts that nothing else could touch, and broke the captive's chains, which justice, and prayers, and tears, had in vain tried to unloose? And hence "the glory of Euripides had all Greece for a monument." He too was elevated by the light of other minds. It is said that he acquired a sublime inspiration whenever he read Homer—whose Iliad and whose Odyssey—the one exhibiting the fatality of strife among leading men—the other portraying the efficacy of perseverance—have stamped his name on the roll of fame in letters of sunshine, that will never fade away. No memorial tells where Troy once stood—Delphi is now mute—the thunder of Olympus is hushed, and Apollo's lyre no longer echoes along the banks of the Peneus—but the fame of Homer still travels with the stars.

TIME AND CHANGE.

Time builds on the ruins itself has made. It destroys to renew, and desolates to improve. A wise and benevolent Providence has thus marked its progress in the moral, as well as in the physical world. The tide which has borne past generations to the ocean of eternity, is hastening to the same doom the living mass now gliding downward to that shoreless and

12

unfathomed reservoir. But whilst the current, in its onward flow, sweeps away all that should perish, like the Nile, it refreshes every desert, and fructifies every wild through which it rolls; and, fertilizing one land with the spoils of another, it deposits in a succeeding age the best seeds matured by the toil of ages gone before. Asia has thus been made tributary to Africa and to the younger Europe, ancient to modern times, and the middle ages to the more hallowed days in which we ourselves live. One generation dies that another may live to take its place. The desolation of one country has been the renovation of another—the downfall of one system has been the ultimate establishment of a better—and the ruin of nations has been the birth or regeneration of others, both wiser and happier. The stream of moral light, with a western destinati n from the beginning, has, in all its meanderings, increased its volume, until, swollen by the contributions, and enriched by the gleamings of ages, it has poured its flood on the cis-atlantic world.

ENGLAND.

The fast anchored Isle—the natal land of our fathers, and the mother o our common law—has done much for mankind. But she too has had her scenes of civil strife and of blood—her Wakefield, her Smithfield, and her Bosworthfield; she has had her Tudors, and her Stuarts, her Jeffreys, her Bonner, and her Cromwell, as well as her Sydney, her Cranmer, and her Hampden; and, after ages of reformation in Church and State, her aristocracy still governs, her Hierarchy still prevails, and the harp of Erin hangs tuneless and sad on the leafless bough of her blasted oak.

The British constitution lacks the soul of a fundamental law. It has no other political guaranty or principle of vitality than the pleasure of King, Lords and Commons, in Parliament assembled. An act of Parliament inconsistent with the constitution, is nevertheless the supreme law, and, in the language of Mr. Hallam, the utmost that can be said of it is that it is —"a novelty of much importance, tending to endanger the established laws." The constitution of England, venerable as it is, can be found only in the statutes and political history of that distinguished Isle. Such a government could not stand in such a country as ours, or in any country where there is an approximation towards practical equality in the rights and the condition of the people. And, though in England, the inherent imbecility of which we are speaking has been hitherto, in some measure, supplied by artificial expedients, yet, if her institutions shall become much more popular in their texture, her constitution must become the supreme law, and its practical supremacy must be secured by other guaranties than any now provided, or, otherwise, dissolution must be inevitable. A landed aristocracy, the stock in an irredeemable national debt—the rival interests of the crown, and nobility, and hierarchy, and commonality, cannot always preserve a safe and stable equilibrium. The spirit of this age will, if it go on, require other and more comprehensive expedients. Liberalism and rationalism are abroad in the world; and all institutions of men must, sooner or later, feel and acknowledge their plastic influence.

HENRY CLAY.

In this sacred and august presence of the illustrious dead, were an eulogistic speech befitting the occasion, it could not be made by me. I could not thus speak over the dead body of HENRY CLAY. *Kentucky* expects not me, nor any other of her sons, to speak his eulogy now, if ever. She would leave that grateful task to other States, and to other times. His name needs not our panegyric. The carver of his own fortune—the founder of his own name—with his own hands he has built his own monument, and with his own tongue and his own pen, he has stereotyped his autobiography. With hopeful trust his maternal Commonwealth consigns his fame to the justice of history, and to the judgment of ages to come. His ashes he bequeathed to her, and they will rest in her bosom until the judgment day; his fame will *descend*—as the common heritage of his country—to every citizen of that Union, of which he was thrice the triumphant champion, and whose genius and value are so beautifully illustrated by his life.

THE REORGANIZING ACT.

He never sought office, he never shrank from duty; and shall his country give him up to his and her enemies? Let such folly never mark her counsels—let such ingratitude never sully her escutcheon. He stands in the breach which ambition has made in the constitution; and whenever he falls a victim to your rapacity, his country's cause and his country's welfare will fall with him. Whenever he is immolated to satiate your vengeance, the incense which ascends from the altar of his sacrifice will be mingled with the smoke of a consumed constitution. Around his destiny, in this crisis, that of the constitution is indissolubly entwined. He stands on the last rampart which protects the constitution from your Vandal assaults. If you can strike him down and pass this barrier, you at once enter the citadel and give it up to violence. Your will is then the constitution. At such a catastrophe, the patriot might indeed exclaim, "O tempora, O mores!" And then it would be but right and natural for a Boyle, like Scipio Africanus, in the fervor of a holy resentment, to bequeath his curses to the ungrateful country which he had so faithfully served and so long illustrated, and his ashes, to strangers, in the memorable epitaph, "O, UNGRATEFUL COUNTRY! THOU SHALT NOT HAVE MY BONES!" But he will never be driven to this sad extremity. Kentucky will not be reproached with the ungrateful neglect of a Belisarius, or the exile of an Aristides. Boyle and the constitution will hold out to the last.

MILITARY CHIEFTAINS.

Military renown has been fatal to liberty. Washington was "a military chief"—But there has been only one Washington. The name of our dead Washington is worth more to us than all the living Washington's in the world. It was not his victories in the field, but his victory over himself, that lifted Washington above all other men.

DEMAGOGUES.

His public life illustrates the difference between the *statesman* and the *politician*—between the enlightened patriot who goes for the welfare and honor of his country, in defiance of all considerations of personal ease or aggrandizement, and the selfish demagogue, who, always feeling the peoples' pulse or looking at the weathercock of the popular breath, counts, as the chief good on earth, his own exaltation, by any means, to some office or trust which he is not qualified to fill with honor to himself, or advantage to the public.

She too had her demagogues, and the *"Majesty of the Roman people"* was their watchword. And though she had her Fabricius, her Regulus, her Cato, her Cicero—she had also her Clodius, and her Sylla, and her Cæsars, honored in their day as the friends of the people; and whether Marius or Sylla, Cæsar or Pompey prevailed, the victory was in the name of liberty, the *Republic* was honored with a triumph, and a clamor of approbation echoed from the Forum to the Capitol. Even Augustus Cæsar, absolute as he was, preserved the forms of a Republic, whilst, by the perversion of his vast patronage to his own aggrandizement, he made an obsequious and prostituted Senate the Registers of his will, and, in the name of liberty, fastened a heavy yoke forever on an *applauding* populace.

A demagogue is a sycophantic parasite—a servile tool—a slave at the feet of power. And, though the object of his idolatry is not a titled king, yet he fawns at the feet of a Briarean monarch, an excitable multitude, on whose credulity, vanity and passions, he plays with all the dexterity of an artful courtier. A member of the American Congress should be an American statesman—not, like Burke or Cato, too tenacious of abstract truth to do whatever may be practically best; but—enlightened by proper knowledge, and animated by a true American heart, throbbing for his whole country—always doing that which he believes to be best for that country in all time. Such a public servant is a public blessing and will always be honored, even in exile. The opposite character will be a curse to any people, and his posthumous doom will be—infamy.

THE PEOPLE HONEST.

Motives of ambition may prompt you; the people feel none such. It may be your interest to do wrong; it is always theirs to do right. This is proven by the nature and the very existence of our free institutions, and is fortified by our experience. If these evidences of popular rectitude are not satisfactory to you, allow me to add the authority of a great name. In Cato's letters you may find on this subject the following just and enlightened sentiments:

"It is certain that the people, if left to themselves, do generally, if not always, judge well. They have their five senses in as great perfection as have those who would treat them as if they had none. And there is oftener found a great genius carrying a pitchfork than carrying a white staff.

"The people have no bias to be knaves. No ambition prompts them; they have no rivals for place, no competitors to pull down; they have no darling child, pimp, or relation to raise; they have no occasion for dissimulation or intrigue; they can serve no end by faction; they have no interest but the general interest."

OFFICE SEEKING

With Epaminondas, neither seek nor decline, on account of their imputed dignity, places of public trust; and always remember his maxim that it is not the station, but the manner in which is is filled, which gives dignity and honor.

LAWS YIELD TO MANNERS.

Manners have always governed, and will ever govern laws. The history of all nations and ages of the world echoes the sentiment of Horace, *Quid leges sine moribus vanæ proficient!*—and proves beyond question that, without proper education and moral principles and habits, all the pomp and circumstance of the most magnificent civil and ecclesiastical establishments, and all the laws, however numerous and good, which legislative wisdom could enact, will be insufficient for preserving order and maintaining justice among men. Montesque announced a self-evident truth when he said, that "the laws of education are the first we receive, and should have respect to the principle and spirit of the government we live under." And we need not look to China or Confucius, or to Sparta, or to Lycurgus for an exemplification—we may find it in every age of the civilized world. Plautus and others complained that, at Rome, manners prevailed over the laws long before the destruction of the commonwealth, which fell in the struggle between Cæsar and Pompey for the prize of empire;—and it was not Cæsar, but the degeneracy of a self-confident, luxurious, and flattered

populace that brought the Roman Republic to its fatal end.   We read in
Tacitus that "good manners did more with the Germans than good laws
in other countries;" and in Lord Bacon, that "it is an old complaint that
Governments have been too attentive to laws while they have neglected
the business of education," and gaming, and tippling, and swearing, and
other fashionable vices, is only a partial illustration of the ancient maxim,
leges moribus servient—"the laws give way to manners"

EDUCATION OF THE POOR.

The rich, it is true, can educate themselves; but the poor, and those in
moderate circumstances, must depend, in a great measure, for the means
of information, upon the care and assistance of a parental government.
Hence, the propriety of legislative interposition and patronage   By the
tutelar assistance of the State, many a brilliant mind, otherwise destined
to languish in obscurity, may be brought forth and expanded; many an
humble individual, otherwise without the means of cultivation and improvement, may be rendered an ornament and benefactor of mankind, and
enabled to "pluck from the lofty cliff its deathless laurel."

CONSTITUTION, SHOULD BE INVIOLATE.

This Constitution establishes justice and guarantees civil liberty.   Its
power is altogether moral.   Its efficiency consists in the public sentiment
of its inviolability.   The soul which animates it is the people's reverence.
The cement which holds its parts together is the people's virtue and intelligence.   The citizen should hold the Constitution as the Christian does
the decalogue, sacred and inviolable.   It is worthy of his most sincere
homage, and requires his most resolute and persevering support.   Every
violation will encourage recurrent violations; and thus its value will be
diminished, and its principles rendered inoperative.   As long as the people
and their functionaries venerate the Constitution in all its parts, justice is
secure and liberty is safe; the poor man may live in peace, and work with
the buoyancy of hope and the confidence of security.   But only sanction
or connive at one violation of the Constitution, and it inspires hope and
confidence no longer.   While it exists, its motto is, "*nolo me tangere*,"
(touch me not.)   Like virgin purity, once sullied, it loses its chaste odor
and its charms, and invites its own prostitution.   Extinguish only one
spark of the vestal fire which burns on its altar, and the desecrated flame
is no longer holy, it degenerates into the common element, and is no more
sacred or enduring.   If one violation be tolerated, another is justified by
the example; usage ripens into law; and the whole Constitution is super-
seded.

RIGHTS OF THE MAJORITY.

The right of the majority to control the minority is derived from nature, and is speculatively just and unexceptionable; but not always practically proper. In regulating the affairs of society, the majority has an undeniable right to control the minority, unless when prohibited by the terms of the social compact, or the constitution. But, as in a state of nature the weak man has no security against the violence of the strong, nor the minor against the unjust dominion of the major party, it becomes necessary that government should be established, with such organization as to guarantee the equal rights of all Constitutions are made for the weak, not the strong; for minorities, not majorities; majorities can protect themselves. Hence the necessity of adopting principles which even majorities cannot violate. It is not only the sole object, but the essence of a constitution, that the stronger man, and the stronger party, shall be interdicted from encroachment on the guaranteed rights of the weaker man, and the weaker party. By what system of government this great end could be most certainly effected, without unnecessarily impairing the liberty of the people, has been the subject of discussion and experiment for ages; and it has been reserved for modern times to discover the secret, which is developed in the American constitutions.

A truly free government is one in which justice predominates over power, and right over might. No government is free or equal in which power is justice, and might is right, although that power is the authority of numbers, and that might is their physical force.

CONSTITUTION DEFINED.

A constitution is a fundamental law, fixing the manner in which the public will shall be expressed, and the national authority shall be exercised. An unmixed democracy cannot practically exist. Under such a form of government, the sovereign power will be assumed by demagogues or usurped by force.

Therefore, for the purpose of wisely enacting and justly administering laws, the power of the whole people must be delegated, in some mode, to a part. And the organic law, which prescribes the mode of delegation and defines the power, and fixes the responsibility of the public agents, is, whether written or unwritten, express or implied, the Constitution of the State.

INSTRUCTING REPRESENTATIVES.

But a pestilent exotic has already taken deep root in the heart of the constitution; and, if it live and grow, it will paralyze the organic life of that unequalled political structure. Its germ, planted by ambition, has

been watered by charlatanism, and nourished by egotism.   The Demagogue feeds on it; and, like the serpent's charm, it fascinates and decoys
but too many of multitudes, who do not understand the spirit and object
of the constitution, and have only an imperfect knowledge of the philosophy of organized liberty.   It is called, "the right of instruction"—a popular
name, which imports that it is the political duty of the members of each
branch of Congress to echo, by their votes, the known will of their electors.   The sole argument in support of this seductive heresy, though to the
superficial thinker quite specious, will not stand the test of severe scrutiny.
Its postulate is the assumption that the representative is only the substitute
of his electoral constituents; and the conclusion is, that he should, therefore, as their agent, represent their will.

If Congress must speak as the majority feels, all the wonderful machine-
ry of our National Government, organized for the purpose of regulating the
motive power of public sentiment, often as explosive as steam, would, in
time, be rendered powerless, and the transient passions and delusions of
the majority, instead of their deliberate reason and final judgment, would
reign unchecked, and soon drive to anarchy, revolution, and ruin.   To
avert such a catastrophe was the object, and is yet the hope, of our fundamental distribution and organization of the power of ruling majorities.
But the popular doctrine of instructions is a cormorant in the tree of life,
and if long permitted to live and feed, will surely make it fruitless, sapless
—dead.

The only constitutional power the electoral constituency can have, or
ought to have, over a member, is that moral influence arising from sympathy, and his responsibility to censorship.   They can neither remove nor
otherwise control him during his term.

NULLIFICATION.

Then it is not true, that the States, in their sovereign political capacity
alone, made the Constitution of the United States, and are the only parties
to it—it is not true that, under that constitution, they retain independent
and plenary sovereignty—it is not true that, for deciding between them
and the general government, or any portion of the people and the government, there is "no common judge" provided by themselves in their charter
of Union—it is indisputably not true, therefore, that "each party has a
right to judge for itself as to infractions, as well as the mode of redress."
And, consequently, the first of the resolutions of '98, the only foothold of
nullification, or of secession, evaporates in detonating and pestilent gas.

OBLIGATION OF A CONTRACT.

"Obligation," in the Constitution of the United States, means what it
does elsewhere, and what it imported in common use at the time it was
inserted.   To oblige is to bind, force, coerce, &c.   The derivative, "obli-

gation," is the binding, forcing power or quality of the thing. It is defined by *Justinian* to be the ligament which binds, and by *Pothier* to be "*vinculum juris*," or bond, or tie, or chain of right; a moral obligation or ligament is defined to be that which binds the conscience, which is the *law* of nature; and a legal obligation, of course, that which binds in or by civil law. The obligation of a contract is that which induces, compels, or ensues its enforcement. *It is not the instrument or agent by which it is coerced, but the right which the obligee has to use coercion, that is the essence of the obligation.* This is either moral or legal, and generally both. When there is no municipal law, which will compel the performance of an engagement, that which induces the performance, is the natural law, and is called the moral obligation, which is either internal or external, imperfect or perfect. It is internal when conscience is the only persuasive or coercive power.

The legal obligation of every contract is, therefore, THE RIGHT OF THE CONTRACTING PARTIES TO COERCE EACH OTHER BY LAW, and thereby obtain indemnity; and any thing which WEAKENS, POSTPONES, OR IMPAIRS THAT RIGHT, necessarily IMPAIRS THAT OBLIGATION.

THE COMMON LAW.

The common law is an unwritten code of matured reason, of obscur origin in times of great antiquity, in the north of Europe and in England —the offspring chiefly of the feudal system—the companion and friend of civil liberty, strengthened by age, and improved and improving with the progress of civilization and of human knowledge. It is found only in the reports of adjudged cases, in elementary law books, and in the enlightened judgment of mankind. It is practical reason, rectified and recognized by the experience of ages, and modified by analogies, and by changing circumstances.

EQUITY.

Although law and equity are generally contradistinguished, the one from the other, yet, when considered with proper precision, they are essentially identical in principle. *Equity* is *law*—otherwise it would be inconsistent with that certainty and security in the administration of civil affairs which the supremacy of laws can alone ensure. *Equity* is *justice* too; but it is justice in a peculiar and technical sense; not variable, like the changing sentiments of the chancellor or the multitude, but as constant as the fixed and rational principles of civil right and civil law. In a judicial sense that cannot be equitable which is inconsistent with the law of the land. In the proper sense, a court of equity can neither make nor abrogate any rule of law; nor enforce what the law forbids; nor relieve from that which the law enjoins; nor decide otherwise than according to the principle and spirit of established law; nor interpret a contract or a statute so as to give

13

to either an import different from that which **should be ascribed to it by** any other judicial tribunal—the intention of the contracting parties is their **contract, and the intention of** the Legislature is the law in every *forum*, and should, in all, be sought and determined according to the same principles and tests. In all these particulars, and in every essential **respect,** equity is law, and law is equity; and each, therefore, is *justice* according to the principles of civil right and obligation. Equity is but the philosophy of law—the spirit and end of the law; and it may therefore be, not inaptly, defined to be *rectified law* administered in England by the lord chancellor, one of the king's ministers, and by subordinate courts of chancery, and in the most of the States of the North American Union by courts of equity in peculiar modes, better adapted to the ends of perfect justice, than the technical and imperfect remedies but too strictly adhered to in those ordinary tribunals called *"common law courts."*

THE VETO POWER.

The qualified veto here is practically an absolute veto. No President has yet been overruled by the constitutional two-thirds—and no President who knows **how to exercise power** for the sinister purpose of increasing his influence, ever will be. Had our fathers of '88 foreseen or seriously apprehended such a result, they never would have permitted the veto, or left it unmuzzled and omniverous as it may be likely to become. They intended to bridle it so as to keep it in the constitutional track, and their journal and debates show that they intended to preserve Congress from the vortex of Executive patronage, by declaring its members ineligible to any other place of public trust, which could be conferred by the President, during their legislative term. Had they persisted in that determination, and especially had they extended the ineligibility to the Presidential term, they would have made representatives in Congress much more true and faithful to their constituents than many of them have been, or will ever be, as long as a President can seduce them from their duty to their country by the bait of office more profitable or attractive than their seats in legislative chairs of uncertain tenure.

ON THE STUDY OF THE LAW.

Do not repose in confidence, or presume too much on the elementary knowledge you have acquired whilst here. Though you have learned much, you are only initiated into the first principles, and prepared for the successful study of legal science, the most of which is to you, yet a TERRA INCOGNITA, far beyond the range of your circumscribed horizon. You may learn all your lives, and the more you learn the more you will find to be learned. To attain the utmost that can be accomplished, it is important to make a judicious selection of books, to read them properly, and to make a systematic appropriation of all your time. It is not the number, but the kind of books, and the manner of reading them, that will be most useful. The most scientific and approved editions of elementary books should be studied, carefully compared with the cases to which they refer, and tested, when doubtful or anomalous, by principle and analogy—and such text-books as Blackstone, Cruise, and Kent, should be periodically reviewed, as well as occasionally read. The more important of the adjudged cases should be read carefully and compared and collated; and a commonplace manuscript, arranged by titles, alphabetically, would be both eminently useful, by imprinting new doctrines on the mind, and always of great value for occasional application.

But the habit of intensely thinking and carefully writing on the more abstruse doctrines of the law, will be still more useful. Unless we meditate on what we read, and see, and hear, until we rightly understand it, we can never make it our own, or use it properly or effectually. Reading and observation only supply materials for meditation; and intellectual rumination is to the mind what mastication and deglutition are to the body. But it is intense thinking alone that can digest and assimilate, into a congenial and vitalizing essence, the aliment of the mind. Intensity of thought is as indispensable to the nutriment of the mind, as the gastric solvent and vascular labaratory are to animal digestion and life. No man was ever truly great or useful, who did not think much and well; and many have been practically wise without reading books. Patrick Henry's chief book was the volume of nature—but he thought with a peculiar interest and intensity—and thus, the carver of his own fortune, he became one of nature's tallest noblemen. But he did not know much law. To have acquired that science it was indispensable that he should have read as well as thought much. Proper reading furnishes food; right thinking digests it; and careful writing and speaking rectify it, and circulate the vital product. Bacon has said—"Much reading makes the full man, much thinking makes the correct man, and much writing makes the perfect man."

CHRISTIANITY.

In its purity and simplicity—the Christian Religion is the friend and companion of civil liberty—its constant companion—its best friend. It taught man his true dignity, and his true and equal rights. It elevated woman to her just rank in the scale of being; and, even amid the perversions and prostitutions of a wild superstition, it rescued literature and civilization from the ruins of a dark and desolating age. It is not the metaphysical, or polemic theology of the schools, nor the infallible "orthodoxy" of sectarian bigotry, nor the false religion of persecution, nor the bloody religion of Smithfield, and of the Inquisition—of which we speak; but it is that mild, and pure, and holy religion which rebukes intolerance, and dispels ignorance, and subdues vice—that heavenly religion which beams in the pious mother's eyes, and hallows the accents of the pious mother's lips—that religion which proclaims peace on earth and good will to men, and inspires that love to God and to man which purifies the heart and overcomes the world.

It is the prevalence of this last and brightest hope of man that will establish his liberty on the rock of ages. And this it was, pure and unconstrained as it came from Heaven, that the Father of his Country recommended to the people of these United States, when, in his valedictory address, he conjured them, by all they held dear, not only to regard religion as the firmest prop of their liberty and happiness, but to treat, as a public enemy, him who should ever attempt to undermine or to shake it.

ON AN ELECTIVE JUDICIARY.

Popular election may not be the best mode of selecting good Judges. Admitting the competency of the people to appoint Judges, as well as the incumbents of the other departments, when they have proper opportunities of doing so, yet the great reason why they should elect the latter does not apply to the former. In legislation the constitutional will of the people ought to prevail—and, therefore, they should elect their legislative representatives. The same principle applies also to most of the duties of the Executive; but a very different one applies to the Judiciary, whose province is, not to echo the public sentiment, but to decide the law and uphold justice and the Constitution against an opposing torrent of popular feeling. To make Judges of the law representatives of public opinion, like the makers of the law, is inconsistent and suicidal. And, consequently, whatever will tend to subject the Judiciary to the fluctuating tide of passion or of party, is, so far, subversive of the American theory of Constitutional liberty and security. Had the Convention only provided for the election of Judges for a period of ten or twelve years, and declared against a reelection, we would not have opposed the adoption of the new Constitution on that ground alone. But, by reducing the term of office to so short a period as six years, and allowing re-eligibility, that new scheme of Government holds out a bait which must subject the Judiciary to a capricious power, whose will the objects of its creation, and of the Constitution itself, require it often to resist and control.

Who could expect such a Judiciary, by a self-sacrifice, to maintain the integrity of the Constitution against an exceedingly popular act of Assembly? Who would hope, that before such Judges, the poor and rich, the weak and the powerful, the popular and the friendless, the minority and the majority, would have an equal chance of stern and impartial justice? And for what, but to protect those who have not the power to protect themselves, is a Republican Constitution ever made? History tells a warning tale on this momentous subject, and yet tells not—because the historian cannot know—the one hundredth part of the corruptions, the prostitutions, and the oppressions, springing from the organization of such a Judiciary as that proposed by the late Convention. But it does record, in burning characters, the humiliating fact that, even in our gallant sister State, Mississippi, Judges have closed their courts to avoid giving judgments—Sheriffs have resigned to prevent execution—and that, more than once, "Lynch" law has reigned supreme and unrebuked.

With a prophetic forecast, as well as historic truth, Thomas Jefferson, in his notes on Virginia, denounced such a servile Judiciary as the supple instrument of faction and of anarchy, and said, in reference to it:—"*An elective Despotism is not the Government we fought for.*" And echo should reverberate through the whole valley of the Mississippi, "*Such an elective Despotism is not the Government we fought for.*"

ON THE FREQUENCY OF ELECTIONS.

Whilst it (the Constitution of Kentucky) amuses the unreflecting with the semblance of a greatly augmented electoral power, it provides for so many and such frequent elections, and of so many officers, high and low, at the same time, as to prevent the pure, careful, and prudent exercise of the franchise, throw all nominations and elections virtually into the hands of a few busy and selfish managers—degrade the practical government into a trafficing and corrupting oligarchy—and, finally, produce among the industrious and working classes, a paralyzing indifference about voting, and thus operate so as to concentrate the elective power on a class that will make a trade of elections. Is this privilege a boon to be struggled for by wise men?

INSANITY.

Intellectual insanity is not any unsoundness of the reasoning faculty, or derangement of the mind itself, psychologically or spiritually considered, nor erroneous reasoning only, nor violent passion, *merely as such;* but is a morbid delusion of the senses, the feelings, or the imagination, which furnish the material on which the reason acts. As the serene and unchanged sun of heaven reflects, from a deranged atmosphere, unreal and often distorted images, and even such as the beautiful *fata morgana* in the Bay of Naples, so the mind of man, operating through a diseased brain or the false suggestions of unsound senses, presents delusive objects or imaginary facts which have no existence elsewhere than in a diseased brain or morbid imagination. The cause is physical, the effect mental. It is delusion—delusion of a diseased brain or unsound senses. Man is so constituted as to be fitly adapted to the material and moral world around him. He is so organized physically, when his organs are all perfect and sound, as to perceive external objects as they are, and so constituted morally, as to be able, by his reason, to deduce true and right conclusions from existing facts, and to conform his acts to the will of God and the laws of his country. And, when in this perfect condition of constitutional harmony and adaptation, he is, in the legal sense, sane, and is responsible for his conduct.

SLAVERY.

Had this lot been cast in a land of universal freedom, he never would consent that its virgin bosom should be soiled by the tread of slavery, or its tranquillity disturbed by the cry of a slave. Of course, were he a resident of California, he would oppose the introduction of slavery there. But the people of that country, like the people here, should be left free to regulate their own domestic relations in their own way; and, if they should desire to have slaves, Congress—though in his opinion possessing the power to prevent them while in a territorial state of dependence on the unlimited legislation of the General Government—would act unwisely, as well as unjustly, to exercise it, and more especially as, in that case, the act being altogether unnecessary, would seem to be wantonly intended for the political aggrandisement of one section of the Union, and therefore would be the more ungracious and offensive to another section, which, though not quite so populous, is at least as intelligent and patriotic

Slavery in Kentucky is a moral and political evil. The children of slaveholders are injured, and many of them ruined by it; and it has greatly reduced Kentucky's ratio of political power; for whilst she, the first born of the old "13," has only ten representatives in Congress, Ohio, younger in origin and inferior in physical adaptations, has already twenty-one representatives in the same body. But the slaves here are so numerous, and slavery itself is so intertwined with the social or personal habits of the free population as, in his judgment, to forbid the adoption now of any system of emancipation with a rational hope of a consummation either satisfactory or beneficial. Before this can be done, the number of slaves must be considerably diminished, and the people more and more assimilated to the non-slaveholding habits and condition. The experiment of non-importation will soon decide whether Kentucky is destined long to continue a slave State, and will in proper time, we hope, develop public sentiment on that subject. It is the interest of all—the duty of all—to try that experiment. Whatever may be its final results, its operation will be beneficial to all parties—masters and slaves, the pro-slavery party, the emancipation party' and the conservative party.

But heedlessly agitate them on the stultifying topic of slavery, and there will be neither peace nor safety—here, nor throughout this entire Union. Many aspiring politicians, of selfish ambition, and a still larger number of fanatics, on one side of "Mason's and Dixon's line," are striving to consolidate the non-slaveholding States on free-soilism as the paramount test of National party—and there are but too many Hotspur's and ultra pro-slavery men on the other and numerically weaker side of the line, who rashly play into the hands of these "North Men," and encourage an issue which, if ever fully made up, must result in the political subjugation of the South, or a disruption of the Union. It is the interest of Kentucky to prevent that fearful issue; and she can avert it only by abstaining from slave agitation and remaining self-poised, firm and moderate.

LAWYERS—QUALIFICATIONS OF.

In discharging the various duties, incident to your profession, you will find use for all human knowledge and moral power. Sallust doubted whether a higher order of talents and attainments was not necessary to make a good historian than an able General. But can there be any doubt that the *beau ideal* of an eminent lawyer requires more knowledge and moral power, than what might be sufficient to make an able General? Prudence, sagacity, decision, courage—are the chief attributes of able Generalship. The able and honest lawyer must have these, and more. He must have a profound knowledge of law, an acquaintance with general science and polite literature—integrity of principle and character, and a peculiar faculty of speech. Nothing is more difficult or interesting, or requires more variety of attainments, or greater compass or power of mind than a forensic argument, in a great and difficult cause, addressed to the reason, the hearts, and the passions of men, in behalf of truth obscured by sophistry, justice oppressed by power, or innocence persecuted by malice and falsehood. In such a cause, all that is most good and great in moral power may be necessary and will ever be most useful.

A man of the ordinary grade of intellect may, by assiduity, perseverance, and fidelity, become a respectable lawyer, and "*get along*" in his profession. But talents, the most exalted—knowledge, most profound and various; industry, most regular; honor, most chivalrous; and integrity, most pure and inflexible, must all be combined in him who is eminently distinguished for forensic ability.

Talents, however bright—knowledge, however great—will be unavailing or pernicious, without habitual industry, systematic prudence, and perfect honor. What Johnson said of Savage, and Butler of Sheridan, is universally true—"Those who, in confidence of superior capacities, disregard the common maxims of life, will be reminded that nothing will supply the want of prudence, and that negligence and irregularity long continued, will make knowledge useless; wit, ridiculous; and genius contemptible." No lawyer, who neglects that maxim, can be true to his clients, to his own fame, or to the dignity of his profession. And here we deem it not inappropriate to invite your attention to the importance of a peculiar propriety in personal and professional deportment; and also, to the necessity of, what may be termed, forensic ethics.

1st. A lawyer should be a gentleman in his principles, his habits, and his deportment; in fine, a gentleman in the sterling import of the term—else he brings degradation on himself, and helps to reflect discredit on the profession. And to be a gentleman in the true and perfect sense, is to be—what is too rare—a man of sound principles, scrupulous honor, becoming modesty, active benevolence, habitual morality, **and rational,** just, and **polite deportment.**

2d. In his intercourse with his clients, he should be candid, **respectful, patient,** liberal, and just.   He should never advise a suit unless it is the interest of his client to "go to law." If the case be frivolous, or the right **doubtful,** he should advise forbearance or compromise. He should never encourage litigation. When a suit becomes necessary, or is pending, his fee should be regulated by the value of his services, and the client's ability conveniently to pay.   An honest man will never barter his **conscience,** nor will an honest lawyer ever speculate on the ignorance, the fears, or the passions of his confiding clients. A faithful lawyer will never deceive his client nor neglect his business. It is his duty, and his interest too, to **deal** in **perfect candor,** and to do, in the preparation of his client's cause, **all that** he ought **to do;** and that is, all that he **can do** consistently with personal honor or professional propriety. If, in consequence of his negligence, misdirection, or unskillfulness, his client's claims unjustly or im- properly fail, he should **indemnify him** fully, promptly, and cheerfully. He **should** never attempt **success by any** other **than** fair, honorable, **and** legal means; nor should he advise **or connive** at **the** employment of any other means by his client. He is **not** bound by any obligation to the dig- nity of his profession to abandon his client's cause, merely because he may discover that he is on the wrong side; for he might be **mistaken in** his opinion, and might do great injustice **by** turning against his client.   And also, it is his duty, whether in a good **or** bad cause, on the wrong side or the right, **to** present, **in** as imposing a **manner,** as fair argument can ex- hibit, the stronger **or** more plausible points in his client's behalf, without expressing an uncandid opinion.   In no case should **he ever** express, as his opinion, any **thing but his** opinion.   To do so would not only be inconsist- ent with the propriety of his profession, but would surely impair his influ- ence, subtract from his reputation, and render it altogether uncertain when he thinks what he **says.**

3d. **Towards the court** he should be respectful and modest, but firm and candid; **and he should** never endeavor to elude his own responsibility, by attempting **to throw it** unjustly on the court.   The artifice **is but too** common.   It is, however, not only disingenuous, but discreditable and **dis-** advantageous; because it is dishonorable, and tends to disparage the **courts** of justice, in which public confidence is indispensable to a satisfactory **ad- ministration of the laws.**

4th. In his intercourse with his professional brethren, he should be courteous, just, and honorable.   He should repudiate all dissimulation and **low** cunning, and all those common place and humiliating artifices of little minds, which constitute chicanery.   He should desire only an honorable victory; such as may be won by fair means and fair arguments.   If he beat his antagonist by superior arguments, or superior knowledge, his suc- **cess is creditable; but if** he beat him **in** cunning, fraud or trickery, he degrades himself, prostitutes his privileges, and outrages forensic dignity and propriety. Such vulgar game is beneath the pride, and revolting to the honor of lofty intellect. It is the offspring of moral infirmity, and is almost always, proof of a diminutive mind.

5th. A lawyer can hardly be both mercenary and just. An inordinate appetite for gain, is apt to seek gratification in spoliation, fraud, and oppression, and is generally the companion of a cold and calculating selfishness, irreconcilable with the most attractive and useful of the personal, social, and civic virtues. Avarice is also undignified and unreasonable. He, who is not content with a competence for independence and rational enjoyment, has a morbid appetite which this world can never satiate—because it craves to *hoard* and not to enjoy. More than a competency is not necessary for happiness, and is but seldom consistent with it.

> "Reason's whole pleasure, all the joy of sense,
> Lie in three words—health, peace, and competence."

And the Book of books tells us, that it is almost impossible for a very rich man to reach, or, if he could reach, to enjoy heaven; because he is almost sure to be sordid, and to look on ephemeral, earthly possessions, as his *summum bonum*, or supreme good. It is almost as difficult for a rich man ever to become a great lawyer. There are but few who can be stimulated by ambition or taste alone, to encounter the toil and vexation, the sleepless nights and anxious days which must be the price of forensic eminence. And he who desires that his last moments on earth shall be gilded with a firm assurance that his children, whom he has pledged as hostages to posterity, shall be useful and honorable in their day, should not be solicitous to lay up for them, more of this world's goods than barely enough to enable them to give to their moral and physical powers proper means of employment and development. Why then should we court an empty and delusive shadow? Worse—an *ignis fatuus*, that too often lures from the straight and open path of virtue and happiness? for we know how few there are, or ever have been, who dedicate their surplus wealth to its only useful and proper end—beneficence.

ERRATA.

Page.	Line.	For.	Read.
11	30	its subject.	and its subject.
97	31	activity.	actively.
98	32	unquited.	unrequited.
104	31	and.	amid.
104	32	stood.	trod.
105	9	of the crucifixion.	The evidence of the, &c.
118	2	shadows.	shallows.
131	31	misanthrop.	misanthropy.
137	11	opportunities.	importunities.
134	34	floor.	door.
139	36	frequent.	pregnant.
141	11	philosophy.	philology.
150	36	elaborate.	elevated.
173	7	contunence.	concurrence.
174	30	obligor.	obligee.